I0742237

Publisher's Note:

Thank you for purchasing this book. It began as an idea, was shaped by the creativity of its talented author, and was subsequently molded into the book you have before you by a team of editors and designers.

Like all EDGE books, this book is the result of the creative talents of a dedicated team of individuals who all believe that books (whether in print or pixels) have the magical ability to take you on an adventure to new and wondrous places powered by the author's imagination.

As EDGE's publisher, I hope that you enjoy this book. It is a part of our ongoing quest to discover talented authors and to make their creative writing available to you.

We also hope that you will share your discovery and enjoyment of this anthology on social media through Facebook, Twitter, Goodreads, Pinterest, etc., and by posting your opinions and/or reviews on Amazon and other review sites and blogs. By doing so, others will be able to share your discovery and passion for this book.

Brian Hades, publisher

BY THE LIGHT OF CAMELOT

SELECT STORIES CURATED AND EDITED BY

J. R. CAMPBELL &
SHANNON ALLEN

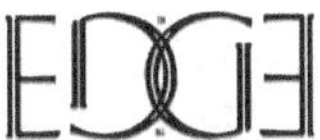

EDGE SCIENCE FICTION AND FANTASY PUBLISHING
An Imprint of HADES PUBLICATIONS, INC.
CALGARY

By the Light of Camelot

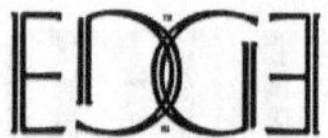

EDGE SCIENCE FICTION AND FANTASY PUBLISHING
An Imprint of HADES PUBLICATIONS, INC.
P.O. Box 1714, Calgary, Alberta, T2P 2L7, Canada

The EDGE Team:
Producer: Brian Hades
Acquisitions Editor: Michelle Heumann
Edited by: JR Campbell and Shannon Allen
Cover Design: Brent Nichols
Cover Art Elements: Fernando Gregory
Book Design: Mark Steele
Publicist: Janice Shoults

ISBN: 978 1 77053 157 4

EDGE Science Fiction and Fantasy Publishing and Hades Publications,
Inc. acknowledges the ongoing support of the Alberta Foundation for the
Arts and the Canada Council for the Arts for our publishing programme.

Library and Archives Canada Cataloguing in Publication
CIP Data on file with the National Library of Canada
ISBN: 978 1 77053 157 4
(e-Book ISBN: 978-1-77053-156-7)

FIRST EDITION
(20180328)
Printed in USA
www.edgewebsite.com

— «» —

Somewhere in the world there is defeat for everyone. Some are destroyed by defeat, and some are made small and mean by victory. Greatness lives in the one who triumph's equally over defeat and victory.

> — John Steinbeck, *The Acts of King Arthur and his Noble Knights.*

— «» —

Contents

Need something new to read?

Foreword

JR Campbell

On either side the river lie
Long fields of barley and of rye,
That clothe the wold and meet the sky;
And thro' the field the road runs by
To many-tower'd Camelot;

— Alfred Lord Tennyson

I was first introduced to Camelot when my grandparents gifted me a copy of 'The Book of King Arthur'. Despite being fairly new to this whole reading thing it was obvious to me this book was going to be trouble. It was filled with words so odd they'd taken the time to put definitions in the page margins. Bad sign that, a book including its own dictionary. One entry in particular stuck in my memory: *Umbril: The helmet visor that covers the face, sometimes called the beaver.* Born in Canada, I knew what a beaver was and I knew that definition didn't make sense. Still, I pressed on. My vocabulary took an odd turn. King Arthur has always been there, a story everyone is somehow expected to know and, having read it, I felt somehow as if I'd caught up. Arthur won a Kingdom, a sword and a wife. Good job, nice story, onto the next. Given how much I would enjoy all things Arthurian later, I wish I could say I fell in love with that book upon my first reading but that would not be true. (When a man lies, he murders a part of the world.) I'd liked it, despite the odd vocabulary, but it contained less mystery and more marriage then I was accustomed to. Glad to be done, my young self sallied forth as a self proclaimed expert on King Arthur. Not only had I'd read the book, I'd also seen Disney's 'The Sword in the Stone', surely I knew all there was to know.

This blithe assumption would go unchallenged for more than a decade but when Arthur and I crossed swords again I was utterly unprepared. The film was 'Excalibur' and the story started with, well, more adult content then I associated with the book from my grandparents. The film had familiar parts but the plot didn't end where I expected. As the movie rolled on it was apparent, even to my teenaged sensibilities, that there was a lot more story in this film than what I had read. The book I'd read featured happy endings for everyone but this film charged right through that part without slowing. There was, obviously, more to King Arthur than I'd known. Suddenly aware of my deficiency, I went looking for more King Arthur books. Did they even exist? It seems a hopelessly naive question to me now but I can't help recalling the wonderment I felt discovering how extensive the field of Arthurian literature was. The seed planted by my grandparents took root and I began a quest leading to the book you now hold.

No doubt your path to Camelot has led you through many books and adaptations as well. In this, we're like all those who came before us. One of the fascinating things about the tales of Arthur is that there is no canon, no detailed timeline or strict continuity such as modern fandoms dote on. The earliest mentions of Arthur proudly proclaim they are taken from books which no longer survive, or perhaps never existed. Writing around 1136 Geoffrey of Monmouth refers to a 'certain very ancient book written in the British language' as his source, likewise Sir Thomas Malory is upfront in his intention to reduce the French tales into English. Each time the story is written down the writers add flourishes of their own, building or altering the tales handed down to them, infusing them with the preoccupations and concerns of their own generation. In an anthology such as this, where authors of differing backgrounds are invited to share one realm, imposing a strict adherence to a particular sequence of events or favoring one generation's descriptions over another seems not just arbitrary but detrimental to the imagination. Enough of the tales persist to allow the reader to recognize the setting but details invariably shift from story to story. This is as it should be, as it has always been, and is an integral part of the charm of Camelot. With each retelling the writer cannot help emphasizing the virtues and perspective of their time and preoccupations. Some stories are more political, others more religious, more romantic, more violent.

The Tennyson quote which started this foreword speaks of the many-towers of Camelot. For Malory, Arthur's realm is less architecturally impressive, focusing more on the years of peace enjoyed under the Great King's rule. Of course, it's not unreasonable to assume Tennyson lived a more peaceful life than the imprisoned knight who authored the eight romances comprising 'Le Mort D'Arthur'. Likewise in an age when timekeeping and detailed records are common and expected, current writers scour historical research hoping to uncover the 'real' Arthur, the man who inspired the old tales, a figure who can be reasonably contained in a historical context.

And yet, whatever the historical truths that inspired King Arthur, it's not fair to expect the ruler of Camelot to be reasonable. What defines Arthur is his unreasonable passion to all that is good and just. A battle-hardened warrior who preaches the virtues of mercy, a High King who designs a court where all are equal, a man of achievement whose most sincere celebrations are for the feats of others, none of these traits are in any way reasonable. To those outside the fascination of Camelot the complaint I've most often heard of Arthur is that he is more archetype than character, a hero too perfect to be human, a literary contrivance stretched over too many themes to have any depth. I'll acknowledge there's some truth to this. The good Arthur always strived towards is more difficult to describe than evil. One generation's view of the happiness of Camelot will clash in details with the generations that follow. Yet I confess that I've always found

Arthur sincere in his efforts to bring happiness and peace not just to his realm but to everyone, friend or foe. For me his humanity speaks from the old stories, the unsure young boy who pulled the sword from the stone not to claim his birthright but to help his brother, the knight whose sword is broken when he puts his pride ahead of the Kingdom's need, the ruler who puts his trust in those who gather to follow his banner. And while Arthur's portrayal in some adaptations can be wobbly, often clearing the stage for whatever the writer wants their protagonist to do, there is always a sense of virtue about him. Arthur's humanity is on full display as the tales come to their conclusion as well, the fall of Camelot brought about not by foreign invaders or magical disasters but due to the very real, very human pain Arthur experiences when betrayed by those he has trusted the most. As I've read the stories, his defining characteristic as always been his striving, his passion, to do what is best and just for all.

This seems like a good place to mention the disservice of the late Victorian penchant to adapt the old tales into children's stories. My first encounter with Arthur was through such telling, suitably sanitized so as not to befuddle young minds with messy passions or divided loyalties. Full of duty, proper behavior and quiet competence, these retellings are near the originals while still missing the point of the older tales. It is amazing to me how these adaptations, more than a century old now, persist in the pop culture memory while events aged years or decades ago fade so quickly from the collective memory. Yet the Victorian, passionless Arthurian perspective stubbornly persists. Still, given my own path to Arthurian literature, perhaps I am not the one to complain about it. The genuine shock I felt when watching a film and learning that Guinevere betrayed Arthur was as puritan and Victorian a moment as I've ever experienced. Reading the more modern and, eventually, the much older versions of the stories, I was continually surprised and delighted with how rich, how human, many of the characters became as each new telling was layered over the previous.

And while the Arthurian themes of inescapable destiny, mad love, just laws and mysterious magic have a natural home in today's modern fantasy genre, it shouldn't be forgotten that Arthurian literature is not just inspiration to these few shelves but to those of all of western literature. While knights such as the love-obsessed Lancelot or redemption-seeking Gawain could step seamlessly in 'A Game of Thrones' or 'The Lord of the Rings', you are just as likely to find shades of them looking back from the text of any book you pull from any shelf, albeit after some costume changes. Like Arthur, everyone wants to do good and, like Arthur, we all struggle to determine what good means.

The most obvious example of Arthur's striving for good is the Round Table. A simple collection of people, all burdened by their own flaws, gathered together under the banner of Camelot and invited to speak their minds openly and freely. Some are welcomed to the table after many achievements, others are greeted just as warmly despite their youth and lack of accolades. More is expected of them than talk, all who gather at the Table are expected to test their ideas against the realities of the world around them. Quests, whether by the command of Arthur or through the practice of knight-errantry, define the Table's reputation. The Round Table expects the best of all who sit there and those chosen rise to the challenge. Long before the terms multiculturism or political correctness entered our lexicon, Malory filled the Round Table with people from an array of backgrounds including a Saracen knight (Palamedes) and a pacifist knight (Servause le Breuse) with knights with names indicating they have arrived at Camelot from all over the known world. Certainly one of Malory's themes is the belief that virtue existed everywhere and that gathering a diverse group together resulted in a stronger whole. The Round Table is very much the world and each who sits there understands that their actions, for good or evil, will reflect not just on themselves but on their fellows, their King and the legacy they leave behind. There are many times when the knights seem fearful their failures will reflect poorly on their fellows but it never seems to hold them back from going forth and attempting great and worthy deeds.

Now we, all who contributed to this book, shall attempt to do the same, adding or embellishing stories to the already storied realm. It's our earnest hope that you, the reader, will find something worthwhile within the pages whether Camelot is a familiar, treasured place in your imagination or you are making your journey to the many tower'd Camelot for the first time.

Enjoy!
— JR Campbell

A Short History of the Table Round

Jane Yolen

Wace was wrong, as he often was.
Merlin did not magic the Table,
It was a wood and nails Breton thing.

There was not just one such,
But three, all equal in area, height,
Though not in décor.

The Yuletide quarrel over precedence
Spilled into the vast kitchens,
Cooks supplying fire, brewers the fuel.

Arthur called for carpenters to make
Dinner seating where none would rise higher,
Lower, though of course,

Anywhere the king sits is the head.
Royalty likes to split such hairs,
We braid them into our tales.

But the great knights sat silent,
And if they grumped, it did not show.
Part of greatness is learning what not to say.

The second round table was for the adjuncts,
Those knights not yet given a nickname
For their deeds by the king's brother, Kai,

A maker and breaker of reputations,
His own included. He knew the value
Of humor being humorless himself.

The adjuncts sulked in their anonymity,
Complained about the low pay,
Hated sitting apart, untenured.

They counted on their gauntlet fingers
Deeds for their imaginary vitas:
Dragons slain, maidens rescued.

(Sometimes the other way around,
Collateral damage it's called in Old English,
Dragons being trickier than maids.)

The third round table was for the squires,
Young, faces pocked with adolescence,
Smelling of misdeeds, unwashed weeks,

Whose deeds were legendary for foolishness,
Those deeds never spoken of again when they moved
Into the sightlines of the king.

— «» —

Jane Yolen, often called "the Hans Christian Andersen of America," is the author of over 360 books, including *Owl Moon*, *The Devil's Arithmetic*, and *How Do Dinosaurs Say Goodnight*. A graduate of Smith College, with a Masters in Education from the University of Massachusetts, she was recently named an unsung heroine of Massachusetts (though she says, "Hey — I'm sung!") Her books and stories have won an assortment of awards — two Nebulas, a World Fantasy Award, a Caldecott Medal, three Golden Kite awards, three Mythopoeic awards, two Christopher Medals, several Rhyslings, a nomination for the National Book Award, and the Jewish Book Award, among many others. She was the first woman to give the Scottish St Andrews University's Andrew Lang lecture since the lecture series was started in 1927.And the first writer in the Connecticut River Valley to win the New England Public Radio's Arts and Humanities Award. Six colleges and universities have given her honorary doctorates. She is a Grand Master three times: for SFWA, SFPA, and the World Fantasy Association. Also worthy of note, her Skylark Award — given by NESFA, the New England Science Fiction Association, set her good coat on fire. If you need to know more about her, visit her website at: www.janeyolen.com

Brannon and the Raven

Fiona Patton

Long ago, the south-west coast of Cymru was a gray and hostile place in winter, the cold, dark sea below, a mirror to the cold, dark sky above. Snow was rare, but rain was common; a harsh and driving rain that scored the cliffs in sheets of icy enmity and fog so thick it dulled the eye and tricked the ear of any mad enough to risk the narrow path that lead from head to heights. High above, a manor house, once fine and strong, now falling into ruin, stood silent sentinel alone. No candles lit its windows, no sound of laughter filled its halls, its once proud crest above the lintel, now so worn and battered that it hardly could be seen beneath its withered mask of moss and ivy. Its family too, long slighted by the Fates, had grown both sad and still, as clad in dust and shadows as the now forgotten honors on the walls.

On the days the sun's attempts to cast a few, pale strands of light across the landscape made some movement possible, the youngest child, a boy of thirteen or fourteen would scour the beach for driftwood thrown up by the nightly gales. His clothes were patched, his boots in need of cleaning and repairs, but his countenance was clear, as yet untouched by age or anger or regret. From time to time, he'd pause to listen for the sound of waves against the rocks that marked the tide's approach, then either carry on his search or flee, his bundle awkward in his arms, the rising water snatching at his heels.

The tide had almost caught him once. He'd been standing staring at a solitary tern wheeling high above his head and forgot to listen for the sound of waves on rocks; forgot the danger of the tide, forgot the driving rain and the ever-growing fog, and the risk of drowning in the cold, dark sea. The loud and sudden cawing of a crow upon the heights had alerted him in time but only just. He'd made the cliff, his bundle lost, the rising water dragging at his arms and legs. He'd sworn he'd not return, but the fires needed tending and there was no one else to do it and so, each day, he risked the fog and rain and tide to bring his family light and warmth.

This day he picked his way along the stony beach and smiled. It was unusually mild for winter, bright and clear, although the host of thunderclouds on the horizon threatened rain to come. He'd gathered several bundles of dry driftwood, tucking them partway up on the path for safety and, with luck, he'd get at least one more before the tide came in.

The tide.

"Stop being such a coward," he said between clenched teeth, his heartbeat sounding loudly in his chest. "It's barely afternoon."

He moved purposely away from the security of the path. With luck he'd find a fish or two trapped in a shallow pool, abandoned by the tide.

The tide.

"I said stop it!"

He jumped. He hadn't meant to shout. "And stop talking to yourself," he added with a nervous laugh. "Or mother will think you've gone mad and she won't let you leave. Finish your task. You almost have enough to keep the fires lit while you're away."

He reached for a piece of wood half again as tall as he was, then froze as a strange sound came to him above the crashing of the waves.

"What was...?" He shoved a lock of thick, black hair behind one ear and turned. "Was that ... tapping? What could be tapping?"

He closed his eyes, straining to catch the sound again. "Yes," he murmured. "Tapping, coming from ... the east."

He followed it.

He walked for nearly half a mile, pausing now and then to reacquire the sound and finally, came upon a huge, black raven, cracking its sharp beak against two rocks. At first he thought it might have found some creature for its dinner, for spots of blood were spattered everywhere, but then he saw the bird was trapped, one leg bent, the other driven deep inside a narrow crack between the rocks. It struggled, beat the air with outstretched wings, then slumped, beak open, breathing with a ragged, panicked hiss.

Water slapped against his boots. He froze.

The tide.

The bird.

The. Tide.

"It will drown," he told himself. "If you don't help it, it will drown."

But with no gloves, he saw no way to free it without bringing his hands so close he risked his fingers to its stabbing beak. With such an injury, he'd never climb the cliff and, if he couldn't climb the cliff, then he would drown.

He watched the raven raise its head, then drop it down again against its breast, exhausted, and knew he couldn't leave it there to die.

He squared his shoulders. "So, help it, and with luck, you won't both drown."

He stepped forward and the raven snapped its head around to stare at him, its black eyes, glassy and unfocused.

"Easy now," he whispered, trying for as calm a tone as he could manage around the pounding of his heart. "Easy. I won't hurt you and, if you don't hurt me, I'm sure that I can help you," He took a few steps closer. "My Granny always said that ravens were intelligent, so I'll just keep on talking, and with luck, we'll both come out of this unscathed." He took another step and then another, fetching up against the rocks a moment later. The raven's feathers ruffled in the wind, but otherwise it held itself immobile as he knelt and studied the rocks carefully. "I think that I can see a way," he said. "If I can move this rock back just a little, you can free yourself, but I must bring my hands close to your beak, so if you wouldn't bite me..." Laying his palms flat against the rock, he slowly inched them forward. "...I'd be grateful." The bird swiveled its head almost upside down to get a better look and the boy froze again, then swallowed hard and, forcing himself forward until, just out of reach, he took a long, deep breath. Narrowing his eyes so all he saw was the bleeding leg, he drove his fingers in-between the rocks and pulled, all the while expecting to feel the bird's sharp beak stab down across his knuckles. The bird jerked free, nearly toppling over backwards, and the boy scrambled hastily away.

Hopping on one foot, the raven hissed in pain, then straightened. "Thank-you, Brannon ap Emyr," it said, bowing low, its wings outstretched as if it held a cloak aloft.

The boy blinked, more from the raven's familiarity with his name than from its ability to speak.

"How do you know me?" he asked.

"I've known you all your life, from the time your mother named you for our people," the raven answered. "And I've watched you growing, day by day, and year by year."

It glanced up at the cliff face, and then back. "Tell me," it asked, its casual tone belied by the sharpness of its gaze. "Your family is a noble one, ancient, proud and powerful; why do you gather firewood each day as a pauper's son might do?"

Brannon bridled at its words. "My family is a noble one," he said. "We once ruled all these lands between the mountains and the sea." He shrugged. "But Fate has not been kind to us. I do my part to keep the fires lit and, one day, I will be a knight and win glory, fame, and honor for my family and we will rule them once again."

"Will you now?" the raven chuckled. "Well, that's a worthy quest, indeed, and one I hear, that may soon come to pass. The young King Arthur and his court are wintering at Caerleon, are they not?"

"They are"

"And you will travel there in three days time?"

Brannon nodded. "With my brother, Tegid, whom I serve as squire. I'm to be presented to the King."

"Well then, your path's assured and you seem assured to set your foot upon it," the raven noted. "You know what lies ahead, that's plain, but do you know what lies behind?"

Brannon stilled. "I do," he answered quietly. "Six of my brothers have gone questing to prove themselves worthy of King Arthur's court and so regain the glory of our family, but all have come to grief. The first, my eldest brother, Rhys, now wastes away, unable to take food or drink but what little can be pressed upon him by our mother. The second, Gofann, was carried home upon a litter, and sits and stares out at the cold, gray sky, reliving memories he cannot share. The third, Caswall, has become a drunkard and no longer has a generous word or gentle glance to give to anyone where once he was the kindest of them all. I have never met my brother, Pwyllin. I'm told he wanders in the wilderness, forever seeking something he can never find, and Llenac, my fifth brother, cares for riches only and has turned his back on chivalry and family."

He fell silent.

"And the sixth?" the raven prompted.

"The sixth is Tegid," the boy sighed. "He carries some dark secret deep within his breast that makes him so ashamed, he cannot look us in the eye. He will not speak of it and so it eats away at him."

"And if you could change all that?" the raven asked. "If you could save them all or even one, what would you do?"

Brannon straightened. "All that I could do," he answered.

"Even if it meant traveling paths they traveled, braving dangers that they braved, and risking ends they risked?"

"How could I do less?"

"Even though they failed?"

"I will not fail."

The raven swiveled its head sideways. "You're not a man yet and I'm loathe to set this quest before you at such a tender age, but time is short. You are the last of your great line, and if you journey to King Arthur's court before we speak, my chance to aid you will be lost." It shook its feathers out and sighed. "Your brothers would not heed my words and so they fell and all that I could do was see them home again. But still, it's only fair that you should have your chance." It set its injured leg upon the ground, then drew it back up with a harsh croak. "But first, I need to rest." Settling itself into a shallow pocket in the sand, it dipped its head to indicate that Brannon should do likewise The boy glanced worriedly at the sea, then sat with his back pressed against the rocks where he could keep his eyes on both on the raven and the tide.

"My family is noble one, as ancient, proud and powerful as yours," the bird began. "And there was once a time when we too ruled these lands, but such responsibilities grew burdensome, and the strength of our great people, which is found in council and in frolic, not in earthly power, waned. So, on a cold mid-winter morning long ago, the greatest of our kin, the Raven King, made as bargain with a man, Mabrad ap Morfran was his name. For the gift of lordship over all these lands, when all was fast secured, Mabrad would set aside his power and serve the Raven King, content to know his family ruled with strength and honor through the years.

"Mabrad agreed and, with the gift received, he soon defeated all his enemies, but when the Raven King came to him to fulfill their bargain, Mabrad refused. The lands were not secured, he claimed, his son too young to rule. Grant him one more year, he promised, just one more year to ensure his line's survival. And so the Raven King withdrew. One more year it granted him and then another, and another. Mabrad had strong sons who had strong sons and every year his power increased, but every year he claimed the lands were not secured; each year, he asked for one more year, until at last, he died, the bargain unfulfilled.

"The Raven King went then to Mabrad's grandson, Amathell, now upon the throne, but his grandfather had kept the story of their bargain secret, claimed the rising of the family's fortune as his own, and so the Raven King was turned away. He took his own court with him, never to return, and so the power of Mabrad faded 'til his latest heir now rules a cold, empty hall while his youngest gathers firewood like a churl.

"But for helping me this day," it continued before Brannon could respond, "I offer you a gift and then a choice, a gift to help you raise your family's fortunes once again, and a choice that may be freely made without unwilling service and without regret or fear.

"Far to the west there is a place of power halfway between the cliff top and the sea. There are steep steps, some fifty-two descending, though more returning, and in that place there is a well in which the waters are the purest in the land and a seat of stone cut deep within the wall. Drink from the well and pass behind the seat and there you'll find a tight crevasse that seems at first to be impenetrable, but if a boy, both thin of frame and stout of heart, was to creep within it, turn about three times and make a wish!" The raven jerked itself upright, meaning to beat the air with wings outstretched, only to squawk in pain as the motion pulled against its injured leg. "Bran's blood, that hurts!" it rasped. "Make a wish and all might come to pass as he most dearly wants it to," it finished, more subdued.

"Do I wish for my brothers to be healed?" Brannon asked.

"Well, yes, you could..." the raven answered with a sly expression. "...and trust that such a vague request would result in happy endings all around, but is that how such matters usually transpired in your grand dame's stories?"

Brannon's shoulders slumped. "No."

"No. But if you were to, say instead, wish for leave to journey to a secret cavern deep within the cliff and there to chose a single treasure that might see your family's fortunes well restored, and come away with it, back to this very time and place, with luck, as you so often say, that just might do the trick."

"It seems a rather complicated wish."

"Landing in the sea a thousand years from now is infinitely more so,"

"Yes, I suppose that's true." A chill breeze swirled about them. Brannon shivered. "Is it far?"

"As crows fly, no. As boys trudge through a land of fog and wind and rain, perhaps. But I'll come with you as a guide and, if you heed my council, you just might get there and back before you have to leave for Caerleon."

It stood, setting its foot down, then shook its feathers out again. "But come, we must away, the tide draws near."

Brannon scrambled to his feet and would have fled but for the raven's outstretched wing.

"Meet me at dawn tomorrow by your father's gate," it said. "Tell no one of your quest and bring nothing with you but your knife: no sword, no shield, no food, nor drink, no blanket and no lamp to light your way, and we will see what can be made of you."

It leaped into the air and, circling once above his head, it gave a loud, triumphant caw, then disappeared above the cliff and Brannon took off running.

Fear compelled him and he made the path in time, the rising tide just slapping at his heels. His back pressed hard against the cliff, his breathing pained, he stared up at the sky, but nothing could be seen and, finally, he straightened.

"Get up," he said. "Get up and to your work. The fires still need tending, whatever comes to pass."

He shouldered the first bundle, and ignoring the loud pounding of his heart, began to climb.

The next morning, he met the raven as agreed. The bird stood on the gatepost, tearing at some creature, but looked up, entrails dangling from its beak, as he approached.

"Did you heed my words?" it asked.

"I've brought no food, nor blanket," Brannon answered. "And I have no sword..."

"But...?"

"But..." He gave the raven a beseeching look. "I met my mother on the stairs. I didn't tell her of my quest, but she guessed and pressed me to bring a flask of water at the very least if I was to go wandering about the wild on some fool's quest and get myself eaten by wolves and break her heart..." He trailed off.

"A mother's request is not too lightly set aside," the raven noted with a sage expression. "You must do as you feel right, but if you will take my council, a flask can be a hindrance if it catches on a rock and causes one to lose one's footing."

Brannon looked from bird to flask, then set it by the gatepost with a sigh. Finished with its grisly meal, the raven rose into the air, and landed heavily on his shoulder, beating at his head as Brannon jerked back in surprise.

"Steady on!" it scolded. "I'm still injured!"

"You startled me."

"Did you think I was to fly to journey's end?"

"I… yes."

"The more fool, you."

"But—"

"Time is of the essence, Brannon ap Emyr. We have but two, short days to make it to the cavern and it's going to rain. Do you plan to stand here arguing all morning?"

"I… no."

"Then let's begin." The raven poked his head quite sharply with its beak. "The path is that way."

With a sigh, Brannon set off walking.

They soon left cliff and manor house behind. A fog that had begun as mist soon closed around them and Brannon would have lost his way but for the raven's council.

"How did my brothers fall?" he asked after they had walked a time in silence. "You said you could only see them home. Did you set this quest before them too?"

The raven sighed. "I could bring your brother, Tegid, neither quest nor council, for he fell at the first hurdle," it answered sadly. "He feared my beak and so he did not aid me when he came upon me trapped and helpless in the rocks but turned aside and regrets his actions to this day."

Brannon hung his head. "I also feared your beak," he admitted quietly.

"Fear was the challenge, not the deed," the raven answered. "You overcame your fear and so won through. You have nothing to regret."

They continued on, again in silence, into a forest of tall, dark trees until they saw a pale light shining in the distance. As they drew closer, they came upon a clearing, ringed with torches. A golden mantel lay spread upon the ground and on it, a great feast was laid: oysters, poultry, fish and joints of meat with loaves of bread were piled on silver plates, beside deep pots of thick, dark honey, and tall, wide cups of wine and milk. Blue plums, bright cherries and green pears with piles of rosy apples lay beside great rounds of cheese and bowls of nuts as big as Brannon's fists. On a low table, egg pies, seed cakes, furmenty and custards steamed, with odors rich and varied. Brannon's stomach growled and he was suddenly aware of how far he'd traveled and long it had been since he'd last eaten.

At that moment, a host of revelers appeared between the trees. They were clad in glossy robes of iridescent black, their hair was long and dark, and their black eyes shone with both a bright and merry light. One shouted greetings as he spotted Brannon and the boy took a step forward but halted as the raven's talons dug deep into his shoulder.

"Go," it said. "Take food and drink, but heed my words, for this is how your eldest brother, Rhys, did fall. Drink only of the purest water, and eat the simplest fare, no matter how you're pressed and, when your hunger and your thirst are slacked, you may rest, but only on the ground or you may sleep too long and come too late to carry on your quest."

It took wing into the branches of the nearest tree as Brannon moved into the glade and was swallowed up by the revelers.

How long he sat among them, listening to their singing and their tales he couldn't tell. The company pressed him to partake of every delicacy but, remembering the raven's words, he drank only from a flagon of clear water and took a plate of simple meat and fruit until a girl his age, her hair as black as his, her eyes unfathomable and inviting, knelt before him and offered him a cup of wine. Looking deep into her eyes, he took it from her, fingers trembling, but as he bent his head to drink, he heard a harsh and guttural cry and, dropped it with a startled jerk so that it splashed against his hand and burned. The girl just laughed and swirled away.

The night wore on and, finally, the gathered drew him to a bower spread with furs and bade him rest a while, but the welt upon his hand blazed suddenly and he curled up beside it the ground instead, his arms wrapped around himself for warmth, and tried to sleep. When he awoke, the bower was empty of both revelers and feast.

The raven peered at him from within a nest of breast feathers. It glanced once at the burn mark on his hand, but said nothing, merely returned to its perch upon his shoulder as they headed through the trees.

Eventually, Brannon glanced at it. "That was your warning, wasn't it? The cawing in the distance?"

"It was," the raven answered.

"And if I had drunk the wine?"

"You would have desired it above all else, and craving it so badly, you would have hunted for it every day in every glass you found."

"As Caswall does," Brannon breathed in sudden understanding.

"As Caswall does," the bird agreed, real sadness in its voice. "Choice is always set before you. Choose the path of idleness and plenty if you wish, but know the price you pay to do it. Sometimes it's higher that you think and when you look back upon your life you may regret the path you chose too late."

They continued on their way, Brannon deep in thought, the raven dozing, its head cushioned in its feathers. Eventually, the dappled sun gave way to mist and then to rain. The wind picked up and, in the distance, Brannon though he heard a strange and feral sound above the rustling of the trees. He froze.

"Was that ... baying? What could be baying?"

"The questing beast," the raven answered, and Brannon jumped, unused to having someone with him when he spoke.

The sound grew closer, filling all the spaces between the trees with a yelping, howling roar, until a great, dark beast exploded from the mist. It had a serpent's head, a leopard's body and its flashing hooves were like a deer's. It launched itself at them and Brannon scrabbled for a sword that wasn't there. He drew his knife instead and, as the baying filled his ears, the beast attacked. Brannon stumbled backwards, slashing blindly as he fell and sending the raven flying upwards with a startled squawk. The beast passed over him like smoke, carving a thin line of red across his cheek, then twisted in midair to become two. They spun about and charged.

"What do I do?" Brannon shouted, throwing himself to one side as the beasts passed over him once more, carving another line, this time across his other cheek, then turned and became four. They crouched like cats after a mouse, weaving back and forth, then coiled and sprang.

"Use what skills you have developed to face the dangers of your life so far," the raven shouted back.

"Skills? I have no skills, I've faced no danger!" Brannon dodged behind a tree, feeling the hot breath of the four beasts across his neck and one sharp tooth across his forehead as they passed.

The four beasts split apart, became eight beasts, and crouched again.

"You face the danger of the tide each day! Use what skills you have developed there!"

As the beasts leapt towards him, Brannon forced himself to stand, listening for the sound of their approach as he'd listened for the tide. He heard the baying hounds, the pounding hooves ... then struck, driving his knife into the belly of the central beast. It screamed and staggered, then flung itself away into the trees, trailing spots of blood behind it.

Brannon sank to his knees, his breathing loud and ragged.

"My brother, Gofann ... he gasped out.

"Feared to leave his weapons on the wall," the raven answered, returning to his shoulder. "He faced the creature bravely, but could not slay it, no matter how hard he fought, striving to cleave each creature as they charged, believing he fought many and believing he could slay them all."

It pecked the line of crimson trickling down his cheek. "This challenge was not of solitary arms," it said as Brannon brushed it absently away. "And not everything is as it seems. Look and listen, think before you act. Use what skills you have to win the day.

"Your brother Pwyllin, discovered its true nature, dealt it a mighty blow and drove it off, but eager to defeat it, he pursued it through the woods and pursues it to this day, his quest forgotten in his need to have the prize of battle won."

"So Pwyllin's near?"

"Perhaps," the raven answered, digging through its feathers with indifference. "If you pursue the creature through the trees, perhaps you might meet up with him and hunt it down and bring him home." The raven trailed off, watching the boy intently. "Was this your quest, to find your brother?"

"No, but..."

"Then you must choose," it interrupted. "To alter course, abandon quest, and seek him out. The creature's blood lies fresh upon the ground along the western path. Our way leads east. Decide."

Brannon thought long and hard. "This challenge was to think before I act and use what skills I had to win the day," he echoed. "I have not yet the skills to find my brother in this place. And if I run off thinking only of the battle's prize, my brother, and not consider all, I might lose myself as surely as he did."

He looked over at the raven, his eyes tight. "I will not find him, will I?"

"No. It would be bravely done and with the best intentions, but ill conceived and so doomed to failure from the start. When to fight and when to wait is a hard and bitter lesson in this age of chivalry."

Brannon scrubbed the blood across his forehead with his sleeve, then struggled to his feet and, turning from the creature's trail, headed east, the raven clutching at his shoulder as he ran.

Eventually, his grief gave way to weariness and the trees to open ground, and finally they came to a high cliff, a set of ancient steps, well worn and slippery from the rain, leading down into the mist.

Brannon took a breath, then began a slow descent and came at last to the stone seat and ancient well midway between the cliff top and the sea.

The raven dropped and pecked about the shifting pebbles, catching up a snail and banging it against the well with a familiar tapping sound.

"Here you may refresh yourself," it told him, spattering small bits of shell across the ground, "before you venture further."

Brannon peered into the well. The water sparkled and, as he dipped his cupped hands in, the shock of the cold water almost made him gasp, but drawing up a handful, he drank deeply, the water flowing down his throat in icy solace. He drank another and another, almost frantically, but straightened as the raven pecked him sharply on the ankle.

"A belly full of water will impede your progress just as surely as a flask," it scolded. "And time is short; the light is failing, or do you wish to find the crevasse in the dark?"

"No."

"Then start your search."

The raven jabbed a wingtip at the wall behind the seat and Brannon left the well with true reluctance. He found the crevasse easily enough, but frowned at it in doubt.

"It's very tight," he noted.

"Then it's well you carry nothing that might impede your progress."

When Brannon hesitated still, the raven hopped onto the seat and glared at him. "Do you think that I have brought you here to fail?" It grated.

"No."

"Then trust that it is possible or choose to leave this place, your quest unfinished."

"But—"

"Surely one who's faced the peril of the tide each day and stood his ground before the questing beast would not be so afraid to hazard such a test as this?"

The raven's tone was so dismissive that Brannon blushed, and casting it a baleful glance, he took a breath, and letting it full out, he pushed into the crevasse.

Somehow, he gained entry and even turned around three times without quite strangling in his clothes, but it was close.

"Now what?" he asked, his voice a plaintive muffle.

"Make your wish."

"But I can't hardly breathe."

"Is that your wish? To make your breathing easier?"

"No."

"Then speak the words I counseled you to speak, both carefully and clearly."

Brannon closed his eyes, and gathering his thoughts, he spoke.

The crevasse opened up so suddenly that he fell forward, throwing out his hands and skinning both his palms and knees. Winded, he glanced up and saw the raven, suddenly before him. Beyond lay a tunnel lit by torches with no smoke nor blackening on the walls. He rose and, pressing hands against his chest, as the raven took its place upon his shoulder once again, he began to walk.

How long he walked, he could not tell. He started counting footsteps, and lost count, then started counting heartbeats, breaths, then torches and lost count. Finally the tunnel opened up to a vast cavern lit by silver lanterns hanging from above. The air was filled with music. Suits of armor stood by swords and spears and lances on the walls between rich tapestries depicting scenes of hunting, battles, courtly halls and deep, dark forests. Strewn about, as if by random chance, were treasures wondrous and magical.

"Choose," the raven whispered. "One item to restore your family's fortune, but beware. It's easy to get lost amid such riches as your brother, Llenac, did."

Brannon moved into the cavern, his eyes so wide they ached. Before him, he saw cauldrons, hampers, baskets, horns of plenty, all with exotic foodstuffs spilling from their depths, piled beside crocks and dishes of the finest porcelain. Golden bowls and silver cups were stacked on trunks of ebony and teak polished to a mirror finish.

"Choose," the raven said.

Coracles and boats of every size were pulled up, side by side. A golden halter lay beside a silver chariot. A spinning whetstone stood beside a spinning wheel, a red-hot forge and anvil by a working loom that wove, unraveled, wove again a scene of wandering and loss. He ran his fingers over raiment soft and shining, coats and mantels, girdles, boots and sandals, skins of seal and fox, of wolf and bear, and cloaks of feathers: swan and peacock, owl and eagle. Mighty chests brimmed high with rings and bracelets, crowns and circlets.

"Choose," the raven said again.

Golden harps and silver flutes played without musicians while a golden chess board with silver pieces played without opponents. By one wall, he saw beds and chairs which grew long, grew short, grew wide, grew tight. By the other, he saw statues of lean hounds, fine stags, vast dragons and wild boars, and one great leaping salmon. He saw chains of thorns and chains of bones and chains of gold and silver. He saw a large, smooth stone on which a spear, a sword, and cauldron lay. Another held a broken sword, a dripping spear and dish. A shadowed corner held a scepter, ampoule and a crown, and in the very center of the cavern by a well of silvery water, was a cup enshrouded by a mantle of pure light.

"Choose," the raven whispered. "Choose."

Finally he stood before a wall adorned by two large shields. The first to his amazement held his family's arms, the second showed three ravens, looking left and right and straight ahead.

"A gift and then a choice," the raven said, perching on a dark green mantle covering a massive axe. "A gift: To journey to a wondrous cave and choose one item to restore your family's fortunes, then a choice that may be freely made without unwilling service and without regret or fear. Take up the left hand shield and accompany your brother to King Arthur's court, live out your life as knight of the Round Table and make the name your own strength of will and arm and heart may make. Your family will sing the glory of your deeds and know some little comfort and no loss of fortune 'til you rest in quiet crypt beside your ancestors.

"But, take up the right hand shield and no one will ever know your name or sing your praise. You'll have little comfort, rare respite. Jewels will not adorn your brow, no comely maiden grace your arm, but years of great adventure, deeds of daring and of challenge will be yours. All will hear your stories, although none will know your name. Your family's hall will ring with children's laughter, fill with warmth and tranquil harmony, but you will not be there to share it with them.

"Either is a life of honor.

"Choose."

Brannon stared from one shield to the other.

"It was a raven," he said suddenly. "Not a crow, that saved me from the tide that day. It was you, Your Majesty."

He turned to see a tall and stately man with flowing hair and eyes as black and bright as in his raven's form. He wore a crown of stones and shells which glittered in the lantern-light, a cloak of iridescent feathers that merged from black to blue to purple as he moved, and a bore a silver sword within a jeweled scabbard.

"It was," he said.

"Why?"

"Why did you free me from the rocks?"

"I couldn't leave you there to die."

"Could I do less?"

"Because of Mabrad's debt?"

"His debt is not your debt, his Fate is not your Fate. That was expunged upon the beach."

"But all of this, the feast, the questing beast, these riches...?"

"Are no more, no less than what I told you, challenges to see what could be made of you. Now made, how you might be wielded? Mabrad's bargain can be yours. In my service taking up these objects, each a riddle, each a challenge, test, or quest for those who claim the name of knight or hero, heroine or king. You would be every unknown knight or maiden, crone or ancient man to come to Arthur's court in challenge or in supplication, bringing honor to those you face for many times a hundred years or more.

"Choose."

Brannon stared at the two shields, his expression torn."If I take up the left hand shield, my family will know my Fate, if I take up the right, my family, my mother, will wonder always if I came to grief and weep for me as often she weeps for Pwyllin."

The Raven King swiveled his head sideways. "This boon, I'll grant you. Take the right hand shield and your first test will be for Pwyllin. Win his freedom from the questing beast and he'll return to hearth and home with word of Brannon's fate."

Brannon turned back to the shields.

"Agreed," he said, and took the right hand shield.

The Raven King clad him in black amour, his youthful frame becoming a grown man's. He set a cloak of iridescent black upon his shoulders and a closed helm with black features on the crest upon his head. A belt of fine, black leather went around his waist, hung with a silver raven's headed sword in a black scabbard. Then, with a swoop of wings, the Raven King became a raven once again, and perched on his shoulder, Brannon found himself upon the south-west coast of Cymru once again. High above, a manor house, stood sentinel, no longer silent nor alone, with six large birds perched high upon its battlements.

"The tide is out," the raven said. "It's time to go."

— «» —

Fiona Patton is a fantasy writer who makes her home in rural Ontario. Her works include the four novels of the Branion Realm series and three novels in Warriors of Estavia, available from Daw Books, as well as a number of short stories in different markets. Fiona has also confessed to a love of Arthur, quests and especially ravens.

Loyalty of a Thousand Years

Wendy N. Wagner

Boris closed the apartment door behind him, hung up his work jacket — first checking the embroidered dancing rats and cockroaches for loose threads —set his boots on the rack beside the radiator, and went straight to the nearest calendar to make his daily notes. He kept a calendar in every room in case he came seriously unstuck in time, and he updated each one every few hours. He couldn't remember when the days started bleeding together, but a written record seemed to help.

For a brief stint before he'd started up the extermination company, he'd given up and just lived on the street. Time didn't matter much there, and no one cared if a middle aged homeless man suddenly started fighting the street art or began speaking medieval French at the soup kitchen. No one much cared about anything he did. But he'd found it wasn't in his nature to drift. Boris appreciated hard work and cleanliness. He relished his weekly shave and haircut at his barber.

Not that he led a life of luxury, he thought as he went from the mostly empty living room to the tidy kitchen to the spartan bathroom, adding the word "termites" to the 25th box on each calendar. Returning to the kitchen, he jotted down "tuna casserole" and began setting out the ingredients. He no longer knew which days should be fast days, so he'd mostly cut meat out of his diet. The Church seemed to have forgotten, too.

The phone in his pocket rang.

"Boris Bors."

"Boss." Gretchen sounded angry. Boris eyed the clock on the stove. 4:52 pm. No wonder she was mad — her kid's after-school program wrapped up at 5. "We've got an emergency call from a 'plex over by Lloyd Center. Some kinda snake in the basement."

"It's probably a rat," Boris soothed. "Tell them we'll have somebody over in the morning, then call Paulo and have him hit the place on his way to the house with the ant infestation."

"The manager sent over a picture. It's not a rat. It's white, and there are definitely scales. They're already talking about calling CaliPest."

His sense of chivalry kept him from swearing out loud. She was right, of course. Those bastards from California had already picked off three of his regular apartment complexes. He couldn't afford to lose this account, or worse, get a bad Yelp review.

"All right. All right. I can be there in," he glanced at the clock again, "an hour. Traffic's going to su—slow me down."

Gretchen chuckled. "'Suck' isn't even swearing, Boris, and you don't have to protect my delicate ears. I'll call the client. You need me to stick around?"

"Naw. Rita's waiting for you."

She hung up, sounding pleased.

Boris went to his nearly empty bedroom and opened his top drawer. A creepy white snake. He'd been working in extermination on and off for fifteen hundred years, and if he'd learned one thing, it was that you didn't mess with a reptile without God on your side.

He put his largest silver cross around his neck, and on second thought, rooted through the socks for the dagger Guinevere had given him.

Snakes.

He should have moved to Ireland instead of the US.

— «» —

As he'd expected, traffic on the four-oh-five barely crawled along. The steady red blink of taillights worked like a soporific in Boris's head. He fought the press of memory, and failed.

Red. It was Italy, just before the invasion of Libya. Even the rain smelled like grapes. The woman holding his hand kissed his cheek, her lips soft even if her hand felt work-roughened. She led him into the little cottage and shoved him onto the bed.

Red. He crouched beside the lake, his armor piled in a heap beside him. The black water refused to show him his own face. Somewhere in the distance someone sang, their voice neither male nor female, barely human in its quavering. "Tell me Arthur will return," he begged. He slammed his fist against the surface of the water. "Tell me he will!" A tendril of fog sped across the water, twisting around his fist.

Red. The Saxon pinned him to the ground, his eyes wild, his beard gore-spattered. Boris pawed at the ground, feeling for the sword he'd lost or the dagger the wild man had chopped out of his hand. The barbarian closed his hands around Boris's throat.

Then a bright steel flashed and the Saxon's head flew off its neck.

"How'd you get yourself into this mess, Sir Bors the Younger?" Arthur tossed the spurting body sideways and held out his hand, laughing.

With a gasp, Boris stomped on the brake. He'd nearly rammed the Prius in front of him, his head so lost in the jumble of memories that he'd forgotten he was driving. But it had all felt so real, more real by far than this comfortable life he'd built for himself. He could even taste the blood and mud of that field in Cornwall.

He muscled the truck across two lanes of traffic to get off at the next exit, client expectations be damned. He needed a coffee, the hotter and sweeter the better.

The girl at the coffee stand posed alluringly in her bikini top as she took his order, and he had to look away. She reminded him too much of the woman in Italy. He had loved her, whatever her name had been. He wasn't sure what hurt most — losing her, or losing track of the memory of her. The snippets that came to him flitted through his mind like bits of mist chased by the heat of the sun. Or in this case, the scorching rays of time.

He squeezed shut his eyes and breathed deep the scent of espresso. He hadn't learned to drink coffee until Starbucks began colonizing the world. The smell felt safe, felt solid. When he had coffee in his hand, it grounded him to his life in the now: the small company he'd built from the ground up, his apartment, the occasional class he took at the local community college. Every Sunday he read the newspapers of four different countries, looking for signs he was no longer alone in this cold, uncanny time. Every Monday, he brought donuts to work to share with Gretchen and Paulo.

"Pumpkin spice latte."

He blinked at the barista a second and then held out a twenty. "Keep the change." He turned the engine back on, then stuck his head out the window. "And check out Starbucks. They help pay for college now."

She just stared at him.

Sometimes he couldn't help trying to save people. They never seemed to appreciate it, but he couldn't stop himself.

— «» —

Boris rang the bell marked 'Manager'. A dog barked someplace in the depths of the building. He hitched up his belt; the sweet coffees weren't helping his waistline any. Setting rat traps and spraying for roaches wasn't the same kind of exercise as swordplay or working in the grape fields. Not for the first time, he wondered if he could afford to stable a horse someplace. Jousting — that had to burn calories.

"Yeah?" The blonde woman standing in the doorway looked as if she'd been waiting for a response for far too long.

Boris cleared his throat. "Boris Bors Extermination. Heard you've got a snake problem."

The woman shifted her little dog to her other arm. The pair looked disconcertingly alike, with masses of fluffy hair threatening to swallow their face. The dog wriggled in her grasp. He wrenched his eyes away from its struggles to focus on the woman.

"—basement," she was saying. He hoped the coffee kicked in soon, because the time slippage was killing his concentration.

He followed the woman to a door marked 'Boiler Room'. She fussed with a ring of keys for a moment, finally giving up and putting the dog down on the ground. It skittered in a circle around Boris' boots, and when the door opened, shot down the stairs with improbable speed.

"Bunny!" The woman stomped her foot. "Goddamned dog. Probably going to get eaten."

Boris reached for the light switch at the top of the stair. "This time of year, a snake's usually in torpor. Bunny ought to be fine." A current of warm, dry air drifted up the stairwell.

The woman crinkled her nose. "Do you need anything else?"

He raised his toolbox. "I'm sure I've got what I need in here. Snakes are sort of my specialty."

With one last, hopefully comforting, smile, he hurried down the stairs. But of course, he didn't mean snakes. He meant wyrms.

— «» —

The abbey lay in smoking ruins, and the novitiate who had guided Boris could no longer talk. The boy had already vomited twice, and now his shoulders shook with mute terror and sorrow. Boris stepped over a limbless torso and peered down the hole. He was probably looking into the remains of the abbey's wine cellar. A sulfurous stink rose up from it now.

"I'll need a lantern," he said.

The boy let out a whimper.

Boris put his hand on the boy's shoulder. "It'll be all right, lad. Did you not pray to the Lord for help, and did He not send you to the very inn where I, Bors the Younger, waited? Now buckle on your faith and help me find a lantern."

The boy wiped his nose on the back of his hand, nodded, and then ran out of the half-demolished kitchen.

The knight turned back to the pit, reaching for the rosary he wore around his neck. "Dear Lord," he murmured. "Infinite is your wisdom, and I live to serve. But a wyrm? Again?"

— «» —

A steady yipping brought Boris back to the boiler room. He pulled out the Maglight on his belt. "Where you at, Bunny?"

The lone light bulb at the bottom of the stairs failed to penetrate the gloom of the crowded space. Shelves of cleaning supplies and stained paint cans lined every wall, and bags of mysterious chemicals sat in saggy heaps all around the floor. At the far end of the room, the boiler sat, big enough to heat the entire apartment complex and perhaps one or two of the neighboring houses. The smells of dust and heating oil nearly covered the faint, crisp stink of sulfur. The little dog gave a fierce growl.

"There you are." Boris put down the toolbox and stooped in front of a shelf, stretching out his hand to the little beast. "Come out, you little rascal."

Something white flashed behind the shelf, and the dog darted out. It stopped behind Boris, barking vaingloriously.

Boris's free hand went to the cross at his neck. "In nomini Patri—"

"Oh, don't start with that rubbish." The voice was as dry as the rustling of its scales. Boris couldn't make out more than a sliding movement of white, but it seemed the creature moved back toward the hulking giant of a furnace.

He took a cautious step to his left, following the creature's movement.

"I was raised atheist," the wyrm said, and then broke into a volley of laughter like a series of dry coughs. "What I mean, since my kind is abandoned to hatch ourselves, is that I've *eaten* mostly atheists. Everyone is these days. Even your weekly mass-goer doesn't really believe."

"I believe."

"But you're not like most people, are you?"

Boris caught a quick flash of green in the darkness behind the furnace, like light playing over emeralds. He tightened his grip on the cross. "What do you mean?"

"You tell me. What do I know of the world, after all, slithering through the basements of this small city, keeping always to the shadows? Even the other snakes fear me and keep themselves scarce."

Boris moved the flashlight to his armpit and reached behind him for the toolbox. "Pity the monster, so sad and alone," he mocked.

With a hiss, the thing raised its head high enough for Boris to catch a glimpse. Its head was the size of maybe two Bunny's. It couldn't be a very big wyrm, certainly no more than twelve feet long.

"You're what, twenty years old?" Boris asked.

"What's a year but more darkness and a different sewer to explore? What is time beyond another stupid human screaming at me or another exterminator spraying their wretched sprays? I have spent all my life hunted and knowing I was destined for something better."

Boris released the catch on the toolbox and felt for the dagger he'd stowed beneath the top tray. "Awfully pathetic for the kin of a dragon."

The green eyes flashed, very nearby. "You know my kind."

"I've killed many. I once killed three wyrms with one slash of my sword. I even faced down one of the last true dragons and ate a slice of its black heart."

"What *are* you?" the wyrm breathed.

"I am Bors the Younger, a knight of Arthur's table. That is all."

"You are as much a stranger in this place and time as I am," the wyrm declared. "Even in the places I have lived, I have heard of Arthur."

Boris found the dagger. He wasn't surprised that the wyrm knew something of the tales. The stories, like Boris, had diminished over the years, but every generation had its Arthur. Boris rarely figured in the newer tellings, although sometimes someone remembered the story of Galahad and the Fisher King, and the great, long quest for the Grail. Boris wished he had another coffee. The sulfur made his head spin. If he let go of his cross, he might spin right out of this basement and back to England.

"What are you doing?" the wyrm asked sharply. "You've gone awfully quiet."

Boris played the flashlight's beam along the edges of the room, confirming his guess at the wyrm's size. He caught a glimpse of a vestigial hind leg, a fragment of black fabric still caught on one filthy talon. Probably the remains of some poor homeless person. These things always hungered for human flesh — dragons, sea serpents, wyverns, wyrms. They never forgave humanity for their exile from Eden, despite their own complicity in it.

"It's been close to a hundred years since I've seen or heard of a wyrm," he mused. "I wonder just how you got here."

The rustling came from behind him,and he spun around just in time to see the thing dart back under cover. He wasn't the only one taking the other's measure.

The beast chuckled. "Don't worry, sir knight. I am still interested in your tale. You're not in any danger — yet."

And its eyes sparkled again in the glow of the flashlight.

— «» —

"Don't worry, sir knight. You're safe here." The girl wiped his forehead and eased him back down on the pile of furs. Her golden hair circled her head in a crown of ribbons and braids, and her smile crinkled the corners of her blue eyes.

"Where am I? Where's Galahad?" He struggled to sit up, and she pushed him back down as if he were no stronger than a kitten. His head throbbed.

"You stepped on an adder. Galahad has gone to Merlin for a cure. But I think you shall be well long before they arrive. I have tended you most expertly." She stood up with the grace of a lady. He recognized the insignia woven into her girdle — the green fish, the golden chalice, the symbols of the Fisher King.

"Are you a witch or a princess?"

She laughed and reached for a wineskin on the shelf beside her. "Do I look like a witch?" She poured a stream of golden wine into a small clay cup. "Now, drink this."

He stared at the cup. A strange ruddiness seemed to come out of the clay itself, staining the fragrant wine.

"It will make you well," she said, in her sweet, kind voice, and he lifted his head. The cup felt warm against his lips.

He drank.

— «» —

A fierce pain in Boris's legs wrenched him out of the past, and Bunny gave a yelp as Boris shook him off.

"So why are you here when Lancelot and the others are long gone?"

The wyrm's head floated directly in front of Boris's face, its tongue flickering. Boris lashed out with the dagger, striking sparks off its scaled snout. The creature darted back, chuckling.

"You're so *broken*! So utterly, enchantingly broken!"

Boris took a step backward. Hadn't he himself thought the very same thing? Every year it was harder to stay grounded in the now. It was as if every new memory added depth to the pool of a thousand years of living, his struggles to stay afloat growing weaker every passing season. No one was meant to live forever, to *know* forever. It was simply too much.

"Yes, it's true," the wyrm mused happily. "The last of Arthur's knights, broken and hallucinating in the bowels of a shabby apartment complex, barely able to fend off the predations of a creature such as myself. The irony is delicious."

The wyrm began to circle the room, its spiral drawing closer and closer to Boris' feet. The scales rustled and hissed hypnotically.

"Have you been waiting for Arthur to rejoin you in this world?" It gave a snort. "I can see by your face that you have! Oh, patient knight, so stupid and loyal. Like a dog waiting for its master to return when the man himself is long dead and gone."

Boris trembled. Hadn't he thought something like this a dozen times, a hundred times, in different years, in different accents? Now in French as artillery fire echoed off the banks of the Seine. Now in Portuguese as he walked away from a failing sugar plantation. Now whispering it to himself as he crouched in an alley behind a Salvation Army shelter. Yes, he was still waiting for Merlin to come out of his cave and for the Lady in the Lake to deliver Arthur back to the world. To save them all and bring back the days of magic and heroes. To make him a knight again.

The wyrm twisted around his legs, its coils lapping higher and higher up his body, squeezing tighter and harder. Bunny yipped in a panicked voice.

No, Boris did not belong here or now — no more than did this stinking, vicious wyrm.

He drove the dagger into its side.

The creature shrieked. A tiny flame sparked on its fetid breath, just hot enough to make the hairs on Boris's skin smoke. Boris twisted the blade, forcing the steel through bone and muscle toward the creature's faithless heart.

"I was given a gift," he growled. The wyrm went rigid as the dagger hit home. "And if I must wait a hundred *thousand* more years for him to return, then I will."

The creature slid off Boris' blade and hit the floor with a thud. Bunny bounded over to sniff at it. The little dog wagged its tail.

The door at the top of the stairs opened with a rush of fresh air. "Hey, are you done yet? I was thinking about making some coffee."

Boris blinked up at the silhouette in the doorway. He hadn't noticed the woman's faint Welsh accent before. It reminded him of someone that right now he couldn't quite remember. He wondered what color her eyes were.

"Coffee, did you say? That sounds good."

— 《》 —

Wendy N. Wagner is the author of Skinwalkers and Starspawn, both Pathfinder Tales novels, and An Oath of Dogs from Angry Robot. Her short fiction and poetry has appeared in over three dozen venues. She is the managing/associate editor for Lightspeed Magazine and Nightmare Magazine and served as guest editor for Queers Destroy Horror! And the nonfiction editor for Women Destroy Science Fiction! and Women Destroy Fantasy! Wendy works, lives and prepares for the zombie apocalypse in Portland, Oregon.

Before All Else

Shannon Allen

Caledwynn sat on the edge of his bed and watched the soft pink light of dawn creep across the floor. He raised his arms over his head pulling the tightness from his body. The night had been long, his dreams dark and unsettled. He ran his fingers through his hair as he walked to the wash stand. The coolness of the basin's water felt good as it scoured away the last of his unease. A walk, he decided would do him good. As he dressed the smell of bread baking in the kitchens wafted through his window, making his stomach rumble. Tempting as it was, he would grab a loaf on his way back. Right now, he needed to feel the fresh air in his lungs and the ground under his feet.

Soon, he was on the path leading to the Glen of the Cauldron where Fergal was standing guard. He was proud of the boy, the youngest to join the Brotherhood. Someday he would tell him, someday. Caledwynn stopped. In his musings, he had not realized how quiet it had become. Not a single bird sang. He stood as if he were stone. Here between village and glen, nothing disturbed the silence but the odor of brimstone lacing the air. It was the scent of only one thing. Arkin and his Black Hounds. Caledwynn's blood turned to ice as he realized where it was drifting from. He broke into a run covering the last of the path to the glen. His calls received no reply. Small clouds of dust marked his passage as he burst through the tree line ready for whatever awaited him. Neither beast nor raider greeted him. Instead it was the one sight he had hoped not to see. Three strides took him to the darkened form. Caledwynn dropped, his knees dampened by the ground next to Fergal. Gently turning him over the wounds of a guard, who had held his post and his oath to his last breath, were laid bare. All Caledwynn could see was the boy who had followed him everywhere, who had been constantly underfoot with his play sword and shield. A boy who had grown into the guard he had sworn into the Brotherhood only yesterday.

He took Fergal's sword from his hand and laid it upon his chest. He stood, knowing what he would find when he entered the cave Fergal had died defending. He would look all the same. Passing through the opening he walked into the main chamber where his fears were confirmed. The Cauldron of Resurrection was gone.

— «» —

Standing by Fergal's funeral pyre, now nothing more than embers, Caledwynn watched as Viviane, Lady of the Lake, seemed to glide along the path towards the ridge upon which he stood. As she drew closer he watched as the silken tendrils of night played in her silver hair, the only real sign she was slowly aging. Cresting the pathway, she silently slipped in beside him and placed her hand upon his arm.

"He was too young. I should have made him wait." Caledwynn's voice was so quiet the wind almost took it away.

"It was all he ever wanted. To be like you."

"I should have…" Caledwynn straightened "I will bring the Cauldron home, make Arkin pay for what he has done."

Viviane moved in front of Caledwynn. "And the Brotherhood, what of them?"

"I gave orders that they are to wait. I will send word when I know which way he's gone." With the Mistress of the Cauldron gone from Avalon for years, many of them have been guardians in name only for too long. Should Arkin return, every man will be needed to protect Avalon from what could be unleashed. The loss of Fergal was enough.

He leaned over as Viviane reached up and gently kissed his damp cheek, both knowing the unspoken end to his statement. She stood there a minute longer before turning to leave.

"Safe journey, child of my heart." The last of her words faded.

Caledwynn knew she wouldn't turn for one last look as she left. Just as he knew that the tears now on her cheek were not for him to see.

— «» —

Caledwynn stopped on the trail looking for the next sign of which way to go. Nothing. Arkin was making this difficult, he moved as if a ghost, leaving very little for him to follow. It had been four days of tracking a thief who crossed the countryside like a madman, Arkin had to be somewhere with a goal in mind. If Avalon had been it, he would have attacked already. No, Caledwynn thought, he had bigger plans. During the days he had followed Arkin, Caledwynn had come across small deserted villages, beasts and food stores gone. All signs of raiders moving across the country side. If Arkin was with them, there was no indication. Deciding to head south he gave his horse a nudge. It pushed back at the request. Leaning over he ran his hand down the horse's neck as he looked to the trees. The horse stomped.

"All right boy" he leaned over and gave the horse a firm pat. Dismounting he headed towards the source of the horse's distress. As he pushed the last of the branches away to enter a hollow, he saw them. Dropping the reins, he ran to the men. He stopped at the first one, who lay on his back with youthful eyes gazing blindly at the sky. Death had come quickly to this one. Caledwynn closed the man's eyes before going to the next. These men, warriors all, had fought together, each falling in moments to some foe; one so vicious that they were all but torn apart. Their shields had stopped nothing. Caledwynn took hold of the man closest to him and turned him over. He recognized the wounds, Fergal had bore the same ones. These men were from somewhere, they would have people who cared for them. People who would want to know their fate. He looked about. There in the grass was the edge of a broken shield. Turning it over he carefully brushed grass and blood from the deeply wounded surface to reveal the remnants of a crest. The bearers of theses shields were no ordinary men. These men were of Camelot's Round Table.

—— ⟨⟩ ——

Caledwynn wiped his face with the back of his hand.

He had spent the last of the daylight burying the four men, marking each grave with their swords. A single horse, now calm, returned and was now tied up with his own. In the morning, he would tie the shields to its saddle and head for Camelot.

—— ⟨⟩ ——

At the edge of the trail, Caledwynn reined the horses to a halt and took in the view in front of him. Sunlight kissed walls of stonework. Elegant gates were swung wide open, allowing people to come and go. It was truly a sight to behold. Where Avalon was open to the air, the Veil her protection from the world, Camelot was enclosed in stonework. Magnificent stonework, but solid walls all the same. He sat for a few more minutes in the coolness of the trails edge before heading down to the main road. Delaying any longer would not change the nature or burden of his news.

As he rode closer to the gates he noticed people upon the road move to the sides, men removed caps. These shields were recognized. The men who had owned these held the trust of the people. His news grew heavier each time people moved or children ran ahead to give him way. Drawing closer to the walls, he looked to the ramparts. There a tall pacing figure abruptly stood still, leaned over the stonework, then disappeared. His pending arrival within the walls had been noted. He adjusted the trappings of his horse as he passed under the portcullis.

Caledwynn dismounted and waited for the two scurrying guards. "I have news of these men's fate. I wish to speak with Arthur."

A third man with confident strides now stood in front of him. "You speak with me."

"I speak with Arthur." Caledwynn looked over the burly man but gave no quarter.

"I am Kay, foster brother to the King, you speak with me. How did you come to have these?"

"In pursuing a man who killed one of my men, I found four men slain by vicious means. I buried them in the glen where they fell."

"How far from here?" Kay's shoulder's drooped.

"Three days north. "

Kay took the reins of the shield bearing horse and waved at a boy. "Take this horse to the stables then bring the shields to Arthur in the Great Hall and you?"

"Caledwynn"

"You will wait in the outer hall till I speak with Arthur. He will decide when he is ready to speak with you."

— «» —

Caledwynn had grown tired of waiting. Walls such as these stifled him. The air did not move, it clawed at him with fingers of subjugation. He headed to where he had entered, striding past a page before he could be stopped. To his right light leaked from under a door, he took it. Once clear, he found himself in a courtyard open to the air. Small it may be but the air was sweet with herbs and in the center stood a fountain, water dancing down into its basin. The simple song of the cascades drew him. Passing his hand through the cool water he noticed a moving carpet of black about a door in the far corner. The sunlight caught the mass reflecting a blue-black hue he recognized. Ravens. How odd that they would collect about a single door, maybe someone there feed them. He paid them no more than a glance until he realized they were coming towards him. He moved to the other side of the fountain, they took flight and landed in front of him. He dodged and twisted to no avail. No matter what he did the damned birds came down in his path. Taking a step backwards he found a solidness stopping him. Looking over his shoulder he saw he was at the door he had noticed just minutes before. The birds would not move so he knocked and entered without waiting for an answer.

"Come into the light and let me look at you. I want to see if I can find the boy in the man."

He had not expected to find anyone. When his eyes adjusted to the dim light he could see the bearer of the request. Caledwynn came forward but stopped just short of the old woman's reach. She raised herself from the chair. Leaning on a walking stick, she stepped into the window's light.

"I see you still carry the weight of the world. A promise made in the dark, a promise hidden in the dark, a bargain unfulfilled. He has no idea, does he?"

"Who?" Caledwynn drew a step closer.

"Merlin of course! Silly fool, he thinks he has the one, his prophecy." Cackling she moved to sit down, her legs giving out on her just as she found the seat. "He is wrong."

"You are mistaken. I am no one."

"Oh, but the marks on your shoulder mean you are."

Caledwynn found his hand start to raise to his shoulder, then he dropped it. How did this old crone know about them, when only one other did?

"Those marks your mother, Igraine, put there the day you were born. Then, kissing you on the forehead, she wrapped you in her wedding cloak and told me to take you to Viviane. In the trees beyond the castle I found her waiting, ready to answer her sister's call. Ready to take you, first born son of Uther Pendragon, away. Your Mother hoped to keep you from the scheming of men, in that she succeeded. Only fate can play cruel tricks, just as I returned, your mother birthed a second son. This time Merlin was waiting for the promise owed. You, child, are on a different path than the one Merlin schemed."

Caledwynn came and stood directly in front of the old woman. "That means, Arthur...."

"Is your twin brother, two sides of one coin, one fair, one dark. Of this Arthur knows not. Uther was ever watchful, so to keep you safe I stayed with your mother to make sure you stayed a secret." She took his hand in hers. "Now life has brought you to a crossroad."

"I am..." Caledwynn could feel his tunic dampen as the room started to spin. He pulled back his hand.

Laying her hands in her lap she drew in a haggard breath. "Listen to what you have been taught as it will serve you in good stead. Don't listen and the Cauldron will stay lost to you. For all of us, don't let it stay lost." She reached for him and he saw it. A faded blue crescent moon on her wrist. He knew the mark and knelt in front of her.

"Mistress of the Cauldron, you have long been gone from Avalon. Your apprentice and Avalon await your return."

"I have been away too long and I am old. A new Mistress will be named soon enough." Her hand brushed his cheek. "I am glad to have laid eyes on you one more time. I can see so much of your mother in you. I don't think Viviane has ever told you that."

His lungs refused to fill with the stale air. The words pulled at every corner of his mind. He trusted neither her words or his memories. He needed out. Giving the old woman a quick nod, he turned and clambered out the door. Eyeing the fountain, he quickly went to its side and plunged his head into its depths. Raising his head, he let the rivulets of water find their own way to the ground. His hands gripped the fountain's edge, fingers digging into the unyielding surface. Wood scraping stone rippled through the air causing him to look up. From across the courtyard a figure approached. This was no mere page. He recognized the man he had seen once as a boy hiding in the shadows of Viviane's hall. He stood and waited.

"King Arthur and the Lady Guinevere send their gratitude for the news of Camelot's knights. You are asked to stay, rest as the court grieves the loss of her noble knights. You will be sent for in a few days." Giving a nod, Merlin turned and headed towards an archway.

"I need to see him now!" The tone of Caledwynn's words caused Merlin to stop but not turn.

"Your knights went looking for something, my guess is the raiding of villages I have seen these last few days. They died as a result. Let me talk to Arthur now. There is much he needs to know. The scourge your knights faced out there and my quest are the same. We face a common foe."

"You have the message, you are to wait" A hand waved in dismissal.

"The Cauldron's gone." Caledwynn saw Merlin stiffen. "A man named Arkin, once one of the Brotherhood, has taken it. His evil has been growing for years, his goal was to possess and wield its power. Now that he has it he will unleash his darkness on us all."

Caledwynn waited, breathing the only exchange. After a moment, Merlin raised the hood of his cloak and vanished under an archway.

From outside the small wooden doorway a raven took flight.

— 《》 —

The air felt cool and clean as he drew it into the very depths of his lungs. Slowly he let it out. He drew in another greedily, his body once more in control as he pushed out the stale air of court and reveled secrets. He had ridden blindly out of the castle, he cared not for direction if it was away from the old woman's words and Merlin's indifference. Only the words had followed him. Thoughts crashed as if waves upon his memory. Why had Viviane not told him any of this? Igraine was her own sister. Did Igraine even know of his fate? Why had she never come, she could have passed through the veil at any time. One fact kept coming back, he had a brother, one who had also been pulled away and raised in shadow. Only Arthur had been able to return to their mother, know her in her last years. Something he had been denied. His breath became labored once more. He slid off the horse and wandered through the trees wiping leaves from his hair and face. He stopped. The tranquility of the place filled him and stilled his heaving chest, his fingers peeled from his sword hilt. Slowly he looked about and saw a raven watching him from a thick branch of an oak. So, Viviane knew. He would camp here then. Let her come.

— 《》 —

Caledwynn sat watching the flames lick the bark in hunger devouring each log in turn.

"So, you know." The words floated across the campfire.

He raised his eyes to meet hers. She stood there, alone. The trappings of the Lady of the Lake left behind. She was in this moment just a woman with her heartache laid bare.

"You should have told me."

"When Caledwynn? When you were five running around our rooms with wooden swords saving us from spiders. When you were ten, wishing you were fourteen so you could start training for the Brotherhood." She stopped, straightened her shoulders and walked through the fire. Gone was the woman, The Lady of the Lake in all her glory now stood in front of him.

"I took a sister's oath to keep you safe. To keep you out of the schemes of men. Till her dying day, your mother held onto that comfort."

Standing Caledwynn met her gaze. "If Arthur is my twin, why didn't Merlin see that?"

"Merlin sees what is to become, not the many paths to that end. His prophecy saw a son, so he only sees one. Never did he think the duplicity of his magic that night at Tintagel would cleave in two."

"By right, I could be King" Caledwynn let the words hang in the space between them.

Viviane picked up his sword. "Arkin is openly on the move in the north leaving suffering and destruction in his wake. The realm of men and Avalon are two sides of one world, just as you and Arthur are." Viviane held out his sword in front of her, "The weight of choice is now yours." Caledwynn reached for it and as his hands touched the blade Viviane faded into the moonlight.

Dawn wound its way through the trees and danced about the now cold fire pit. He hadn't moved all night, the sword still in his hands. He had tipped its weight from left hand to right and back again in rhythm with his mind's thoughts. Now, with the day's first light breaking, he knew it was time to return to Camelot.

Caledwynn could see him on the ramparts as he neared Camelot. Merlin's moving figure cast a stark contrast to the unmoving armed men. Had he been there all night? Caledwynn had a feeling that he had. As he passed through the arched gateway, no one stopped him. Yet, no one greeted him either. Stabling his horse, he headed for the one place of tranquility in the chaos of people within these walls. He had not been in the small courtyard long when the door at the end announced an arrival. Caledwynn looked up and did not see the expected figure walking towards him. He stood as tall as Caledwynn, a lightness in his step that his size contradicted. He saw fleeting reflections of his own face in the dark framed one now looking at him.

So, this must be Arthur.

"You have returned!" Arthur extended his hand. As Caledwynn extended his, the blue crescent upon his wrist was exposed. "So, you are a son of Avalon."

"A son and one of the Brotherhood that protects her."

"But even there, treachery lurks. Merlin tells me the Cauldron of Resurrection has been taken. Such a thing is in this world and I knew not. Why has it been in Avalon and not here under my care?"

"It did once reside here in the hands of one clan or another but as men grew in their lust for power, darkness leached into the land. Holding the means to bring back the dead, giving one an renewable army, corrupts one to the core. A solider named Galen saw the tentacles of darkness engulf his Liege causing a once kind man put power and greed above honor and valor. So, one night, Galen stole it hoping to rid the world of such a terrible thing, to free his Liege and the land. As he held no shades of darkness in his heart he had the ability to pass through the Veil and enter Avalon where he entrusted it to The Lady's care."

"People arriving at our gates tell of such horror. They tell of men cut down in battle only to be put into a silver pot to emerge alive as if demons. It is truly a thing of nightmare."

"But as with all things not of this realm it asks a price to be of service. Arkin paid the price with his soul and the soul of every man he puts in her depths. By all that I am, I plan to stop him."

"May I have your sword?"

Caledwynn unsheathed the blade and handed it to Arthur who dipped it in the fountain before facing him once again.

"Men of honor, men such as your Brotherhood, are the pillar of all we hold dear. They are our strength in times of need, our guiding light when we are lost. Above all, they are our brothers in arms who ask not the price but only to serve something bigger than themselves. I feel you are such a man Caledwynn. If you are, take a knee in front of me."

Without a moment's hesitation, Caledwynn knelt.

"Do you swear, Caledwynn of Avalon, to me Arthur of Camelot and all I uphold that you shall do no violence without purpose, you will shun murder and treason and give mercy when asked. To hold love, loyalty, duty and your oath above all else. Do you swear to protect those who cannot and defend all that is just in this world?"

Hand on hilt Arthur placed the sword tip to the ground in front of him, Caledwynn placed his hands lightly to the blade. "I do so swear."

"Now Sir Caledwynn, we have plans to make if we are to stop the plague that threatens to blanket all we hold dear."

— «» —

Caledwynn along with three other knights rode in the morning sunlight, each lost in their own thoughts. Caledwynn had told Arthur all he had learned from Viviane about Arkin's location. It was the hope of all of them that Arkin had not drawn many men to his twisted cause. If the numbers were still small, they had a chance to defeat him before they reached Camelot. If not, Arthur, his men and those of the Brotherhood would be ready.

By early afternoon the forest grew thick, any sound of men moving was stilled by the great trunks that surrounded them. They all tried to keep each other in sight, soon the crowded terrain made even that impossible. He called out. The trees threw his words back. Not knowing if the other knights were in front of him or behind he felt that pressing in what he hoped was north was the best option. His hope was that when the trees thinned he would have a better chance of finding the others before pursuing Arkin and his men.

Caledwynn finally broke free from the grip of oak and elm. He drank in the breeze that blew past. Only it assaulted him. A stench permeated the air like daggers, making it painful to breath. Arkin's black hounds were near. Taking in short bursts of air, he scanned the tree line for any sign of the others. Nothing. Deciding to see what they would be up against, he moved amongst the thinning vegetation towards the odious vapor.

He worked his way through a small stand of trees, flattening himself to the ground, when he heard voices. Not far off men came out of the trees entering the small field before him. In their arms, they carried leaves and moss which they dumped upon a small fire, probably Caledwynn thought, in hopes the plumes of smoke would dissipate the smell. It was also something that could work in his favor. Not far from the men he could see two large carts loaded with the spoils of raids and a smaller one beyond with Arkin's black hounds sprawled about the wheels. That would be where Arkin had the Cauldron, he would not trust its care to anyone but himself or his hounds. Caledwynn changed direction and crawled towards the smaller cart, watching every moment for signs of movement from the beasts. He stood and took a few cautious steps. He could now see the pitch-black paws larger than a man's head, razor sharp nails shimmered in the light. Slowly an eye opened and Caledwynn could see death and despair reflected in its orb. These were beasts of unnatural order and needed to be banished from this world and Arkin's control. Calling on all he had he drew his sword and swung, catching the first beast under the chin as it raised its head, removing it. The ground trembled as the body slumped to the forest floor throwing Caledwynn off balance. Black flashed in front of him as the second hound barreled down on him. Getting to one knee and tightening his grip on the hilt of his sword he drove his blade up as the beast leapt towards him. His hands were wrenched from the hilt as the beast rolled taking him along with it as it plunged to the ground. He lay there, gulping what air he could into his straining lungs. Working his way clear of the beast's hind legs he heard voices, yelling mixed with the din of sword meeting sword. Tenderly he pushed himself to his feet to survey the scene in front of him. Flashes of steel cut the air, horses in halos of silver charged. The knights had arrived.

Men raged against the pride of Camelot as Caledwynn sprinted to the field. His sword showed mercy to those who yielded and swept away those who did not. He surveyed the field for the one man he so desperately wanted to find. Arkin was nowhere to been seen.

"Coward!" Caledwynn bellowed. "You hide behind men and hounds! You slither through the night and take what is not yours. Show yourself and answer for what you have done."

From behind him there was a scream of a sword being drawn. Pivoting he barely blocked the blow meant for his back. Metal rang as the two men fought, determination etched on each face as they moved towards the heart of the battle. Swords locked. They now stood face to face.

"Your guard tried to stop me that night," Arkin hissed "Pity he was so young, untried it would seem. My hounds would have liked to play a little more."

Caledwynn saw nothing more than a darkness, a plague standing in front of him, one that needed to be eliminated. Twisting his body, he wrenched the hilts to the side throwing them both to the ground dislodging both swords from their grip. Arkin regained his footing and weapon first. Caledwynn, sword nowhere to be seen, reached into the debris of battle where his hand wrapped about a shaft. Planting both feet firmly on the ground Caledwynn drove the lance through Arkin driving him to the ground.

"Fergal, his name was Fergal."

As the last wave of life left Arkin, a slow realization seeped throughout the field. Arkin was dead and so too were his promises of wealth and glory. Fear gripped them, fighting only long enough to flee the battle. In minutes, stillness wrapped all left. Wounded lay upon the ground. Others begged for a mercy they had never given others. The knights stood battle bruised, but alive.

"We need to make room in the carts for any wounded who cannot ride. Those wounded who can, try to find any of the horses who have run off. The rest will walk. We will give the food to any in need we meet on our way back." Caledwynn beckoned one of the knights. "Come with me. We need to retrieve the Cauldron." The one closest, Sir Elyan, joined him.

Rummaging through the contents of the small cart Elyan's hand hit a rag pile that did not give way. He reached for it, the weight making it hard to lift so he jumped into the cart and dragged it towards the end where Caledwynn stood. As he pulled, the shifting rags drew back exposing the Cauldron. Elyan's hands grabbed a hold of the rim. Caledwynn watched as a shadow crossed the man's face.

Elyan's voice quivered as his grip tightened. "There is so much one man could have with this. I could have Camelot and all of her riches at my command."

Caledwynn slapped the trembling hands away then swiftly pulled the Cauldron to the ground. Kneeling beside it, he placed his wrist to the Cauldron, crescent moon to rim. Closing his eyes, he drew on the grace of Avalon and the goodness of Camelot. Calmness surrounded him, he knew what to do. A man, living and whole, asking not for himself but for the people, accepting whatever fate was to exact, stepped into the Cauldron. Before anyone could stop him, he drove his sword, etchings radiating from hilt to tip, into the heart of the bowl. Screeching voices lashed the air as the cauldron turned to dust in front of them. Caledwynn looked to dusk-laced sky.

"Let the soulless now be at peace."

Silence radiated over field. The magnitude of what just happened taking minutes to sink in.

Caledwynn turned and faced the knights, "We must return to Arthur."

—— «» ——

Moving past the open doors Caledwynn could see Arthur pacing, the clips of his heels echoing on the stone floor. Merlin sat at the table, fingers drumming on the rounded edge. Knights milling about the edges of the room turned from Caledwynn's gaze.

"I am here at your request" Caledwynn did not kneel. "Our discussion is for us and us alone."

Red crept above Arthur's collar. "In this hall, around this table, you may speak freely."

"Be that as it may, I humbly ask, as one protector of truth to another." Caledwynn saw Arthur straighten 'It is matter concerning your mother. She and the fate of the Cauldron are intertwined. If you choose to share it with your knights after, then let it be your choice."

Arthur narrowed eyes and took in a deep breath. There was something about this man, a bearing not held by his other knights. A code that bound him to something more than even he understood. He would at least listen.

"Brothers, leave us" A few of the knights hesitated then turned and left. Merlin sat still.

Caledwynn eyes meet the challenge in the old mage's gaze. "You are right to stay as you had a part in all that stands in front of you now."

"Speak now, for my patience runs thin, the Cauldron was to return to Camelot."

"In the world of men, the Cauldron was not safe. A mere touch and a knight is tempted to break his vow. What of a King? What dark shadows would it draw? Here in your kingdom there are many with seedlings of betrayal in their hearts. I will not have them grow. By my sworn oath, I could not have that darkness here. I made a choice."

Arthur's fist hit the table. "A choice you had no right to make!"

"This gives me the right!" Caledwynn pulled back his tunic exposing the marks on his shoulder. "Firstborn son of Uther Pendragon."

Merlin bolted from his seat. His fingers hovered above the ridges of the scar.

"This is" Merlin stammered.

"The front of our Mother's medallion. Lay your hand upon it Merlin and know the truth of what I am"

Merlin hesitated, looking deep into the man who stood before him. He flattened his hand. The image glowed under his fingers, light seeping up Merlin's arm to his chest. Drawn to Merlin's side Arthur saw that acknowledgment.

"It was the only piece of jewelry she ever wore. I asked her once why, she told me it was the key to the lost part of her that could never return. On her death-bed she asked to be buried with it. I carried out that wish by wrapping it in her hands the day we laid her to rest." Arthur sank into the nearest chair.

"This is some type of trickery, I was there. Only one son was born."

"But you were late Merlin." The words floated across the room. They all turned. There in the doorway stood

Viviane. "The trickery was yours that night so long ago at Tintagel."

"Lady," Arthur quickly stood, turning the vacated chair. "You must be tired from your journey and there is much we need to discuss."

"Yes, the shades of our past must be put to rest so we may have a future." Slowly she lowered herself into the chair, never once letting grace and beauty slip from her movements. "Caledwynn, come out of the shadows you are trying to slip into and sit here just in front of me."

Caledwynn strode across the room, pulled out a chair but stood behind it, his heart still conflicted between duty to the Lady who stood before him and the brother looking at him. Viviane waved her hand for Arthur to sit next to where his brother stood. When he had, Viviane took Arthur's hand and reached for Caledwynn's. He moved around the chair taking her offered hand. In that moment, as he wrapped her hand in his, he knew. He knew the gift of choice was his. Viviane pulled them closer to her and leaned her head towards theirs. A calm filled the room. Viviane raised her head.

"Merlin, come and join us."

In the deep gray before dawn Arthur stood and raised a sword from the polished surface of the table. He let the weight of it sink into his hands before he walked over to stand in front of Caledwynn. There, in his extended hands, lay Excalibur. "Truth is a powerful mistress, one to be treated with a prudent mind and an insightful heart."

Caledwynn unsheathed his own blade and laid in upon Arthur's open palms. "We are a balance within this world. Something our Mother triggered when she separated us. I have seen darkness and felt betrayal, you believe in all that is good in men's hearts. That is your gift Arthur. It is what drives men to be better than themselves, to protect the weak and uphold the vision of a better life. Be that man. Be their King. Inspire greatness and grand ideas." He closed Arthur's fingers around the two blades.

"Before all else Arthur, I am your brother but my heart is held by Avalon. I will stand with you and for you. I will always answer the call of Camelot. To protect all that is good and banish all that is evil. And when the sun sets on the reign of Arthur, I will be the boatman to take you home."

— «» —

Shannon Allen's short fiction has appeared in Enigma Front and Enigma Front: The Monster Within. A long time fan of all things Arthurian, Shannon lives with her husband Lloyd just south of Calgary, Alberta.

The Terrible Knitter

Simon Kurt Unsworth

Arthur was dead.

Of course, Arthur had been dead for over six hundred years but for the first time he *felt* dead, as though the things he had represented and the things he had embodied had finally collapsed to the earth and were rotting down to nothing alongside him. The land wasn't even ruled by an Englishman any more; the Norman interloper *Williame*, William the Conqueror, had killed Harold at Hastings and then split the country into baronies that had been gifted to his friends and allies. The barons lived apart from their subjects in hugely constructed castles, monuments to the English defeat and subjugation, sending out laws and instructions as they felt fit, and now William the Conqueror, William the Bastard, spent his time on the continent, leaving the land without a figurehead and without a heart. It was so bad that Dysig had even met people who didn't believe that Arthur had existed, so far from his memory had the land and its inhabitants traveled, so far into this new fractured reality had they slouched. *And thus are we cursed and fall,* he thought, and wanted to weep as he rode.

Dysig was in the north, his travels having taken him without plan towards the colder, darker parts of the country. The land here was harsh and the weather harsher, the people stunted and poor and sometimes barely human. The light that fought its way through the clouds was bleary and weak, but it didn't matter *where* he went, only *that* he went. Not hardship nor cold nor loneliness nor continual failure would stop him, because he had a quest, as they all did, those who remained loyal to Arthur; find the Grail, honor Arthur's memory and repair the dark and splintered thing the land had become.

And so he rode, chasing stories. Last month he had been on the coast following a rumor about a man who held the grail in a cave, the month before in the central flatlands chasing a dream of the grail half-drowned in a salt marsh, the month before that rooting through the cellars of a castle because the grail was supposedly hidden in a chest of mouldering women's clothes. None of it ever came to anything. They, he and the other remaining Knights, would come together on midsummer's day night, as ever, gather under the stars or the rainclouds and hope that one of them had been successful. Until then, Dysig rode, and he listened and he asked, and he visited towns and villages, sleeping mostly in fields or forests, bathing wherever he found water, and always he looked and always he was disappointed.

Now, Dysig was on the trail of what he assumed another will-o-the-wisp tale. Earlier that day, he had been told about a place, about a person, by two of the local soldiers. They had challenged him as he rode past their keep, a ragged motte and bailey thing, trotting out to stop him and demanding to know his business in the area. Two jumped-up lackeys wearing ill-fitting leather armor bearing the insignia of their lord, they had laughed when he said he was hunting the Grail, but had let him go after he had after he paid a 'passing tithe'. It was the older of the two, the one whose accent still held traces of his Norman heritage, that had told him about the place where questions might be answered. He had been serious when he spoke; his partner had grinned.

This was not, Dysig thought, a happy or easy place. There was a keep, but there didn't appear to be a town anywhere nearby. He had passed numerous dwellings, scrappy huts made of mud and shit, churned earth around them showing the passing of feet both human and cattle. The whole area was farmland, long swathes of greenery grazed by the ugliest, filthiest sheep and scrawniest cows he had ever seen, and it stank, of animals and waste. It was hard to imagine the grail being found in a place like this, but then, Excalibur had come from a lake and England's current king had come from France, so anything was possible.

"Cross the bridge by Cherchebi", the older soldier had said with a glance at his companion, "and then find biggest of the drovers' trails and follow it back along the river. After less than a day's ride, when it reaches the village and splits, take the left hand path and follow that for another day until you reach the village with the hill behind. There's a woman, and she can answer things. She lives in the oldest of the huts in a village that looks like it was shat out of the Devil's arse." *Cherchebi,* the guttural Norman word for the church by the river, another part of England being lost to this creeping colonisation. *Soon, everything will be gone, or changed so that no one can* recognize it, thought Dysig, *and then what will we do? What will I do?*

The bridge was wood, a ramshackle thing, wide and bleached by the sun and rain. It had low railings to each side, and its surface was covered in the prints of animals and people. The ground at the bridge's feet was a torn mess, wetly black soil exposed through the wounds in the skin of grass, and all over was animal excrement, mounds of it, streaks of it, its odor pungent and sour. The church was by it, small and squat and gray. It looked miserable and Dysig turned his back on it gladly, guiding his horse over the bridge. The animal's feet made hollow echoes against its span as they crossed, empty applause to encourage Dysig on his way whilst below him the river muttered to itself in a voice that was low and secretive.

The trail was wide and well-used and Dysig rode along its outer edge to avoid getting too bogged down or muddy. His horse, which he had never named but always just called Horse, was already worn to tiredness by their quest and its legs were caked in dirt. The river here was too fast to enter, but at some point before bedding down he'd need to let the animal bath and drink. He'd find a tributary or stream, or the main flow that he was now moving along would widen and slow. He'd never be too far from water on a drovers' trail, as they'd keep the cattle near places to drink whenever they could. They used the land, and the land kept them alive; it was how it had always been.

The two soldiers watched him from the other side of the river, and even after the trail curved around a hill Dysig felt they were still staring after him.

He reached the fork in the trail a few hours later, just beyond a small village that one of the inhabitants told him was called Sedbergh, a place that existed to give the farmers of the area a space to cluster together for warmth and protection. It was a small, huddled place at the foot of a range of hills that were behind him as Dysig moved past the last of the dwellings, and the sky above him was gray and leaden with cloud. It was colder here, wetter, but there was a keep on the hill on the far side of the town that looked as though it dated from about the time of Arthur. Dysig tried to take it as a good omen.

The new trail moved away from the full river and traced alongside one of its tributaries instead, and Dysig let Horse bathe and drink his fill. Now, the landscape was opening up and the trail peeled away from the water and made its ways out into a bleaker space. They were rising more sharply, moving along the flanks of another range of hills, smaller this time and to the east, whilst to the west the land dropped to form a gorge, a great split in the earth that ran parallel to the hills. It was thickly wooded and from Dysig's vantage point above it looked like a great patchwork of green and brown wool. The exposed grasslands of the hills around the gorge were a pale green, dotted with rocks and low, wind-bent bushes. Here and there, sheep and cattle grazed, silhouetted against the sky on the brow of the hills or closer, trudging through the grass and mud.

It was getting late, the air graying down towards night. Up ahead was a small level area surrounded by rocks and Dysig headed for it. He tethered Horse to one of the low bushes so that the animal could graze and then went down into the gorge; the slope wasn't too steep and the tree cover at the bottom meant that the fallen wood that covered the ground down there was relatively dry. He made two trips, gathering armfuls, and then set his fire but didn't light it. A third trip brought rabbits which he skinned and cleaned, throwing the guts back down the hill so that stray dogs or local wolf packs wouldn't bother him or Horse. Spitting the creatures, he finally lit the fire and roasted the meat, eating without thought as Horse stood stolidly to his side, head down and resting. The flesh was tough and stringy, like the land, and it was full dark by the time he had finished.

It was time. First, he put several more pieces of wood on the fire, making it blaze up like a beacon so that anyone for miles around could tell where he was camping. Then Dysig took his sheet from the bag hanging over Horse's rear, a huge stitched mass of fur and skin that he could fold double and wrap himself in to sleep and be relatively free from the damp. He folded it over by the fire, filling it with other things from his bag. Where his head would be if he was laying down he put one of his water bladders. Standing back, he was satisfied that, on first glance at least, the deception he had created looked like a sleeping man wrapping in animal skins keeping warm by a fire. That part of things done, he looked around.

There was a rock on the far side of the flat area that was almost half as tall as he was, and equally long. Its far end was buried in the earth and its exposed surface was covered with ragged, scarred striations and a crack that ran all the way around it horizontally at its midpoint so that it looked like the head of some great slumbering reptile that had been asleep so long its body had been covered in dirt and grass and was being slowly swallowed by the ground. Dysig walked over to it. It was snug to the slope that rose away from the flat area and sitting behind it he would be entirely out of view even to someone descending the hill towards his makeshift camp. It would do. He went and put more even wood on the fire, so that it burned higher and brighter, and then gathered several handfuls of smaller, fist-sized rocks and went to sit behind the snout.

He didn't have long to wait.

It was the grin that had told him, the younger one's grin as the older one had given him directions, as though he was party to some private joke that Dysig could not hope to understand. They came, as he thought they might, from the gorge, emerging several lengths back from the camp by climbing over the edge and clambering up onto the trail, practically invisible in the darkness but lazy in their noisiness. They clanked as they came, the sound of weapons drawing and feet trying to creep over damp earth. At one point one of them, the younger one he thought, slipped and muttered a loud curse, the other one shushing him almost as loudly. They became quieter as they came close, as though that would help them, skirting Horse widely so as not to disturb him, and then approached the blanket on the ground. One of them raised a weapon and, without warning, slashed down at the bladder. There was a splitting sound and then a gurgle of liquid and a cry of triumph. If he'd genuinely been asleep there, he'd be dead. Enough. Time to end this charade.

Dysig stood.

They were beautifully illuminated against the fire and Dysig's first rock flew true, crashing into the assailant's face with a noise like tearing cloth and splintering twigs and sending him staggering back and over. His second caught the other man in the neck as he turned, dropping him to one knee. Dysig covered the distance between them quickly, drawing his sword. He snapped his wrist and hand about in a sharp arc, bringing the flat edge of the blade around hard against the kneeling man's temple. With a groan, the man puddled down, crumpling to the earth.

Dysig tied them with strips of cloth cut from their own clothes and then sat them near the fire so that they'd be warm. Both men were unconscious but neither was in any danger, although the younger one would wear his nose wide and scarred for the rest of his life; Dysig's rock had turned it about and spread it into a misshapen mess. It seemed a small price for him to pay for attempted murder. Their weapons Dysig put out of reach, in a pile by Horse, and then he sat opposite them and dozed, knowing he'd wake when they did.

It happened just before dawn. The young one suddenly rocked forwards and made a noise somewhere between a sneeze and a groan, blowing a mess of dried blood and snot from his deformed nostrils. He started bleeding again and his fresh blood spattered down his face and across his chest, obscuring his lord's emblem. The noise woke the other, who gazed around woozily before focusing on Dysig.

"My master won't be happy that you've attacked two of his men," he said, wincing. His Norman accent was thicker now, rising up unguarded from the center of his pain.

"I wonder how happy he'd be if he knew that two of his men were deliberately sending travellers down lonely paths so that they could then attack and rob them? Travellers who, I might add, had paid a passing tithe? Indeed, I wonder if he knows about the passing tithe?" The man remained silent.

"Your Lord is called?" asked Dysig.

"Gillemichael," said the older man after a moment.

"Gillemichael? Excellent. What do you say, then? Shall we saddle you and your friend on the back of Horse here and go back to your Lord to ask his opinion?"

"No," said the man, and now his voice was more controlled, the accent fainter. In the firelight, Dysig could see that the side of his neck had swelled, an angry knot the size of a fist bulging out above his collarbone. His companion's eyes were already swelling and discoloring above his damaged nose.

"What a sorry looking pair of fuckers you are," said Dysig, keeping his tone conversational.

"Fuck you," replied the younger, his voice nasal and thick. He spat after he spoke, expelling another thick wad of blood and crust that looked like it might have teeth in it. It landed in the fire and sizzled.

"I should have killed you but it wouldn't have been that chivalrous, I don't suppose," said Dysig. "It'd be like a dog killing a rat. A stupid rat at that. A tip: when you want to ambush someone in the night don't make it so obvious what your intentions are when you first speak to them, and for the Lord's sake don't keep glancing at each other and nodding and grinning like simpletons. Then, when you do attack, try and keep the noise down. I assume this has worked before but mainly on rich merchants or farmers? Never on a knight?"

"A knight," said the younger man, giggling despite his obvious pain. "You're a knight? Like Galahad or one of those other round table cox combs? Lancelot or one of them?"

"No," said Dysig. "I'm nothing like them. I'm a mere shadow of the light they cast, those *cox combs*, but I'm a knight nonetheless, and I search for the same thing they searched for."

"What's your name then?" said the younger man, his voice a sneer. "They all had names, didn't they? 'The Pure', 'The Chaste', 'The Noble', that kind of thing, so what's yours then, knight?"

"Dysig," said Dysig. "Dysig the Ugly." The man roared with laughter, then groaned as the movement made his nose bleed afresh, new spatters joining the dried and drying streaks down his chin and chest. Dysig watched without feeling; he had had the name for many years now and it had ceased to hurt when people laughed. And besides, he was ugly; there was little point in denying the evidence of his own eyes when he saw his reflection.

"You're serious?" asked the older one, softer now. He looked at his companion, frowning, shaking his head, quietening him. "How can you be a knight? I thought William had stripped all of you of your titles unless you agreed fealty to him?"

"He can't strip me of anything that he didn't give me in the first place," said Dysig, "and my fealty will only ever be to Arthur and his descendants. I'm a Knight of Arthur and his table, and nothing but death will stop that. So, a question. The woman? Is she real, or just a thing you made up to send me out along this lonely road?"

"What's in it for us if I tell you?"

"My silence. A promise that I'll never call on Gillemichael and tell him stories. That's me handing you back your life and freedom, isn't it?"

Neither of the tethered men replied for a long time and then, after glancing at each other, the older said, "We have your word?"

"The word of Dysig the Ugly, Knight of Arthur, yes."

"Then we agree." His accent was back, strong, now. Dysig waited.

"The woman's real," the man said finally. "She's in a village on the other fork of the drovers' trail, in a place called Dent. She knits answers." Dysig drew his sword again and the man, seeing him, went on hurriedly.

"It's true, you have my word. You take her yarn or wool, anything, and she knits things that answer your questions. She's in Dent. It's less than a day's ride from here. God's truth!"

Dysig sheathed his sword. "Less than a day?"

"Half a day if your horse is good," the man said as the younger one nodded an eager confirmation, "but Dent isn't a good place, sir."

"More stories," said Dysig.

"No, sir, no. It's wild, so wild that William's auditors wouldn't go there for his great recording. Dent is an unrecorded place, a closed place, and the people are odd. Most of them can't speak, or only do so rarely, and they look wrong. It's not a place people like to go."

"Well, I'm going," said Dysig. Dawn was tracing its breath along the top of the hills, which meant he could see to ride. He stood, picked up his blanket and folded it back into his bag along with the other things he had used to make the false him. Horse, sensing movement, raised his head expectantly and Dysig rubbed his nose as he untied him and fitted his saddle, speaking to him softly. He and Horse had come a long way together, and would go further yet. Then he took the men's weapons and threw then down the slope so that they tumbled towards the bottom of the gorge. Tied up, it would take the two men some time to crawl down there and retrieve them and to then free themselves once he'd gone, and he hoped the effort would make them think twice about following him. He did leave them some of the rabbit, though, so that they could eat once they were free.

As he was climbing onto Horse the older man said, "Be careful of Dent. People go there and don't come back. Some of the people, they don't sleep at night, and they're the kind of pale you get in the bellies of fish. It's a bad place."

"Most are these days," said Dysig and wheeled Horse about and started back down the trail. Behind him, the men started to slither across the mud towards their weapons.

— «» —

Dysig didn't push Horse so it took them most of the day to reach Dent.

He had checked several times but no one followed them. This was a place of repetition, of more of the same, and after a while Dysig ignored the landscape through which they traveled except to give it only the most passing of glances. It was simply more mud and grass, more twisting, low bushes and trees, more cattle and sheep and the occasional hut. This was the England of poverty and dirt, of a scrubbed existence wrenched from the earth in exhausting handfuls, of people who might live their lives only ever speaking to the few other people that lived in the same valley or village and who farmed the same fields or grazed the same slopes every day of their lives. This was the place of the small, broken England, and Dysig wished it were different, because England could be, *should* be, so much more.

The trail had crossed the river several times, once via a bridge but the other times at fords where the water was slower and shallower, its grasp less strong. Each time, Horse drank and rested, and Dysig let him; this quest had been his whole adult life, and he could let it stretch a few more hours if that's what was needed. Always assuming, of course, that this was to be the end of the quest. The grail had danced ahead of him, unseen and out of reach, for every step of this journey and for every moment of his existence, and he had little reason to trust that it would change now. It glimmered in his dreams, capered at the edge of his vision, and sometimes he thought that that it was grinning, wide and savage, as it did so. The cup of Christ, that had held His wine or wafer, the purity of God Himself but he sometimes wondered, what if like everything else it had become corrupted since Arthur's death? What if it had tarnished and blackened, was a dark reflection of its more perfect self, and it not being found was deliberate?

What if it did not exist?

No. *No.* Arthur had tasked them, had had faith, and he must have faith too. He would find the Grail and all would be well because its purity would seal things and make them whole again. Arthur had said this, Arthur believed, and he and the others were Arthur's memory and legacy and could not fail him now. So Dysig coaxed Horse on, and finally came to Dent as the sun finished its tired path across the second half of the sky.

It was another hovel village, a collection of low huts clustered around a central green built, as the soldier had said, on a flat place by the side of the river. A place chosen, Dysig suspected, for convenience more than any other reason. These were homes built by the people that lived in them, mere shelters for the workers of earth and beast to retreat to when their work allowed. Perhaps half had smoke trailing from gaps in their roofs, and less than that looked to be in good repair. The river here was dirty too, stank of ordure and blight. The midden behind the village was overflowing, rank with the stench of rotting food, piss and sweat.

Dent looked *wrong*. It was hard to say exactly what it was, but there was something not quite true about it. Perhaps it was in the angles of the buildings, which were not simply sagging but appeared to have been built that way, in these strange folds and bends, or perhaps it was in the smell of it, which was not simply rotten but somehow foreign, as though the food cooked here was brought in from some other place where tastes were baser. Even its sounds were odd, the air full of clicks and taps and little sucking sounds as though mouths and tongues were toying with rotten teeth, pushing and prodding and poking at things half decayed and half dead. Looking at Dent was like looking at a thing stuck on the skin of the world, both too far away and too close at the same time, a picture of a village drawn by someone that had only ever had a village described to them but had never seen one and whose ability to draw was hampered by limbs that could not easily hold pencil or brush.

Dent was a wild place, the Norman had said, and he was right; this was the wildness of the untamed and the unknown.

Despite this, and despite his caution, especially after the incident with Gillemchael's men, Dysig could not wait and rode straight to the farthest hut. It was the smallest and filthiest, just as the Norman had told him, but its door was open and heat came from inside, where shadows danced across the walls in orange shadowfire jumbles. As Dysig dismounted Horse, a man came out of the hut.

He was, as Dysig expected, odd looking, taller than most people and thinner, his face paler, although this paleness was framed between a huge beard and a mass of long, thick matted hair. What exposed skin Dysig could see was covered with a myriad spatterings of dirt that looked old, crusted and ground into the pores like the makeup the noblewomen at court sometimes wore. His eyes were gray and the lips behind the beard were dark and narrow.

Seeing Dysig, the man mumbled something in a language that might have been English but that was so heavily accented that Dysig couldn't understand so that he had to shake his head to show his ignorance. The man sighed and said, more slowly and clearly, "You want an answer?"

"Yes."

"You have yarn?"

"No."

"Must have yarn, must be yours, otherwise the question cannot be asked." The man reached into a bag hanging by his side and pulled out several balls of coarse wool, held them out to Dysig. "Here. Sleep with this to make it yours, then come back tomorrow and ask."

Dysig took the wool and reached for his purse to pay the man but his offer was waved away. "Make it yours," said the man, "then ask. Pay then, if you want. Now, fuck off."

Dysig took the yarn from the man. It felt rough and greasy, left a scum across his fingers, but he put it in the bag hanging from Horse's saddle and remounted the animal. He wouldn't sleep in Dent, he decided, not in this warped and warping place. He trotted Horse back downstream, eventually finding a place a where trees grew by the river that might give them shelter if it rained or the wind picked up. There was wood on the ground for a fire and Dysig caught birds and burrowed out roots and berries to eat and managed to make a meal that tasted almost good despite its paucity. He couldn't remember the last time he hadn't been hungry; several months ago, maybe, when one of the old families still loyal to England, the England of Arthur and not the bastard thing it had become, had given him shelter for a few nights. They had given him a warm bed, he remembered as he rolled into his blanket and put the wool under the sheet under his head to act as a pillow, a warm bed and a daughter who had warmed the bed for a few wonderful hours before he had set on his way again, and sleep found Dysig with a smile on his face until the sound of Horse nickering and then screaming woke him.

Dysig rolled out of his blanket and had his sword in his hand before he was properly awake, was running to where Horse was tethered before he saw the pale thing clamped into the animal's neck, and was screaming along with Horse before he heard himself.

The thing on Horse was long and thin, a central trunk laying along the horse's side with tendrils coming off it that clamped around the animal's neck and belly, and then Dysig realized it was a person, impossibly white and terribly, awfully thin but a person nonetheless, a distortion of a person. It was naked, its flesh almost glowing in the night's faint light, and it was clinging to Horse, its face buried into the poor creature's flesh just below his jaw. Horse bucked and neighed and kicked helplessly there was a sound, a sound of slurping and swallowing and then Dysig was there grasping the attacker.

Its flesh felt like old, rotten wood, slimy and damp and cold, and as Dysig yanked it seemed to flow around his fingers, away from him so that he couldn't pull them off. He dropped his sword by his feet and pulled again, this time with both hands, and managed to yank the person's head back. It came free from Horse's neck with a tearing sound, exposing a ragged wound that dripped blood. Dysig pulled again and the attacker lost more of their grip, turned to face him and snarled. Its face was moon-white and round with entirely black eyes and a mouth like a lamprey's, needle teeth slick with Horse's blood behind lips the color of cooked offal. Dysig pulled again and the thing fell off, hitting the ground with a noise like loose turds escaping, and started to slither away. Horse reared as far as his tether would allow and stamped on the thing as Dysig retrieved his sword and slashed at it, slicing away one arm. It split with no resistance, as though there was no bone within the flesh, and rolled away leaking liquid that, in the light of Dysig's ember fire, was black and which steamed and stank.

He slashed again, this time at the thing's face, slicing through the mouth with a clinking sound as the blade struck teeth. The creature mewled as Horse stamped down again, this time landing squarely on its center and puncturing it. Strings of saliva swung from horse's nostrils as his hooves ripped into the flesh, scattering more of the dark liquid that smelled, Dysig realized, of earth and mulch and slaughterhouses and age and corruption.

When Horse reared again, Dysig used his sword to impale the thing, simultaneously dragging it away out of the animal's reach and pinning it to the earth. It writhed, the split in its face leaking and flapping as Dysig said, "What are you?"

The thing didn't reply, instead trying to turn despite the blade impaling it, managing to flip almost all the way over and starting to crawl, body tightening and tearing around the sword. It hissed again, spitting blood and something darker across the earth, single hand reaching forward and clutching at the dirt and trying to pull itself forward. It had shit itself, Dysig saw, and the mess coated its thighs and buttocks, and thick urine spilled on the ground below it.

Dysig pulled his sword back and stabbed down again, slashing out more of the foul liquid, then again and again and then he was chopping and slicing and by the time he was finished the thing was in more pieces than there were stars visible above them and the breath was ragged in his chest and the smell of it was in his nose and the monsters were real and if monsters were real then the grail must surely be real too, he thought, because one would balance the other. Wouldn't it?

Wouldn't it?

When it was light enough to see, Dysig tended the wound in Horse's neck, which thankfully wasn't too deep, and then went to the river to wash himself and his sword. While he was there, he let out the vomit that had been boiling in him these last hours, spewing it into the river and watching as it tumbled away in long strings. Finally, he went back to the thing's corpse but found that it had dissolved down to a few clumps of a gelid, white scum that trembled in the morning breeze and smelled of sweat and putrefaction. Patting Horse, he tethered him further away from the noxious mess, where there was fresh grass for him to eat, and then looked up. The sky looked back, impassive; the quest remained. Dysig took the yarn and walked back to the farthest house in Dent.

"You met one?" asked the man in his guttural English.

"I killed it," said Dysig. "What was it?"

"Just a man," said the man again. "They live here and do not sleep and sometimes their hunger drives them out at night. This place is poor and thin and cursed, and they are part of the curse."

"Where was it from?"

The man didn't reply, looking at Dysig as though he didn't understand the question. Finally he said, "Here. We are all from here. You have a question to ask?"

It was too much to think about, and he was too close to what might prove to be an answer to stop now or to be distracted by abominations or things in the night. He put the white thing from his mind and said, "Yes," handing the man his yarn. The man motioned him in.

The hut was tiny and the man had to stoop to move around inside it. Dysig, shorter, could stand straight but could feel the top of his head brush against the rough roof and automatically lowered his head to avoid collisions. Things hung all around the walls of the hut, pots and tools and skins, all coated with skin of old smoke and dirt.

An open fire burned greasily in a pit at the room's center and the woman was sitting next to it. She was old, ancient, her face crumpled like rotting apples, her belly huge and distended and Dysig wondered what she ate to be that fat.

Her eyes were milky with age and she was, if not blind, then almost sightless, the orbs rolling helplessly in their sockets and watering from the smoke from the fire. Her hair, what he could see of it under the cloth pulled tight over her head, was gray and thick.

The woman's right hand was held out, grasping, and the man put the yarn into it and then went to sit against the hut's wall. Easily, the woman found the end of the wool and looped it around a needle, wrapping another section around a second needle attached to her belt, one that jutted up and bent slightly towards her like a sharp cock.

"Think of your question," said the man.

So Dysig thought, of Arthur and the Grail and the quest, and the woman began to knit. She did it one-handed, the needle in her hand clacking against the belt needle as stitches formed and dropped, the wool held taught across the backs of her fingers so that it flowed into the emerging cloth without hindrance. Sometimes, the woman would stop and use her other hand to add in new sections of yarn or to tease free a tangle, but mostly this hand tapped arrhythmically against a small table by her side, creating a discordant tattoo that filled the hut. The heat of the fire made Dysig sweat, the smoke stung his eyes, the smell of her and the man turning in his nostrils, but it was somehow hypnotic to watch her, to watch the answer he wanted form at the end of her fingers.

Dysig watched as the wool was knitted into a cloth in which vague images and intimations could be seen. Although most of the thread was a single shade of dirty brown, the woman used different stitches to create patterns in the garment, sometimes doubling or trebling the thickness as though in emphasis. It took her most of the day to finish, and by the time she was done Dysig was weary with the temperature and the smell and was glad to take the cloth and leave the hut. Again, he offered to pay before he went and again the offer was refused.

The woman had made him something that looked like a scarf, long and narrow and filled with odd half-formed pictures and things that Dysig could almost recognize but which seemed to slip from his vision when he concentrated on them. His eyes itched as he looked at the scarf, and he wasn't sure it was simply the smoke from the hut that was causing the sensation because when he looked away from the material the things on it seemed to move, to slip from place to place, leaping back into their original position as he looked back at them. Although the yarn he had given the woman was brown there was a thick blue vein knitted through the center of the scarf, undulating and uneven and impossible.

The man followed Dysig outside the hut and took the scarf from him, holding it up to the light and saying, "The answer is over in the forest. See, here are trees," pointing to a series of ridges in the pattern that might conceivably be trees just past that impossible blue mark of the river.

"How does she do this?" asked Dysig, still unsure if he believed or not.

"Because Dent is thin. My daughter sees truth in the cloth that we cannot see until she exposes it, just as others here feel a truth in the tonic of drinking blood. This is just Dent."

"Daughter?" said Dysig. "But she looks..." and stopped because how could he say it, that she looked a single shuffle away from death and the man looked many years her younger?

"It takes a toll," said the man simply. "It is a terrible thing she sees and a terrible thing she does. People's answers are rarely what they want, and that burden lays heavily on her. One day one of the pale ones will visit her, I think, and she will welcome them and on that day I shall weep and rejoice at the same time. Now, go. The answer is ahead."

Dysig went.

— «» —

He left Horse tethered near the camp because the trees were too thick on the other side of the river for the animal to move through.

The walk back to the river from Dent had been unnerving. Dysig had felt people watching him, as though unseen eyes were tracking his every step. Once, he glimpsed something glimmering white in the open doorway of one of the huts but it had gone when he turned to look at it, and as he reached the outskirts of the village he was sure that someone far too tall and dead-tree skinny had peered at him from behind the last hut, crouched low but their head still on a level with the top of the wall. They, too, were gone when he looked around. He imagined more of the pale people slipping through the undergrowth, keeping pace with him as he walked, imagined mouths opening and lips pulling back to reveal teeth like needles.

Teeth like knitting needles, attached to belts of gum, thin and curved back to better hold the threads of flesh they tore loose.

No. *No,* he would not allow this place to scare him. He was Dysig, Knight of Arthur's court, Knight of the Round Table even if they had no table now and simply sat in a circle on the ground when they met, and he would not be defeated by the phantoms and imaginations of a place worn sheer. *This is not England,* he thought as he reached the river, *not my England, but it will be again.*

Dysig entered the river slowly and crossed the river with care, feeling ahead with his feet across rocks that were slippy and rolled under him, moving through water that was cold and tugged at his legs. It was shallow, though, never coming above his waist, another reason Dent had accreted at this place he supposed. But why, he wondered was it cursed? Why was it so thin here?

Because they tend the earth but no one tends the land, he thought. *When Arthur prevailed the land prevailed, when Arthur fell the land fell. There's no one here but Norman lords and careless soldiers and barely half-human laborers. No one cares for the land beneath the earth, and it's crumbling.*

Dysig had been to other places were the walls between this world and the others felt more fragile, places where the shadows seemed longer or darker, places where the daylight less powerful, but never somewhere where the others had actually broken through. Was the thing he had killed even truly a man? He couldn't tell, even thinking back over it now. It had appeared human-like, certainly, but had it been male? Or female? And if not, then what? He knew that the land contained more than the things than could easily be seen, of course, but something so wrong? Had anything like that ever made it into the world before?

Whenever they gathered, fewer and fewer of them each year, they each of them had tales about the increasingly wrong things that they had seen or heard or sometimes fought. There was a huge cat stalking the land somewhere south, he had been told, that took children from their beds after calling to them in the voice of their mothers, and an island somewhere up near the top of the country populated by flying women who swept out over the sea during storms and snatched sailors from boat decks and ate them still living in the skies so that their screams joined the moans of the wind. Giants still lived in caves in Wales, and dragons swam in the sea, sometimes fighting huge fish with teeth like curved blades, and there were bodies of water in which worms lived that could borrow into your gums and fill the entire inside of a man's head, but he had never heard of a thing that drank blood and that dissolved into jelly when cut.

"Another of God's miracles," he said out loud as he reached the far side of the river and climbed out, although the pale thing seemed an affront to God as much as a creation of His, more evidence of the dark and suppurating flesh of the wounded world.

Dysig approached the trees, and prayed for the healing power of the Grail.

They were old trees, gnarled and twisted, their branches above him forming a solid canopy through which little light fell. The air was warmer here, damp and humid, with tiny fragments of leaf and dust floating in the haze about him, insects buzzing and flitting amongst the motes. He drew his sword, holding it loosely by his side, wary. He still didn't understand why he might find answers here but the knitted cloth with its swirled and ridged patterns, now tied around his wrist, gave him hope.

Arthur gave him hope.

Dysig moved further into the trees, threading his way between trunks the color of old iron, ducking below branches and stepping over hunched, raised roots with care. This place smelled, of blood and something else, the smell of the air after lightning strikes, sharp and vibrant and yet wrong, so very, very *wrong*. Each step on this side of the river, Dysig thought, was a step further away from the world, away from the things he knew, a step into the unknown and unknowable, but this was the quest, this was the purpose of it all, and he would go wherever he needed to achieve his end.

Another step. Another.

Something was moving through the trees at his side, keeping pace with him.

When Dysig looked around he could see nothing, but it was there nonetheless. He could sense it, feel the delicate shifts of the air as it moved somewhere beyond the nearest trees. Was that the gentle soughing of a foot stepping on twigs and damp earth? The sound of body brushing past a trunk? Was it on his left side or his right?

Both?

There was another noise, this time from behind him. He turned, seeing the trees but nothing else. Another noise, this time from in front, a low snuffle like something sniffing and searching. Dysig turned again, still seeing nothing. Something pale flitted in the edge of his vision, definitely on both sides now, low and sinuous like snakes made of smoke. The snuffling sound came again, closer, wet and deep.

He sped up, slipping between the trees which were growing together more and more thickly so that passing amongst them was becoming harder and harder. Branches scratched at him, clawing fingers that dragged in his hair and snagged at his legs, slowing him, and all the while the sound of other things moving grew closer. The air was filled with a snickering, a series of snorts and giggles, high-pitched and clear and mocking. White flickers danced around him, closer and closer, circling. The branches were so thick that he could not see anything in front of him and he waved his sword ahead of him, attempting to cut a path through the branches but somehow his arm was caught, could not move. He tried to push forward, tripped but did not fall, held by the branches and punctures.

Something ran a hand along his back.

Something, not someone. The hand felt too long, the fingers almost like tentacles, the skin a cold that he could feel even through his leather armor and woolen underclothes. It was gone almost as quickly as it came, but then was back almost immediately, it or another like it, stroking his side. He twisted, trying to break free from the trees' clutches but couldn't, getting instead more tangled. His clothes were twisting around him now, making it difficult to breathe, and another of those touches came, this time tickling his feet through his boots. A branch pressed against his face and his mouth was suddenly full of leaves, thick and wood and with edges that scored his gums and tongue. He spat, but had nothing to spit with, couldn't get his mouth free.

Another touch, across his forehead, but so tight was the grip of the branches that he could not raise his head to see what it was, only move his eyes which revealed the edge of something white and semi-transparent and long and languid. More giggles, another little snuffle.

He twisted again, seemed to be raised even further from the ground, felt thorns and edges dig into him and now his nose was blocked and things were scratching at his face and he'd be even uglier if he ever got out of this. He felt the knitted cloth rip from his wrist and twisted again, a last time, to try and grasp at it. It dropped below his fingers, the woolen stitches tantalizingly close, and then it was gone.

Another touch brushed across him, this time along his belly towards his balls and he twitched away from it but still couldn't move. Then it was grasping him and squeezing and the pain was a white burst of agony. Something wrapped around his throat and tightened and he tried to call for help, knowing that there was no help for the helpless but trying anyway and nothing except a rasp came from him, hemmed in by the suffocating trees and in that moment, when the air was lost to him Dysig heard a voice.

"Do you want to stop?" It was the soldier, the older one, his Norman accent thick now, turning the words into something new and strange.

"Just let go," the soldier carried on. "Accept that it is not to be and all this can end," and it would be so easy to just stop, to let go, to stop searching and to collapse to the earth and be buried by leaves and grass, to turn into a rock that looked like it might once have been a Knight and have people sit on him whilst he spent eternity in blessed, resting awarelessness.

No. He had spent too long, come too far to quit now.

He swung his sword again, using what felt like the last of his strength, felt it move slightly and connect weakly, felt its blade edge dig into something and then he was sawing, hacking, making any movement he could to loosen his jail. Something gave slightly ahead of him and his upper half jerked forward, dropping slightly. The movement seemed to open up a little space and he used his weight to fall into it, shifting again, opening a gap up. He spat, this time managing to clear leaves from his mouth, gagging on the taste they left behind. His sword arm managed to swing further, this time chunking the blade into something more solid.

Another slash with his sword and this time he fell further forward, the grip around his neck loosening, the touches falling away from his sides, and he managed to crawl through a space that was opening up ahead of him between two trunks. His free arm managed to hook around something, branch or root, and he pulled hard, his head emerged and then his shoulders into blessed light and he was half out now, arms swinging, and then he managed to press a foot against a root and push himself further so that he was out to beyond his waist. He twisted, falling onto his back and pulling his legs after him, still spitting, still gagging, feeling blood well from the cuts on his exposed skin.

He was in a clearing, and the forest around it was just forest. The trees were not close together, and there were few branches emerging from the trunks, none sharp enough to puncture or thick enough to hold him. Dysig caught a glimpse of the white things flitting away, still unsure of what they were. *More overspill from this place's thinness*, he thought, another wrongness like the trees that could close together and then appear so opened out. He had to find the Grail, had to fix this, to fix the land.

"It can't be fixed," said a gentle voice from behind him.

Dysig rolled and turned, coming up to his knees and thrusting his sword out, expecting another attack. Instead, he was confronted with a bearded, smiling knight holding a shield on one arm, his other weaponless. He was dressed in old fashioned armor, battered and dented although well cared-for, and his eyes were kind. He crouched, holding his free hand out to help Dysig up. Dysig warily took the proffered hand and clambered to his feet. He ached, and where the strange touches had pressed against him his skin had started to burn.

"Who are you?" he asked

"I'm your answer," said the knight. "I'm what you wanted to find. You've done so well, my son, so very, very well."

"No, that's not right. I want to find the Grail, to make things right again."

"You never wanted to find the Grail, not really. You wanted to find me, to bring me back. I'm Arthur, my child. I'm what you sought."

"But the Grail," said Dysig and then trailed off.

"There is no Grail," said the man, said Arthur. "There was only ever me. I am the Grail, come to you at last." And Dysig understood, because it was true, finally understood the one mystery that he had avoided investigating before, himself. All these years being one of the last knights of Arthur, cleaving to the dead king's values and beliefs in the hope that they could fix an England they had never really known, loving him like a father, like the father of all things, and when the time had arrived for him to complete his quest he had failed because he was weak and ugly and had believed in the wrong thing.

"There, son, there," said Arthur. "There's no shame in not understanding. This quest was always hard, was always going to winnow out the weakest, but you've come so far, done so well. I'm here."

"I've failed," said Dysig.

"Yes," said the thing that claimed to be Arthur. "You and all before you. We will ever be a fractured place, Dysig the Ugly, because once fractured not even bones or lands can be properly fixed."

"I don't understand,"

"Of course you don't," said Arthur, smiling kindly. "You've spent years searching for the wrong thing. How could a grail ever hope heal the land? You were always searching for me, child, for the person that once united this place into a single whole, and found me here where the skins between worlds are weakest but I cannot help. The answers to the present are not in the past, and they never were.

"I'm dead, Dysig, and this land cannot be fixed."

Arthur dropped his shield and held out his arms in a gesture of embrace. Dysig, feeling the thinness all about him, seeing white shapes gathering amongst the now densely packed tree trunks, fell to his knees and as Arthur took him in his arms he wept for the fractures that would never be fixed and the grail that had never been.

— «» —

Simon Kurt Unsworth was born was born in Manchester and is the author of many short stories, including the collection Quiet Houses. His short fiction has been nominated for the Edge Hill Short Story Collection award and the World Fantasy Award. His novels The Devil's Detective and The Devil's Evidence are available from Penguin Books.

House of the Knight's Nail

R. Overwater

Singeth ye of good knight Oswin, dost ye know?
Of suster's strength 'twas house 'ere built
With forge and ferrier and lordes own nail?
—House of the Nail: traditional ballad

The campaign against King Idres went badly and Mathie avoided eye contact whenever the soldiers rode through. They always came this way — the shortest ride to their own encampment was through hers — and the grim resignation on their faces left a cold feeling in the center of her stomach.

This time, one of them caught Mathie's eye before she could look away. He stared back and she wrapped her tattered shawl tighter, shielding herself from his penetrating gaze. He kept on staring until his horse stumbled. Mathie could tell it was going lame, hooves cracked, lower hocks covered in open sores.

These new men were different. They scowled at the grubby camp followers, the ratty tents, the battered carts, pigs rooting in the mud. The front men, resplendent in holy clothes with large crosses on their chests, pointed their noses at the gray sky. The next ones were sullen, vicious looking, their once-colorful tunics brown and torn. Two soldiers in gleaming mail brought up the rear. Large shields ornamented with engraved copper hung on their backs.

Mathie wasn't sure if Father would have liked seeing the shields, or been saddened. Copper-smithing had been his whole world, and he'd delighted in showing his children the trade. But now King Ban fought on the side of Arthur and this new life, scrabbling as a food gatherer in Ban's camp, stung Father's pride. Perhaps she wouldn't tell him about the shields.

The three old men who tended the camp's meager herd pressed in, shoving her aside. "They're Christians," one said, pointing at the men as they passed. "The one-eye says they sailed here to demand that Arthur to renounce the old gods."

"Bah," said another. "Everyone knows his army depends on Christians and the old gods alike."

The old men smelled like sheep dung. Mathie wrinkled her nose and inched away from them.

Well behind the foreigners, a single rider followed on a gray horse. Clothed in a billowing cloak, his cowl blocked all sight of his face. When the procession slowed, so did he, keeping his distance.

Mathie tried to get a glimpse of his face when he passed. She wished she hadn't. The man stopped and looked down, focusing on her from the shadows of his cowl.

She swallowed. She'd seen this strange man before. Sometimes he circled the camp on horseback, watching everything. Once, when she and her brother Oswin helped Mother carry firewood, she was sure he was observing them in particular. "Do not stare," Mother had said. "That man is Myrle, the eye of Arthur. Consort with him is forbidden unless you have King Ban's blessing."

Mathie swiveled around, hoping the man was gazing at someone behind her. Her eye caught Oswin, working his way toward her through the crowd. When she looked back, the unnerving figure was riding away.

Oswin pushed through, his broad chest and shoulders making it easy to clear a path. Helen, the vinegarish hag who kept tally of the camp's provisions, fell to one side. "Look out," she shouted. "It's the daft one!"

Mathie bit her tongue. Helen was old and she knew Mother would scold her again about the way she spoke to her elders. God bless Oswin though. He never got angry at the way people treated him, assuming he was slow-witted because of his clumsy speech. More often, he was embarrassed because Mathie spoke up and made a scene over it.

Oswin ignored Helen, sliding past to Mathie. His eyes streamed with tears. Seizing her by the forearms, he dragged his sister through the crowd.

"What? Just tell me," Mathie said, trying to wriggle free. He didn't answer, tugging her toward a gaggle of people at the camp's edge, in the clearing just before the willow thickets.

Two men in rusted mail stood on either side of a flat cart covered by a large sheet stitched from cowhide scraps. One grasped a tall pole. On its end, the green standard of the local earl snapped in the breeze.

A graying, hunched man in a green tunic came around from the back of the cart. "Come to claim the last two?" he said. He pulled back the cowhide. "Look closely!"

A necklace of swollen bruises wrapped her mother's throat where the rope had dug in. A noose was around her father's neck. Mathie choked. She placed two fingers on her mother's forehead. It was cold, clammy to the touch. Loose articles of clothing, mismatched boots, a scarf, lay near them. They weren't the only dead borne by the cart today.

"The Earl has a message," the old man said. "He knows of this young King Arthur, who supposedly we will all someday kneel to. He knows King Ban fights for Arthur and the Earl can't stop him from marching on these lands. But you all" — he waved his hand in the direction of the camp — "are nothing more than looters. Stay off his hunting grounds."

The last thing Mathie felt was Oswin's hands, catching her as the world fell away.

— «» —

Pain shot through her as a stick came down across Mathie's neck. "Get in there," someone shouted. A hand pushed at the small of her back. Across the circle of children, three girls — the ones who'd mocked Mathie about her size on the very day of her fourteenth birthday — were bawling as someone thrust them out from the crowd. A fat man in sackcloth struck one above the ear and she fell to the ground, squealing. Today, no matter how many times they'd called her "Beastie," Mathie couldn't summon her usual contempt for the trio.

She struggled to focus on the adults around them. *Cruel. Pig-headed.* Yesterday, Oswin had put on a brave face, but she'd hid in their tent and cried all night. Then men burst in, divided up their possessions, and hurled the two out onto the damp grass.

To her left, a man in a leather apron with shoulders like an ox yoke ran his hands up and down Oswin's muscled arms and poked at him. The burly man called out and, seemingly from nowhere, Myrle, the cloaked man walked up.

Mathie couldn't make out the words the two spoke to her brother. Oswin replied and the big man in the apron squinted. Gripping Oswin by the jaw, he pulled his mouth open, frowning when he saw the cleft palate. He shrugged and took Oswin by the arm, leading him away. Myrle followed behind.

Mathie stumbled as hands seized her from behind, jerking her around to face in the other direction. She tensed as the hands lingered, already guessing who it was. The man, a horrible red hole in his face where his right eye had once been, walked around her. The way he looked Mathie up and down made her squirm.

"Helen!" he shouted. "Keep this one?"

Helen walked over from the girls she was assessing. Hands on her hips, she eyed Mathie suspiciously. "Her parents are dead. And the orders from King Ban are clear," she said, turning to the one-eyed man. "Arthur and his knights join the campaign within a fortnight. If they see miserable orphans all about, it will go badly for Ban."

The one-eye chewed his lip. "And then Ban will blame you and I. We should drive her out with the rest."

Mathie was a good head taller than Helen and the woman had to crane her neck to look up into her face. Helen pinched her waist and seized one arm, holding it aloft. "She's a brute like her older brother. Perhaps stronger than the other girls?"

"That just means she'll eat too much," the one-eye said. "Away with her."

"Wait," said Mathie. "The soldiers need food and firewood. I can find it every bit as good as anyone."

The man glanced at Helen, who was already walking away. He leaned in. "You'll risk swinging like your parents?" Mathie nodded.

"Alright then."

On the north side of the clearing past the trees Myrle, Oswin, and the giant in the leather apron walked up the small hill that separated the followers from the soldiers' camp. Mathie prayed they weren't taking Oswin all the way to the battlefront.

She wandered in the woods, dazed, crying, not searching for food. At nightfall, she stole shelter in a straw cart back in the camp. Drawing her knees to her chest, she sobbed until she shivered so badly from the cold, she could no longer cry.

— «» —

The first mornings had been the worst, and the weeks that followed weren't much better. Clothes soaked with dew, cold biting so deep into her bones it hurt, she'd lie in the straw and wonder how she could possibly move. Fleas bit her constantly.

Mathie's stomach growled, knotted from more than a month of constant hunger. What little food she could scrounge in the countryside went to the soldiers; it was the luckiest of days when she dared keep any for herself.

A whiff of meat drifted up, worsening the pangs. She rolled over and poked her head up to see where the scent came from, feeling a lump beside her. Fumbling through the straw, she pulled out something wrapped in oilcloth.

A small gourd and a piece of cooked meat, still on the bone, fell out as she unwrapped it. She glanced around. No one was watching.

Mathie ducked beneath the straw, biting off pieces of the meat, swallowing them without even chewing. She sucked at one end of the bone, drawing out as much marrow as she could. Pushing her thumbs into the squash, she broke it in two and scooped out the insides of one half, seeds and all. A grunt escaped as she pushed the juicy pulp into her mouth.

Shudders wracked her body. It was the most she'd eaten at once in some time and she clenched her jaw, forcing herself to hold it down.

Where could she hide the remaining bit? And — the question hunger had overridden — where did it come from?

She sat up part way, peering above the straw. A hooded profile stood among the other carts. *Him again. Myrle.*

A week ago, she'd mustered the courage to ask the one-eye about him. If she found the cloaked man, maybe she could learn where they'd taken Oswin. A blow to her head was the one-eye's only answer.

Mathie slid down off the cart, crawled around its corner and peered past the wheel. A silhouette, hard to make out in the morning sun's glare, continued past the carts, out of sight.

Taking a deep breath, Mathie summoned the nerve to follow. She wished she hadn't just thought about Oswin — it made her think of Mother and Father too. Mother, brushing Mathie's hair late into the night when she'd finished cleaning the lord's house. Father, standing behind her in his workshop, gripping her wrist and showing her how to hammer soft copper into fine shapes. The memories made her ache, and she forced her concentration back to the man she followed.

They neared the Christian camp, at the southern edge of the clearing. Just before a line of embroidered, luxurious-looking tents, the man paused.

She froze. He went around the tents, out of sight.

Mathie scratched at a fleabite on the back of her neck, unsure. She shuffled closer.

The sound of argument erupted. She kneeled and spied around the corner. A rotund man in luminous, white robes leaned into the cloaked figure's face. "Your King is but one of the Lord's sheep," he spat. "He holds no sway over us. He can see it when he meets with me in person."

"I am the King as far as you need be concerned," said the voice from within the cowl. "Much is at stake. Let me see it."

Behind the fat man, guarding the tent, the horseman who'd gawked at her the day her parents died stood with his feet planted wide, one hand on his sword hilt. Nearby, his horse nipped at a patch of overgrazed turf. Its hooves were cracked worse now and it favored one leg as it moved.

A second guard approached. He spotted Mathie and pointed. As the others turned to look, Myrle quietly side-stepped toward the tent opening.

The fat man noticed. Repositioning himself between Myrle and the tent, he shouted "Guards!" Keep a close eye on this man!"

Mathie ducked around the corner, pressing her back to the tent-cloth, holding her breath. Had the fat man in white robes not seen what the guard was first pointing at? If he had, running wouldn't save her. They'd catch her in the wide-open space between the camps. Unable to think of anything else, she stooped, lifted the lower wall, and slid into the tent.

Two candles flickered and something glinted. An ornate golden box sat on a table, its carved lid beside it. It was beautiful, with long strings of engraved words punctuated by red jewels. The candlelight, dancing upon the gold, gave the impression of flowing liquid.

The box's contents, a simple iron cross, sat in contrast. Dotted with flecks of rust, the cross bore no jewels or filigree. Such plain a thing, in such a rich setting.

Her heart pounded, her skin tingled and the sudden impulse was overwhelming. She ran up to the cross and lifted it from its box. It was cold to the touch. She tucked it beneath her shawl.

Voices rose up. The flap over the tent doorway rustled as a hairy hand came through, grabbing its edge, stopping short of pulling it back. She crawled under the back of the tent and ran as fast as she could.

No one noticed Mathie coming back to the followers' camp, huffing in the late morning sun. Her side ached from her awkward gait, one arm pinning both the food bundle and the cross under her shawl.

When she got to the trees, she opened her shawl and threw the cross to the ground. How could she be so foolish?

The smartest thing would be to get rid of it, bury it perhaps, but Mathie couldn't bring herself to abandon it. She carried it all day, removing it from her shawl after she burrowed into the straw cart that night. She was starving. There would surely be no more mysterious packets of food, and as autumn approached the cold was becoming unbearable. Without food and proper shelter, she knew she could die.

Perhaps she'd stolen the cross out of desperation. The decision to take it or not take it was one of the few choices she'd been presented with in some time. But now she was a thief. They would do to her what the local earl had done to her parents. She closed her eyes and tried not to think about it.

Angry shouts and the stamp of hoofbeats awoke her. The Christians, swords drawn, roamed the camp, kicking things over, storming in and out of tents.

"You!" someone shouted. To her left, the one-eyed man pointed at her as two swordsmen ran up. One grabbed her hair, dragging her out onto the ground. The other scooped armfuls of straw out of the cart. Stooping and reaching down, he shouted.

One-eye crowded in, blocking Mathie's view. When he turned to face her, he was holding something. "You've been somewhere you shouldn't," he said.

Mathie pictured her parents, lying on the cart, bruises around their necks. She could flee, but there was no clear way past the men. The one-eyed man pushed his face into hers. A minute trace of clear liquid seeped from the eyeless gap.

"This," he glowered, "is from the knights' own provisions." He wagged the bone at her. Confusion paralyzed Mathie's tongue.

"Arthur might inspect this camp at any moment. It's bad enough you look like a hungry wretch. Do you think King Ban wants Arthur to find thieves about too?"

Someone could make broth with that bone, and might let her have some. Feeling heat rise in her face, she grabbed at it and tried to pull it from his grasp. He snatched it away, looking smug. The two Christians shook their heads and they all walked away.

In the woods, she found a tall tree and climbed high into a crook between three branches. She hid there all day, praying no one would unload the straw cart she'd slept in.

Returning to the cart that evening, she was shocked to find that no one had disturbed it and the cross was still there. She climbed in and lay down, her mind whirling, the night growing darker. It took a long time to fall asleep.

A pair of muscular arms pawed through the straw. One found Mathie's wrist, clamping long, strong fingers around it. Unable to squirm free, she was pulled upright. She tried to cry out, but a hand covered her mouth. Someone emitted a low mumble.

It was the thick, familiar tone of Oswin. He yanked her arm, pulling her away.

"Wait," she said. She reached back into the straw.

—— «» ——

For the next few weeks, Mathie marveled at Oswin's new world. It was loud, hot, smoky and fascinating. From the hiding space he'd made her among sacks and barrels in the sturdy leather tent, she watched a daily spectacle of fire and mystery.

At dawn the large bearded man, the one who'd accompanied the cloaked man as they led Oswin away, would push in and begin shouting. "Rise Oswin! His majesty's horses are waiting!" A trio of coal-boys stoked two large stone hearths and wheeled out carts of cinders. Soon, sweat dripped off Mathie's forehead and the smell of heated stone and metal filled her nose.

She wished sometimes she could sneak out for a breath of air. She was fed and warm, but her hiding place was a kind of prison.

All she could do was spend the hours watching Oswin work. His arms, more muscular than ever, bulged as he raised a hammer above his head, slamming it down onto the white-hot iron, beating it into something new. Swinging and hammering, swinging again, the rhythm was deafening, incessant, hypnotic.

Mathie had never seen a blacksmith work. It wasn't all that different from her father's trade, but she'd never heard of such a thing as this: forging iron pieces for a horse's feet. One morning, Oswin's master — Smith was his name — slapped Oswin on the back and told him these horses were making a difference. He commended Oswin for playing his part.

Despite all this, Oswin worried about Mathie. Hugging her tight and forming his misshapen words slowly, he explained that as long as they had use for him he was secure. But what about his sister?

Over a month ago, he'd learned about Mathie from the foragers who brought firewood. At first, he feared she'd been driven from the camp and was gone forever. When he completed his brief apprenticeship and was given his own tent to work in, he'd made a plan to find her. He'd keep her hidden as long as he could. But how long could that be?

Mathie hugged Oswin tight and just listened when he talked — it was not like him to talk. She kept the story about the Christian camp, the cloaked man and the cross to herself.

Oswin worked in near isolation. Smith and the coal-boys came once a day. Horses, every two days. After a week, Mathie hung a strip of leather across the tent opening, festooning it with pieces of slag and small bits that would rattle if someone unfastened the opening. Oswin observed her as he worked, amused.

Convinced she could hide in time, she walked to the row of hammers and gripped the biggest one she could heft. "Teach me this," she said. "All of it."

The next month went by quickly. Gripping the tongs, forging hot iron into new shapes hammer-stroke by hammer-stroke, she found pleasure in the way it was soft and yielding, bending to her will like few things ever had. Father would have been pleased.

It took practice getting the nails to uniform length, about as long as her little finger. At first she had to heat and reheat each one several times. But, tapping one end to a fine point, flattening the other, she'd eventually finish one and dip it into the water bucket, drawing satisfaction from the percussive burst of steam that signified completion. Soon she was shaping the iron crescents that would become horseshoes.

The sparks burned her forearms. She flinched, dropping nails, missing hammer-strokes, but Oswin's arms were scarred worse and she bit her lip.

When she first tried shoeing a horse, it kicked, grazing the side of her head and leaving her face with a dark, purple bruise. Oswin would hunker down and lift a horse's hoof with brute strength. Mathie discovered she could squeeze the sinewy, ropey bit inside its ankle just above the hoof and the horse would lift it willingly. Squatting just right, she could brace the leg against her hip and summon enough strength to drive a nail through the four holes in each shoe.

Her work became neater than Oswin's. Mathie made sure the nails went in to the thicker outer wall of the horse's hoof and they never limped when she was done. Her shoes never stuck out past the hoof and she trimmed her nail ends off cleanly.

"You've gotten twice as fast," Smith said to Oswin, gathering the reins of some freshly shod horses. "But you are rushing sometimes." The master pointed at a horse Oswin had shod. "This work is acceptable, but why settle for that when you can do so much better?" He gestured to one of Mathie's horses. "The knights argue over these ones. They turn more nimbly."

In her hiding place, Mathie smiled. She wondered if Mother, scrubbing floors every day — before Idres' men and the swords and the fires — would have approved. If this could be Mathie's work, that would be enough for her. But sooner or later this would have to end. And what then?

Almost out of iron, they worked at a leisurely pace the next morning. Mathie was on alert, ready to disappear when new lumps of cold metal arrived. The doorway rattled. She dropped her tools and hid.

A squire walked in, the small boy who sometimes helped bring horses and snuck Oswin extra food — unaware that Oswin secretly shared his own with Mathie. "Today will be the deciding battle," the boy announced, his voice wavering. The King's armorer says he'll beat me if I don't fetch help." There was fear in the lad's eyes as he spoke. "They are short of men everywhere. The mood up there is not good, Oswin."

Oswin nodded. The boy left the tent.

Mathie poked her head back out. Oswin gave her a worried look. He pointed at the tools.

Mathie picked up a hammer. "Please don't leave me here alone too long."

Oswin crushed her in his arms. His eyes were wet. What did a sister mean to an orphan who relied on others to speak for him? She hadn't considered it until now.

He left and she busied herself shaping a rough shoe. A voice thundered through the tent. "Who are *you*?"

Smith stood at the door, anger creasing his face. The tanned apron he wore daily now had a jagged rip in it. Mathie jumped. How—? At the door behind Smith, the string of noisemakers had fallen aside when Oswin left.

"Where's Oswin?" the man asked. Mathie managed to shake her head. He grabbed her and lifted a curled fist. "Tell me where he is!"

Smith's strong fingers pressed through to the bone and the grip was excruciating. "Samuel must have stolen him to help with his shoddy breastplates," he said, stepping back. He put a hand to his forehead. "Even though I threatened to break his neck if he did."

He took Mathie's arm, looking at her burns. Similar marks, long faded to scars, covered his own forearms. Pushing her back, he grabbed a cold nail from her workspace and held it up in the firelight. "You, girl? You've been doing this the whole time?"

Mathie met his eyes, trying not to look frightened.

Puffing out his cheeks, he exhaled. "I have no choice." Smith left the tent, returning with a dark brown mare. It walked haltingly, a shoe on its front left hoof hanging to the side by one nail.

"This is a horse of the king's counsel. I will pay if it isn't dealt with today. Try to shoe it as neatly as Oswin."

Mathie felt a smirk creep across her face.

His eyebrows lifted. "Hmmm," he said, and walked out of the tent.

Mathie lifted the horse's hoof and straightened the shoe. She decided it would be best to pull the last nail and flatten the shoe a bit more. The soft part in back of the hoof was tender and she could afford it a little more protection. When she looked up, Smith was leading the small horse from the Christian camp, the one ridden by the ugly, leering guardsman. It favored its sore leg even worse now.

"This belonged to a guardsman who was beheaded for not doing his job. The Christians have promised to ride for Arthur, but Idres is cutting us down like wheat. We are all short of horses." He stared at it for a moment. "If we weren't, I'd feed this thing to the men and not waste the time."

Mathie tried not to let her hands shake as Smith followed her every step. When she was done, he surveyed her work. He led the counselor's horse to the entryway. "I'll be back for the other one," he said. He paused, looking thoughtful. "When Arthur's meddler asked me to take an apprentice, I was sure we'd already made the best choice. Perhaps not. Do well and maybe I won't chase you out of here."

Mathie strung the noisemaker over the door again. Her gut, still knotted from the visit, didn't loosen any when she realized there wasn't enough iron for the last horse. Oswin had roughly beat out three shoes the previous day, and she had enough for the fourth. But, at most, she could cobble enough bits together for two nails.

Usually, the coal-boys had wheeled a barrow of iron in by now. Where were they? Good fortune had struck; Oswin's master had all but approved of her presence and she needed to protect this opportunity. There was no choice. She had to find the iron herself.

Steeling her nerve, she unfastened the tent flap. Only then did she notice the din that had arisen while she worked.

Screams of pain floated through the air, giving her gooseflesh. Over the rise in the distance, smoke drifted above the followers' camp.

Much closer, Idres' red-striped horsemen rode through King Ban's spearmen as though they were tall grass. The horsemen's swords swung back and forth. Shiny helmets spun through the air, their gruesome contents spraying trails of dark droplets.

A dozen horsemen came from behind her, one carrying the triple-crowned banner of Arthur. They charged the enemy mounts from the side. Before they were close, a cloud of arrows dropped upon them.

A whinnying horse screamed past Mathie, shafts sticking from its neck. Arthur's horsemen lay dead on the ground. Riderless horses milled about.

With the spearmen decimated, Mathie had an unobstructed view of Idres' army. They resembled a moving wall more than a row of men. She spun about to run back to the tent. It wasn't there.

In its place stood Myrle. His back to her, the cloaked man spread his arms wide and the air shimmered where the tent should have been. She fled into the next closest one. It was empty, save a few lengths of rope.

"Come out of there. Now!" A sonorous voice permeated her skull. "We have no time!"

Mathie clutched her head. Her world seemed to grow more confusing whenever this man appeared. Outside, it was madness. Her entire life was madness. If she faced him, perhaps she could make sense of things. She slipped back out of the tent.

He stood holding the reins of a tall white horse now, his other hand in the air, palm upward. In the vaporous air around him, Mathie could see the opening — just the opening — of her own tent. A column of men bearing long pikes streamed past them, parting as they marched. Further back, a group of red-bannered horseman galloped toward them. At their front was a massive figure in black armor.

"Get in there girl," the cloaked man boomed.

Mathie stepped through the tent opening. The hearths were blazing as though she had just stoked them. "The King needs a well-shod warhorse. Now, or there will be no King!"

"But I can't—" Mathie took a breath and gulped. "I have nothing to forge into shoes."

"Have you not? Nothing you might be concealing?'

She knew what he meant. Fetching the bundle she'd tried to forget about all these past weeks, she opened it and laid the cross on her iron work block.

"It is the Cross of Apostles, forged from the nails of early followers who were crucified. The reason we have it is because the Christians bicker in Constantinople. The ones here hoped to offer it to Arthur, if he let them found a church on our soil." The man's voice softened, less fearsome now, more scholarly and human.

"Like all religions, they fumble about, grasping the smallest bits of truth. But they are right in believing this object is special. I mean to use it."

Mathie pushed it into the hot coals. "Thank you for the food that day," she blurted. "But — why give it to me?"

It took until a soft, orange glow crept into the heated metal before he said anything.

"I use my power for Arthur, but I do not possess as much as he thinks. What I do best is find the pieces of a game and set them in motion. That is often all I can do. You are headstrong and impulsive, but not too much so. You are also compassionate. I fed you that morning believing something — I could not be sure what — would come of it."

Mathie pulled the cross from the fire and reached for her customary hammer. He stayed her hand and pushed it towards the large one Oswin favored. "Arthur has nothing but good in him. The holy men — some do, many do not. I have seen the horrors this church will visit upon the world. The magic objects they accumulate would compound their atrocities. Better they are used for our cause."

Lightheadedness overtook her, like the delirium of a fever. The fire slowed, long tongues of flame barely moving now, swaying like flower petals. Oswin's hammer felt no heavier than a spoon. A giant clang pierced her ears when she swung it down. Sparks floated into the air like dust motes in a sunbeam.

She tried to distract herself from the odd sensations. "Wait. You've seen what the Christians *will* do?"

"Time is a fable told from the beginning, middle and end all at once. One of my few true powers is to catch glimpses, sometimes affect how others perceive that fable. You saw that outside, and feel the effects of it now, no? I very much wish I could see the whole thing, what befalls us here. I've seen bits of *your* tale, but ultimately you are the one who must tell it. The story of two children, the son and daughter of a coppersmith; I suspect much will hang on how that ends."

If all this were true, Mathie did not like her own story so far. Neither, surely, did Oswin. And, if Idres' men continued advancing, there would be more children with dead parents. "This horse will help Arthur stop Idres?"

"If it survives. I wish I could have brought two, to have a fresh one should Arthur need it."

Mathie pointed at the Christian guard's small, weak horse in the corner. "But there is not enough metal here for two horses," she said.

Her hammer made the only sound until he spoke. "I see that one. It is scarcely a horse at all. But perhaps you are right. Too much is at stake to depend on one horse entirely if I don't have to."

He reached into his cloak again. Unrolling a swath of lustrous cloth, he produced several shards of gleaming steel. It was obvious they were once part of a long, sharp blade, so finely polished she could see her reflection in each piece.

"This was Arthur's famed sword, Caledfwlch, shattered in his fight against King Pellinore. The remnants may still possess enough magic to be of use to us." He put them in the hearth, rolling coals over them.

Mathie pointed at the hearth, the tools. "Is all this magic?" she asked.

"Very little," he said. "Much of what you are doing here is known to armies across the sea. Arthur's counsel wish me to smite the enemy — as if it were so easy." He made a sweeping gesture. "I have brought this new craft to our kingdom for a reason. These skills can bring an army victory and still be practiced long after I am gone."

She tapped the last nail into the white horse's front shoe. Myrle grabbed the reins. "Finish the last one, bring it outside and wait. Stay near this tent and you will be safe."

"Out *there?*"

He pulled back his hood. A long gray beard flowed down into his cloak. His face was gaunt. The eyes were younger, moist and gleaming, but Mathie could see fatigue in them.

"I've asked much of you." He waved an arm at the tent wall. "If Arthur wins the day, no child may ever again experience what you have gone through. If Idres triumphs, prepare to live in darkness. All that we love out there, it rests with us, and Arthur is the one man I trust to preserve it. Through him, you and I serve everyone."

He led the horse out.

Mathie rolled the softened metal of the broken sword in with some extra bits of iron. An afternoon's work passed through her hands in a few blinks.

The horse stiffened as soon as she tapped in the first nail. Its breaths grew slower and deeper. When she finished, she walked it in a small circle. It no longer seemed lame.

The air still shone as she slid out of the tent. The din of battle was a low, deep murmur and the black rider had merely advanced halfway. Someone new had appeared though: Oswin.

He stood like a living statue. Soot covered his face and he looked bewildered. Of course. He couldn't see the tent, the same as Mathie before.

She led the horse forward, away from the tent. Instantly, the thunder of hooves and the howls of dying men erupted around her. The black rider and his men bore straight at them at breakneck speed. "Oswin!" she screamed.

His head jerked and he blinked. "Mah-ie!"

Standing there would mean dying. The one path that didn't take them into the heart of the battle was toward the followers' camp. Mathie pointed in its direction and considered the fact that she'd never actually ridden a horse. Oswin, however, had steered cart horses before.

"Oswin!" She handed him the reins. "Get us away from here!"

He wrapped his hand in the horse's mane and pulled himself up. Reaching down, he grabbed her hand and swung her up behind him. The horse lurched ahead. Mathie clutched Oswin's arm, sure she'd fall.

A wind crossed her neck as the black knight's sword whistled past her head.

She looked back to see his horse, a massive charger, wheel about and give chase. It snorted, nostrils flaring, and the muscles of its haunches rippled as it propelled its master forward. His visor was up and deathly purpose burned in his eyes.

"He's upon us!" Mathie shouted.

Oswin leaned over their horse's neck and kicked its belly. It shot forward and Mathie caught a fistful of Oswin's tunic in the nick of time.

They rode straight into the other horsemen. The first few wielded lances, and the horse somehow sidestepped them.

Making an impossibly sharp cut to the left, then right again, the siblings threaded through the last of the horsemen and were clear. The black-armored man was still close behind.

Now they were among dead spearmen, dodging the strewn bodies, leaping over two at a time. The first landing caught Mathie unprepared, jarring her, causing her to bite her tongue. When they were through, the horse put his head down, gaining speed until the wind made her eyes water.

Well behind them now, the armored man turned away.

Bodies young and old littered the followers' camp, cut down where they stood. Black patches of ground smoldered where tents had been. A man lay on his back, his head half gone. Mathie recognized the cleaved face by its eyeless socket. *Good riddance, one-eye.* Before she'd even completed the thought, she felt shame for thinking it.

Oswin reined their horse back as they approached a cluster of bodies, dismounting near a crumpled footman. His helmet bore the red line of Idres. Dead fingers still clutched his sword.

Oswin glanced around. He spread his hands questioningly.

Mathie was supposed to be waiting back at their tent with this horse. What to do next?

Oswin's eyes went wide and he took a step back.

"You there," a voice shouted. A hand came from behind and snatched the reins, jerking Mathie and her mount around.

One of Arthur's men sat astride a weary-looking horse. White foam lathered its flanks. Mud covered the soldier's face and red seeped from beneath a gash in the mail on his chest. "A strapping lad with a horse! Do you see that?" He pointed to a swarm of men, mere dots, fighting between them and the Christian camp. Smoke rose from that camp too.

The soldier dismounted and strode over to Oswin. "King Arthur's men fight for their very survival. All good men have been called to take up his cause." He picked up the dead footman's sword and poked the tip into the fallen helmet, flipping it into the air. Oswin caught it to prevent it striking his face.

The soldier gestured at the melee. "Your new King will bring about a better age. But he must prevail here today, or lose all."

The man handed Oswin the sword and remounted. "A man's chance to show true valor, such as you can today if you so choose, are rare. So, then —what will you do?"

Oswin hesitated.

Mathie considered Myrle's words; how things would be better under Arthur, how terrible life might be if not. If she were in Oswin's place, she would go. If she told him to go, he would. He'd always trusted her. But she couldn't bring herself to ask him to do this.

She slid down and walked the horse over. Unblinking, Oswin took the reins and clambered up.

"Follow me," the soldier said, turning his horse around. "And pray to whomever you might pray."

Oswin overtook him immediately. It was probably a trick of the eyes, smoke in the air maybe, but the little horse's hooves barely touched the ground.

The trees far across the clearing were likely the safest place to hide. She was almost there when she heard pounding hoofbeats and the shouts of men, growing stronger with every second.

An armored rider with a red stripe on his shield flew past and then swung about, facing her. An elaborately tooled leather mantle lay across his shoulders and his helmet bore a thick plume. Mathie's heart stopped. She knew it couldn't be Idres, but surely it was someone to be reckoned with. She followed his gaze.

Across the expanse behind her, dust rose above the approaching horde. A man in shining silver rode in and out of the chaos, brandishing a sword and shouting. Well ahead of him, crossing the gap in a blur, was Oswin.

She'd seen the expression on his face one time before; the night the great house burned. He'd crashed through the door and scooped her and Mother up, throwing them over his shoulders. He kicked his way through the flaming wreckage, roaring and shouting — bestial, violent sounds frightening her almost as much as the fires. His face that night had been a mask of fearless, resolute determination — and was even more so now.

Oswin raised his sword and charged at the armored rider. His arm tensed, rippling with cords of muscle accustomed to a heavy hammer. Mathie heard the blade as it landed, splitting armor and prompting a scream of pain.

The rider tried to turn his horse about and flee. Oswin's steed danced around it, blocking escape. Jabbing with his sword, the soldier tried to attack but Oswin's horse sidled just out of reach.

Oswin lifted his weapon for another blow.

Then the galloping horses were upon Mathie, mowing her down in a tangle of legs. She screamed as a horse stepped on her back. A hoof came toward her eyes and next there was nothing.

— «» —

"I admit, my hopes were dashed when you two fled. But you delivered to Arthur a mounted knight on the freshest of horses, just when he needed him."

Mathie heard the voice in the darkness, recognized it, but could not see where it came from.

She tried to open her eyes. One was swollen shut. She could hardly see anything out of the other. It took a moment to realize this was because it was dusk.

The cart she lay in went over a bump, jolting her. Sitting up, she saw the cloaked man, riding the horse that pulled it. Around her, the battle camp lay in ruins. But the tent she and Oswin had called home was unscathed. The cart stopped.

The cloaked man took her hand in the near-darkness. "It took me some time to find you. Come now. The battle is won. Not the war, not just yet — but I fully believe you will change that."

Mathie was steadier on her feet than she thought she'd be. Folding back his cowl, the man smiled.

"There is food and drink in your tent," he said. "Tomorrow, Master Smith will be here with your new apprentice. No doubt, there is more you will learn — but already you have plenty to teach."

Still dazed, she could barely comprehend. This was good news. Nonetheless, pain shot through every inch of her body when she moved. She felt all used up and wanted nothing more than to lay down right there on the ground and close her eyes. "Enough with you," she said. "You fool about with my life as if I were your plaything, and never so much as ask."

His eyes wrinkled around the edges and he smiled. "I do lack manners," he said. "But I promise you, I will be your friend to the last of your days. Your brother's too." He touched her and she winced. "More than ever now, I believe if you let the right people tell their own tale, things will end as they should."

Her head throbbed, but his words jarred a single thought loose: "Oswin."

"We'll know his fate soon." He brightened. "But from what I hear from Smith, there will soon be songs of the girl who shoed Arthur's horse. It is you who won this day as much as anyone. Someday, when they sing of Camelot, when Arthur's horses charge forward to protect that which is good, the kingdom will know your name and praise your part in it."

Mathie was unsure what he meant by "Camelot." Before she could ask, he led her around the side of the tent. A fire blazed and dozens of people stood around it.

A small group of riders approached from out of the darkness. The first's shoulders were slumped and he looked like he could no longer hang on. Wearing the helmet he'd been given, it was Oswin, still on the same horse. One arm hung limply to the side, dragging the sword he'd ridden out with.

A knight in full armor rode up beside Oswin. Unlike Oswin's steed, head high, straining at the reins, this one's head hung down, spent. "Foh Ah-huh!" the knight shouted, a twisted grin on his face. "Fuh Oh-hah!" another knight yelled from behind.

Mathie clenched her fists as the men mocked her brother. She looked over to see Myrle's reaction, but he'd melted into the shadows.

Oswin pushed the too-large helmet back from his eyes. "Ah-huh!" he shouted, raising his sword.

"For Arthur!" the men shouted. As they rode past, several of them whooped and pounded his back.

They *weren't* mocking him.

They dismounted and circled around Oswin. Parting into rows, they removed their helmets and tucked them beneath their arms. And then another rode in, his horse taking high steps and looking every bit as fresh as Oswin's. Mathie noticed the crown before anything — the King himself.

Head-to-toe in silver armor, he rode through the men and they dropped to one knee. Oswin did the same.

Arthur wasn't tall or broad at the chest. Yet somehow, Mathie thought, he seemed larger than everyone. Someone ran up from behind and helped him down. He stood over Oswin. Light from the flames illuminated his crown.

Arthur said something and Oswin smiled. The king laid the flat of his blade on each of her brother's shoulders. The men surrounding them cheered.

When Arthur rode away, the knights walked to the fire, arm in arm, singing. Songs of battle and victory, no doubt.

Whatever had happened — more than she'd seen — Oswin was obviously a hero now. Mathie didn't want to interfere with the men around him, but she edged toward the fire as they dispersed.

The singing grew louder and the sound of instruments reached her ears. Mathie touched Oswin's arm, wrapping her arms around him when he saw her. He kissed the bruise on her forehead.

A group of minstrels sang lustily, three of them strumming lutes. A knight stepped out of the shadows, clasping Oswin's hand. "Aye, you lot!" he shouted at the minstrels. "Tomorrow this young man rides forth as a knight! Sing of *him*, who fought side-by-side with the King and turned the battle!"

The firelight threw splashes of gold onto the knight's armor, reminding Mathie of the light that danced upon the cross in the foreigners' tent months ago. Oswin threw his arm around his sister, squeezing her tight. She winced, but not so much as she smiled.

The minstrels crowded around them and one lifted Oswin's arm.

Another stepped forward and raised Mathie's too, entwining her fingers with Oswin's. Clasping their hands tightly, the minstrel opened his mouth and began to sing.

— ⟪⟫ —

Rick Overwater is a longtime Calgary-based writer and musician. His short stories have appeared in several anthologies covering a variety of genres including weird-west, crime-noir, fantasy, and science fiction. He loves guitars. And short sentences. He has been advised that, when dancing, he should assume *everyone* is watching.

Sir Tor and the River Maiden

Colleen Anderson

Sir Tor cursed and wiped his bloodied hands across the ferns, then tucked his shirt into his hosen and stepped from behind the giant oak. Immediately, he ducked back on hearing a sound like chiming bells, a woman's voice lilting in tune to the falls that plashed nearby. What had she seen? The song stopped abruptly. He peered around the broad, rough-barked trunk and saw a maiden with widened eyes looking around from where she languished in a nature-carved basin. Water streamed from her hair, obscuring all but a hint of bare skin.

There was no sneaking off now. His back against the trunk, Tor called out. "Fair maiden, I meant not to fright you and indeed did not realize you were there."

Her voice rang strident and clear. "Come out now!"

He reluctantly stepped from behind the tree, pushing aside leaves of a soft reddish hue, much like he imagined the blush to his cheeks. Yet another delay to his quest. Moving through the decaying bracken, he looked upon the woman standing up to her chest in the cool river. The falls behind her added a murmur as the water poured over rounded rocks and gurgled down a gentle incline to meander on its way through the forest. How he would have loved to shed his mail and clothes and cleanse the grime of riding from his body. But he dared not.

The maiden stared up at him with slatted eyes, hair tinted by the surrounding autumn colors, no hint of the chill affecting her. The arm covering her chest was as white and slender as a birch. In her other hand, she held a short, leaf-bladed sword. Tor did not recognize the style, and while it looked old, light glinted off the keen edge.

"What do you want, *man*?" Her lip curled as she pronounced the last word and he wondered if she had been beset upon in the past. Her beauty was luminous, her skin looking almost translucent in the late afternoon light.

He held his hands up, away from his own sword. "I want nothing, m'lady. I stopped only to rest before I continue my quest for King Arthur." He had not wanted to encounter anyone. Especially at such a trying time, he had to keep his secret.

She kept the sword pointed at him but cocked her head to one side. "Arthur. I have heard tales of knights and how they treat 'fair ladies.' Some are good and some claim to be good while they force themselves upon those not strong enough to repel them. Which are you, *man*?"

"I uphold the code of chivalry," Tor said indignantly, remembering the tale of how a king had lain with his mother 'half by force.' Who was this wench to question him, though, a knight of the king's court? But he had not long been a knight and indeed was the first made. By his deeds would others judge King Arthur's knights. "Honor, honesty, valor and loyalty is what I believe in."

"I would assist a damsel in need and would never do any harm. I seek only the glory of battle, to go on quests set by my liege, and to right the wrongs that are perpetrated upon the weak."

Her laugh startled him. "Oh, you are such a young knight, are you not? So *noble*. And what quest does your worthy king send you on? Does it involve you using your stick? Would you poke it in any hole you find, whether you know what's there or not?"

She mocked him but he was not sure what she hinted at. Tor pressed his lips together, refusing her goad. "My lady, I apologize for any slight I have given you. But I'm in chase of a knight who stole a brachet from the court during Arthur's wedding."

"A hound? That is your quest?"

He shifted his footing, averting his eyes from her bare flesh. "It was stolen and as such, the wrong must be righted."

"It sounds more the chore for an errand boy. How many of these quests have you taken on?"

He tried not to stare at her, at the clear water revealing a wavering form beneath the surface. "This is my first one, my lady. But knights take many quests, to rescue maidens in need, fight errant knights, find mystical objects, and rid the land of monsters. If you will allow, I shall be on my way and bother you no more."

"Monsters?" Her sword lowered, but the blade still pricked above the water. Then she raised her head, drawing air deep, her nostrils flaring, and closed her eyes. "Ah, you are a young knight, on a virgin quest and I would surmise a virgin too. Tell me, are these monsters just creatures different than you, not as fair?"

She smiled but Sir Tor did not find it friendly at all. He ignored his cramping belly. "It is my first quest, only to bring back the hound. I beg your leave." He took a step back.

"Wait!" Her command stilled him.

She titled her head to the other side. "Does not your code say you will help those in need?"

He nodded.

"Then, good knight, I ask a boon of you. It is a riddle too. Bring me the head of a dwarf, one of your monsters, but without killing him. Should you do this, I will give you ample reward. And ... I will not reveal your secret."

"My secret? What—"

With that, her arms flashed into the air, the sword having disappeared.

"Wait!"

As she dove, Tor saw a flash of breasts, pale and perfect as she disappeared into the water. He had seen breasts before and tried not to think of it. He blinked and looked again but the surface was calm, the maiden gone. He had not had a chance to ask her how capturing a dwarf was something she needed. Glancing toward the falls, he surmised that she must have swum under the curtain of water and now watched him from behind the waterfalls, most likely laughing at his awkwardness.

As he strode back to his horse, angry that he'd been unable to articulate the code of chivalry, he wondered about the mysterious maiden. He had never been with a woman and had indeed tried to keep his thoughts away from such turmoil. Fighting and riding had been all that occupied his thoughts for years, and by focusing on those skills he had kept himself sane and his secrets to himself. His mother had taught him caution early on, and no one else knew what he hid. Had the maiden been toying with him or did she truly know?

He leapt astride his horse, its tawny head nuzzling through brush and meadow leaves. He pulled up on the reins; the horse left off, shifting its head, and Sir Tor rode from the glade, birch leaves falling like golden coins in the sunset.

— «» —

Tor's stomach growled. Knight, he might be but his supplies were meager, and only had the few coins his father had given him. As eldest, he had always wanted more, not happy to just herd and farm the land as his younger brothers had. He had always been different and when Merlin revealed him not to be his father's son, it only explained some of his differences. But Tor believed in his heart in the good of the knights, of the nobility they brought to Arthur's court. He would prove his worthiness and that he was equal.

The maiden had been correct. He was sent to fetch a hound, while the others had been sent in pursuit of the errant knight or the missing lady.

So deep in thought was Sir Tor that he missed the beauty of the autumn painted forest, the slow darkening as the day made ready to leave and indeed hide all the details of his surroundings. It was his horse's sudden rearing back that threw him out of his thoughts.

The horse shook its head from the stave that had smacked it between the eyes.

"Hold up!" came a high reedy voice.

Sir Tor unsheathed his sword, looking around in the gloaming.

"Sir knight," the voice came again and Tor looked down. He first saw a long object and took it for the staff that had hit his horse. A man, small of stature, dressed in rough spun hosen and tunic stood before him. His cap was askew and none too clean, with scratches crisscrossing his face and a bruise purpling his eye.

"What would you dare?" asked Sir Tor. The tiny man was unarmed and surely Tor could not do battle with one half his height.

"You must fight the knights over yonder or you may not pass." The man pointed with the staff.

Tor looked. A pavilion canted to one side, dirt patches visible in the waning light. The undefined pennons hung limply from the top.

"No. I have a quest I must complete." He twitched the reins to send his horse around the small man.

The man shook his head, scowling. "Then you cannot pass."

Tor laughed. "You cannot stop me and I will not battle you."

As he made to go around a weight hurtled him from his saddle. Guttural roaring accompanied his fall to the ground.

Being taken by surprise could have been the end of Tor, but growing up with eleven brothers had taught him other moves that did not involve swordplay.

He grasped his sword tightly, and rolled away as his horse whinnied, shying from the tumult underfoot. Tor came up into a crouch and immediately spun to his left as another dark shape barreled toward him. He brought his sword pommel down on the back of the man, momentarily stunning him.

The fetid smell akin to a pig's wallow assaulted him as a sharp pain seared his belly. For a moment, he thought he'd been stabbed, then cursed his affliction. He took a deep breath and moved into the offensive, toward the first man who circled to Tor's left. From what he could discern, neither wore armor more than a simple padded hauberk. The first to knock him off his horse came back, a spear in his hand, but as he thrust it forward, Tor sidestepped to the right, turned forty-five degrees and cleaved the spear in half with a down-ward swing. He did not stop there but spun a full circle, smacking the flat of his blade hard against the man's head.

An "oomph" escaped as the man slumped to the ground.

The other man roared and rushed Tor, knocking him to the ground, but Tor took that momentum, dropping his sword and grabbing the man's greasy hauberk, pulling them into a full somersault that ended with Tor on top. He punched right, left, right and the man went limp.

The other 'knight' was still down. Tor pushed himself up, picking up his sword and checking his horse while keeping an eye on the two knights.

The small man stood off to the side, watching silently. Tor pointed his sword at him and said, "I'm not going to have trouble from you, am I?"

The man shook his head. "Not for the likes of those two."

Tor walked over to their camp and a poor one it was too. A thin gruel bubbled in a pot. The pavilion might once have had bright colors but was marred more by moss and dirt stains, and in several spots the canvas sagged, revealing rents into a dim and shabby interior. Their benches were logs and they barely had enough bowls and spoons between them.

There were two shields, their arms faded, and a couple of pitted blades. These were knights?

He asked the servant, who had silently come over to watch Tor, "Who are these men?"

The man shrugged. "Gregor and Antelius. Knaves more than knights."

Tor frowned. How could that be? He'd heard tales for years that had fueled his desire to be a knight. The troubadours sang of gallant men, completing great deeds for the needy. These vulgar curs had not even greeted him properly but sprung upon him like varlets. There had been no fair fight, and thanks to a lifetime of wrestling, Tor had come out on top. What had these two done to others they'd met on their path?

Groaning accompanied the two men who helped each other over to their meager fire. Their faces were as hard to see for the wild growth of beard as for the smudges of dirt that married them with the forest more than with any civil nature.

"You are knights?" Tor looked to each of them.

"As it is coined," said the shorter of the two as he rubbed at his matted black curls.

The willowy one snorted, revealing fewer teeth than black gaps. "We still have our horses, and what's left of armor, if that's what you mean."

"But…" Tor waved his sword around him. "You did not follow the code of chivalry, did not even ask my name."

When they sat, they did not even offer him a spot. Antelius, the stocky knight, spat. "You are a young fool, aren't you?"

The other drank brackish water from a wooden ladle. "You'll see, once you've been a knight for a while, without land, without a home. It's not such a wonderful life."

Tor sheathed his sword, but watched them closely, his lips pressed tight. This could not be. The knights of Arthur's court bore themselves with dignity, were clean and held the aspirations of the king. Tor himself may have had only simple mail but he was new and would make sure he did not become a degenerate like these two.

Still … he stared at the two men. Arthur's reign was still young, his reputation forming and it was the duty of the knights of the Round Table to spread his glory throughout the land, to uphold the rights and code that would make the kingdom legendary. But not with tales of wrestling in the woods.

He drew himself up as tall as he could. "I charge you with this duty as I have bested you, though you made it less than a fair fight." They both stopped and looked at him, eyebrows raising. "You will clean yourselves up and present yourselves to King Arthur's court. You will say you met and waylaid Sir Tor on his quest for the brachet and you will say I bested you in a *fair* fight. Should you not do this, when I return from my quest, I will hunt you down and take those scruffy heads from your bodies."

They silently watched him for a full minute, then Antelius burst out laughing. "Of course, me lord." He bowed.

Gregor snorted. "Fool. You'll soon learn quests are never what you think they are."

Sir Tor spun away, cursing under his breath. They laughed at him, just as the river maiden had. He straddled his horse and was about to gallop off when a voice drifted up to him. "My lord, I would go with you, if I may."

"I have no use for a follower."

"I'll be your servant as you seem to have neither that nor a squire. And all knights should." The man looked over to the paltry camp and spat upon the ground. "And I'll work no longer for such wastrels."

Tor stared into the shadows. This was the first person who wasn't laughing at him. "Fine then, but you'll need a horse."

The man put two fingers to his chapped lips and whistled. A small pony trotted over, and he was mounted by the time Tor turned to the trail.

As luck would have it, the sky chose that moment to let loose its belligerence, rain pelting and instantly chilling them. There was no castle, no lady biding him to sup, not even a paltry hermitage. In the end, drenched and shivering, they found the lee of a crumbling grange to keep away the driving rain and wait out the night's storm under sodden cloaks.

— «» —

His name was Owen and he worked without complaint, content to let Tor lead.

Sir Tor let the horse carry him forward, wondering how he would find a hound in the vast woods. And then there was the river maiden's request. Demand.

"Owen, have you traveled far with your former masters?"

Owen snorted and spit. "Far enough and too far. Every mile felt like forever and whether they were hungry or drunk, they took their sport out upon me. Unless, of course, some young fool came along."

Did he mean Tor? "Well, I'm sorry for your pains and swear I will not treat you so ill."

"We shall see."

They rode bedraggled, still damp in the cool air. "Tell me though, have you ever seen mountains filled with gems or gold."

He turned back, halting his horse, for Owen's pony had stopped.

Owen sat with his mouth open. "And just where would such mountains be, my lord."

"That I don't know, but I have a second quest, after I find the hound. And it is most likely I must go where the legendary smiths of lore reside, though I'm not sure how I'll accomplish my task."

Owen clucked to his pony and caught up to Tor. They moved into a glade of pale gorse that crunched underfoot and through the trees now bereft of most leaves they saw lazy curls of smoke. A town to find warmth and dry out, and a good meal were in order.

"What smiths of lore are these that you're seeking?"

"The dwarves, the mountain lords. I am to find a dwarf as part of my quest."

Tor was taken aback when Owen started laughing. Owen drew a breath, looked upon Sir Tor's puzzled face and laughed harder, letting go of the reins, guffawing, and grabbing his belly.

"What's got into you, man?"

Owen's howls vibrated through the meadow and Tor looked around, thinking he had missed some antics. Tears wet Owen's cheeks as he tumbled off his pony. Even after he thumped against the ground, he righted himself, groaning and laughing as he got to his feet. He hung onto his pony's bridle, his mirth finally subsiding as he gasped for air.

"What is so funny?" Tor had a feeling he wouldn't like the answer.

Owen settled his cap back on his head, trying not to look at Tor. He chortled again, then bent over, hands on knees and drew in a deep breath.

"You read a great deal, didn't you? All those tales of fairies, and magical beings? Well there are no mountain kings living on mounds of gold and making enchanted weapons. In fact, you're looking at a dwarf."

"Wha—" Tor shook his head. "What?"

"I am a dwarf, Sir Tor. A man who is small. And there is nothing magic about me." He giggled as he mounted his pony again. "If only I had a mountain full of gems." Moving into the lead, he left Tor astride his horse, his face burning as yet another foundation of his beliefs tumbled down.

The village's meager inn was not more than a thatched cottage, but it was warm and dry. Sir Tor ate his stew quietly, hoping it would lessen the pain in his belly, and looked at the three other men, farmers by the looks, who sat at a table and glanced over at the dwarf several times. Of course, Owen was a dwarf — dwarfed by the world around him. He'd said there was no magic.

Tor caught a mumbled phrase of 'half man'. Owen paid it no heed as he ate and drank. "It's been a long while since I had enough to fill my belly. My thanks."

He nodded, paying little attention, lost in his own thoughts. A half man. Tor bit his lip and stared into his wooden bowl, moving the spoon through the remaining liquid, drawing paths and swirls.

Was Arthur's sword, Caliburn, just the same as every other weapon? Was it not revealed by magic? And Merlin himself was a creature of magic, wasn't he?

He sighed and sipped his ale. Being a knight was not what he thought it would be. All these small events that dragged out his quest, how did they bring glory to the king?

Yet Tor had never wanted anything else. To marry and farm the land was not in his future. What else was there for him to be, but a knight? The alternative quaked his belly.

He quaffed the last of his drink and firmly set the mug down. The world was divesting itself of the dreamstuff with which Tor had woven his tapestry. Nevertheless, his liege had requested he right a wrong. He would be the best he could be, no matter that magic and even the code of conduct was more elusive than he had surmised.

— «» —

Sir Tor scowled at the man kneeling at his feet. Blood dripped down his hand, onto his sword, mingling with the other man's. At least this one had had decent armor, better than Tor's, but why risk life and limb for a dog? He snorted and the man squinted through sweat at him.

Tor's quest had been for the damn hound, to set justice right. And he would have died to get the brachet, ever loyal to Arthur. The woman standing before him, robed in a heavy green tunic trimmed in gray squirrel fur, her hair modestly wrapped in linens, watched closely. She clenched her fists, tears ready to fall.

She said again, "I ask justice, my lord. When my brother yielded to him and I knelt with him, begging for an hour, he did not spare my brother's life, but struck his head from his body, for no reason other than sport. I ask the same to balance justice's scales.

Tor shook his head, looking at this knight. "You would not yield to me when I offered. Yet now you beg for your life? Truly you are a fool. I have no choice and must uphold the code. Prepare to meet your lord."

Tor hefted his sword as the man bowed his head, either not wanting to see the fatal swing or already praying. The severing jarred him back, gore splattering everywhere. The woman now turned away, paling at the execution. Tor hacked repeatedly at the thick neck as the body jerked, drumming its feet against the ground.

He spat in the dirt, clearing his mouth of bile. Grimly, he grabbed the head by the blood-spackled hair and shoved it in a rough woven sack that once had held some food.

He handed it to Owen. "Return to Arthur's court with this and the hound. I will take care of the body and be on my way by tomorrow. "

Owen shook his head, silent and tying the sack at the back of his saddle. He glanced once at the woman, her back still to them, and pulled the pony's reins.

Tor stared into the thinning trees. He estimated there were about two hours until nightfall. Chill crept out of the ground, and the air was sour with sweat and blood.

"My lady, you need not linger. I'll take care of this." He rummaged in the leather panniers, pulling out a short-handled spade. He began to dig off the trail. Would anyone miss this man? Had stealing a dog and thwarting Arthur's rule been worth it?

The woman came over. "Thank you for avenging my brother's murder. I will go on ahead but you must come to our castle and spend the evening. My husband will be glad to meet you and I'll have a supper prepared." She touched his arm, her fingers trailing down as she drew his attention. She gave him directions, then rode away on a magnificent black horse with gold and green barding draped over its haunches.

Tor thought about riding straight on to Camelot but the fight and burying the body left him exhausted and sore. A night's rest would be better than wandering a trail in the dark.

The small castle offered some comfort and the lady's husband was her senior by two decades. Sir Alistair chatted with Tor about castle upkeep and then excused himself early to bed. Tor's limbs were shaky with fatigue and the dancing torchlight begged him to sleep as well, but he couldn't be rude. Lady Richildis still sat with him, sipping mead and talking about her brother.

She refilled their cups and sat close, too close to Tor. He shifted uneasily. When Richildis leaned toward him, her hand on his knee, he leaned away. "You must excuse me, my lady. It's been a long day and I am sore from battle." He rose and went to the simple room they had given him for the night.

With the one taper burning, he prepared for bed, taking off his tunic and chemise. He had just begun to unwind the bandages on his chest when a breeze licked across his back. Whirling, his shirt held to cover him, he saw Richildis standing in the doorway, a candlestick in her hand.

"My lady!" He moved forward quickly, pushing her back through the door before she could close it. "You must not be in here. Please, leave now."

She resisted at the doorway, swaying from the mead's effects, trying to lean in and kiss him. "Don't make me leave." She whimpered. "It has been so long. Alistair is not fit to lay with anymore."

Tor edged the door closed, pushing her out, still holding his shirt up. "I cannot! I am an honorable knight and this would be fair neither to your husband nor the laws of Arthur's land." With that, he closed the door, lowering the latch before she could say more.

His back against the wooden door, Tor closed his eyes, face in hands, trying to still his heart. Had she seen?

The cramps and blood had finally stopped days ago, but he could not hide his physical affliction as easily. He continued to unwrap the bandages, his hated bound breasts coming into view. Quickly, without looking at them he drew on his night shirt and crawled beneath the coverlet. As he waited for sleep to draw its cover over his mind, he hoped Richildis had seen nothing in the low light. He would lose his knighthood if it were ever found out that his body was that of a woman's. How he hated it and the curse that caged him.

He shuddered, thinking of the fate of Richildis' life and the horror that would be his should he ever be discovered. There was no other life for him, besides a convent. All he had ever wanted was to be a knight, but honor, valor, loyalty and honesty were the foundations of chivalry, and he could never be honest. He would be a knight but it would be a sham.

When Tor took his leave in the morning, thanking Alistair and Richildis for their hospitality, neither he nor she would look the other in the eye.

Snow fell thick and fast and within an hour of leaving the humble castle Tor was battling a roaring wind that swirled snow like dervishes. White on white blinded him, freezing his eyelashes to his cheeks, numbing his fingers. Eventually, even the horse faltered against the driving blizzard. Tor jumped down, and pulled the horse toward some trees. While thin, they were numerous enough to block the worst of the storm with Tor hiding beneath his cloak against the horse's flank.

He fell into a state of endurance, all sound insulating him as his mind wandered in the maze of weather. And there he stared at four pillars as he walked out of the mist.

Upon each one was a statue of a knight in armor, holding a flag. One flag showed a lance emblazoned on a gold field, indicating honor. The second knight's flag showed an azure background with a wolf for loyalty; the third flag was a fierce silver griffin for valor, and the last held a silver lozenge, a red heart within for honesty. The knights' visored helms tilted down to watch Tor as he passed. Each one turned his back. The knight holding the flag of honesty broke the staff over his knee and tossed the pieces toward Tor.

The clatter brought him out of his stupor, to discover Owen staring down at him. He yelled through the swirling snow. "I thought you might be lost. I brought this."

A thick rectangular mantle landed on Tor's head. He wrapped numb fingers around it and pulled it close. Owen then handed him a skin. He gulp the liquid quickly, coughing but relishing the whiskey's warmth.

Sir Tor mounted his horse and they moved slowly through the driving snow toward Camelot.

Owen yelled over the wind, "Are you enjoying your knightly adventures?"

Tor ignored his jibe, thinking of how his fantasies had been quashed. Still, he had one last quest to complete. The river maiden.

They traveled for most of a day, Owen explaining that he had not returned to Camelot but had stowed the hound with a reliable friend, not far from the city.

Tor said nothing but led them toward the river. Twice, they had to shelter from the outraged storm, once they wandered back the way they came. Two days later, exhausted, numb and well disillusioned, Tor found the river basin. Branches dropped icy fingers of water down his neck and he slipped in mud once he dismounted. Owen gave him a questioning look and said nothing.

Muffled well from the winter weather, still Tor felt it bite at his cheeks and eyes. There would be no hope of finding the maiden in the river, let alone near it. Near the same broad-backed oak, Owen started a small fire, where he melted water, adding herbs and a splash of the dwindling whiskey to warm their limbs.

He never asked what Tor was doing nor tried to breach the dark pall that had fallen over the young knight. Tor was grateful for that. No matter that he was a sham, more a half man than Owen was, he would still fulfill this quest. Love might never be his, nor the ideals of chivalry but he would honor his word.

They camped the night on the chill ground and stayed the next day. It was only after the sun's chariot began to race toward the far horizon that a ripple in the water caught Tor's attention. He stood up and walked to the bank, his boots squelching through the decaying brown and yellow leaves. Snow held on in the shadows but had begun to melt away.

He leaned over, peering into the dark water, wondering if it was a fish he'd seen. A face appeared so abruptly, right below his, that he jumped back, slipping and falling in the mud.

Laughter, high and clear, filled the area. "You have returned, man. I am surprised."

The maiden grinned up at him, her hair wet and trailing in the water, her limbs only slightly less white than the snow. How could she stand the chill waters?

"Did you complete your quest?"

"Almost." He stood, wiping mud and leaves from his mantle. "The hound will shortly be returned and I have fulfilled your request. Owen?"

The dwarf came over, goggling at the woman in the water. Owen looked up at Sir Tor, puzzlement creasing his brow.

"Here is the head of a dwarf, and as you can see, I have not killed him."

The maiden spun in the water, laughing as if she were dancing at a ball. "Then I must give you your reward, but only you may receive it."

Tor thought of the tricks, the hidden motives that had beset his trial. Nothing ever had been what it seemed, or what he had thought it would be. He doubted she would give him more of a reward than a kiss, if even that. Still, curiosity won out.

He turned to Owen. "I'll meet you where you have kept the hound."

Owen nodded, looking once more at the maiden, then packed his gear and mounted his pony. Tor watched him leave, thinking how only Owen had shown merit of the people he had met on his quest. Turning back to the river maiden, Tor asked, "How can you be in the river without turning blue?"

She swirled her hand back and forth through the water. Grinning, she said, "It's not that cold. There is a natural spring. Try it."

He squatted, leaning forward to touch his fingers to the surface. The water was not warm, but tepid and a better temperature than the air that nipped at him.

"Why don't you join me?"

He pulled back. "I cannot." His secret would be his undoing, should anyone know. Looking around, Tor made sure she did not have other compatriots waiting in the trees.

"You can, Sir Tor. You'll find it pleasant enough."

He shook his head, mutely. "How is it you know my name?"

"I'm sure you told me." She dipped beneath the water, then emerged. "You forget, I already know your secret."

His hand gripped his sword's pommel, the cool metal bringing clarity. "What secret would that be?" he challenged.

As she had done once before, the maiden tilted her head back and breathed deep. "Ah, so young, so sweet, so untouched. You are a virgin, yes?"

Tor's shoulders slumped in relief. That was all. He could live with that secret. "You said you would give me a reward. Are you magical?" He hoped, yet the world was peeling back its skin to reveal what lay beneath and it was not as he thought. If he could peel back his own flesh, he would reveal the soul of a man, his true essence. Yet the world had chosen to play its cruel jest on him.

The maiden looked at him, all mirth gone from her dark green-brown eyes. "What is magic, Sir Tor? Is it finding the heart of a quest? Is it understanding the mysteries of the world? Is it fulfilling the dream of chivalry?"

He turned away, about to leave the river and its denizen behind, suspecting yet another subterfuge. "What does it matter? There is no magic." He turned back, glaring at her, angry. Angrier than he had ever been at what nature had dealt him, at what his real father had done to his mother, at all the lies that were told about chivalry and knights. He clenched his fists, his heat thawing the world about him. "There is only that which we hide from ourselves and from others. There are only lies and half-lies. You sent me to find the head of a dwarf, giving me a riddle that had little meaning but to amuse you. I ask you now my own riddle. When is a man not a man? Well?" He didn't wait and for this one time she did not seem to have the upper hand.

"You don't know the answer? Then I will give you the answer." As Sir Tor talked, he threw off his mantle and mail, undoing his sword, tossing all on a pile upon the bank. He unbuttoned his tunic, stripped off his hosen, and unwound the linen cloth that hid the truth of his body. He turned back to the water and waded in, naked.

"This is when a man is not a man. Will you laugh at me now, make me the target of your jests and your little games?"

The water licked coolly at his flesh, the cleft between his legs, his breasts, and dissipated the anger that had seared away all caution. But what would this maiden do? She would not harm him, yet she might spread word of his true nature.

He stood in front of her and she looked up at him. Her hand, cool and white, touched his cheek. "When is a woman not a woman?"

With that, she leaned away from him, into the water and as her head dipped beneath the river's surface a silvery green fish tail, larger than any Tor had ever seen, flipped up into the air. Her head broke the surface and she dove forward, completing several watery somersaults so that Tor had no doubt that the fishy appendage was her own.

He marveled at the woman, part fish, before him. She stopped in front of him once again and touched his face. "We are both part of two worlds. We may never have all of one."

Her tail whipped the water beneath her and she rose up until they were eye to eye. Then the maiden leaned in and kissed Tor. Her lips were surprisingly soft, not hot, nor cold. Tor had never kissed anyone and another form of heat obliterated any discomfort from the river.

The maiden's hands explored Tor's body, hardened by the labours of a fighter. In turn, he could not stop his hands from reaching forward to cup breasts he would not touch on himself.

"Be happy that you have a body, Sir Tor. And that for a time you can feel this." Her fingers traveled between his legs. Tor couldn't help but moan as shivers having nothing to do with cold rippled through his body.

For the first time, Tor let himself feel. They explored each other, a strange mixture where for one day they became whole. They lay on the rocks near the falls, kissing, caressing murmuring to each other. The maiden said that her body gave enough heat to protect Tor.

The day cooled toward blue shadows and the night began to whisper to Tor. "I thank you for this time. It was indeed a reward, though who knows how much longer I can be a knight. I'm a sham and someday I will be discovered."

The maiden sat on the rocks, her hair drying into long curls, a hint of gold showing in the last kiss of late afternoon. Her laughter carried scorn. "You are more a knight than any that was born a man. Consider that you have held the quest pure. I said I would reward you and the gift of love was not it."

Tor looked at her, puzzled. "Would you give me jewels now, or an enchanted sword."

"No." She shook her head. "I have no riches and while I'm a being of magic, I have very little magic. I cannot give you a man's body but I can take away these. Her fingers slid over the mounds of flesh.

"It is easier to hide what is below. I cannot add to your body but I can take away."

Tor's chest tingled, as if ants ran over the skin. The intensity increased from a light tickle to fiery prickling. He clutched at his chest, gasping. In a few long moments, his chest flattened, showing the hardened muscles honed from sword work.

He gasped, removing his hands, looking down. "How..."

She smiled sadly, tilting her head to one side. "That is all that I can do."

"Some day they will discover the truth and it will be the end of me."

"No, Sir Tor. Some truths need never be revealed. Remember, it is not the flesh that makes the man but the soul and intent that lie within. You are a true knight. Never forget that."

She kissed him long and full, her tongue darting into his mouth. The kiss was so sweet and of deeper mysteries that when she stopped Tor stayed still, tasting the reverberations thrilling his body.

"Remember that. You help create Arthur's kingdom."

He heard a splash and knew she was gone. Sir Tor had come far from being a naïve young man. He would stay a knight and by his hand, he would make sure the tales told of noble deeds, and the secret of the river maiden would never be revealed.

— «» —

Colleen Anderson has been nominated for the Aurora Award, Gaylactic Spectrum Award, finalist in the Rannu competition and received several honorable mentions in the Year's Best Fantasy and Horror, the Year's Best SF, and Imaginarium. Her poetry and fiction have been published in Britain, Canada and the United States. She has attended both the Clarion West and the Center for the Study of Science Fiction (CSSF) writing workshops and has a degree in creative writing. Colleen is a member of the Horror Writers of America and SF Canada.

Ghost Child

JR Campbell

He saw her as he rode, leading the horses among the silver birches. A small girl of no more than eight winters, blonde hair and an expression as solemn as a wandering star. Toryn had been riding alone for days but wasn't so weary he couldn't offer a wave to the small one. The child's frown deepened as she looked silently back at the mounted knight. Her hands remained clasped before her even as her eyes followed the parade of his horses. With a mental shrug Toryn turned back to the trail ahead but something, elusive even to his questing thoughts, caused him to pull back on the reins. Turning to the sombre child he offered words of greeting.

"Well met," he said, an easy grin shaping the words. "Can you tell me, am I near the village of Fand's Shame?"

"You can see me," the child said.

Toryn nodded slowly. When the child made no further response, he felt obliged to add, "Is that strange?"

The child nodded a slow nod. "I'm a ghost."

A rush of questions crowded Toryn's thoughts but, confronted with the child's unyielding solemnity, he didn't voice them. "Oh," Toryn said cautiously.

"How can you see me?" The child asked with a puzzled dignity. "No one else can. Are you a ghost too?"

"Not yet," Toryn answered. "I am Toryn from Camelot. I'm bound for Fand's Shame—"

"Where the children were taken," the child said.

"That's right," Toryn agreed. "I've come to help. If I can."

"Camelot, that's where the King lives. And his knights and their table."

"You're well informed for one so young," Toryn flattered, hoping to trick a smile on the child's face. It didn't work. The child's grim dignity remained undisturbed. She looked at his horses and their cargo, then back at Toryn. Speculation gleamed in her eyes.

"Are you a knight? Of the Table?"

"I am," Toryn admitted.

"Then shouldn't you be called Sir Toryn?"

Toryn leaned back in his saddle, stretching before he answered. Another question. With a child such as this it seemed as close to an invitation as he was likely to get. "I am called Sir Toryn by others. You may call me Toryn though."

"Why?" Suspicion battled curiosity in the little ones eyes.

"I feel we are destined to be friends," Toryn answered. "And friends need not bother with formalities like titles. I believe I heard a prophecy about it back in Camelot, though I may be mistaken. I've been travelling for a while now and prophecies are never as clear as they could be. May I ask your name?"

"No," the child answered. Troubled by the harshness of her refusal, she quickly added. "But you are close to Fand's Shame. It's just a little west."

"That's excellent news," Toryn said. "Do you know the place?"

"Very well," the girl said with a sigh. "It was my home."

"And your parents," Toryn asked."Do they live there still?"

"They do." The child's words were heavy again.

"Then we share the road," Toryn said. "Let me introduce you to the horses." Patting the horse he rode, Toryn started. "This is Avis. She's an ambler and has a very sweet disposition. That is Lune," he waved to the pack horse behind. "Unlike Avis, Lune always thinks we are lost. No faith in that one but she's good hearted all the same. And that brute is Calgacus. He is neither sweet nor good hearted but we are friends all the same. Now, does Lune suit you or will my pretty Avis carry you?"

"Are you trying to trick me into visiting my parents?"

"No," Toryn said. "That is to say, I'm not trying to trick you. Don't you want to see your parents?"

"I'm a ghost," the child reminded him.

"You did mention that," Toryn said. "Don't ghosts visit their parents? If I were a ghost, that's the first thing I would do. And you are going to show me the way, aren't you? I need to find a place to make camp."

"What sort of place?" The child asked, starting to walk down the trail.

"Well," Toryn said, urging Avis after the child. "Ideally it would be hidden but near a field where the horses can graze. Someplace I can light a fire that won't be seen from the village or the main trails. A place where I can think, more than anything else. If your parents had a—"

"No," the girl said firmly. "But I know such a place."

She led him first to see the village, speaking as little as possible. The village was as he expected. Not prosperous but solid, with a forge and miller's, more a cluster of homes that fell together and worked just fine. No signs of soldiers or other trappings of oppression. Once he'd seen the village she led him back into the woods to the cave. It was, Toryn had to admit, a perfect location. Far enough away to be unseen, a field for grazing, near enough he could ride back to the village quickly. He suspected the child was using the cave as her home but he didn't find any blankets, clothes or supplies to support the idea. After unpacking his gear, he lit a fire and started a meal for two before going to rub down the horses. The child watched, unperturbed and seemingly uninterested. She didn't leave though. That was something.

The horses tended to, Toryn came back and finished preparing the meal. He invited the girl to share but she shook his head. He ate half of what he prepared, left the other half out with what he hoped was tempting carelessness. The sun was setting as he settled by the small fire, unpacked his armor and started polishing it.

"What can you tell me about what's happening in the village?" Toryn asked casually, rubbing a rag over the bright metal.

The girl shrugged. She looked at the food, Toryn thought he saw hunger in her eyes but he couldn't be sure.

"I was sent to this place because children have gone missing," Toryn continued. "Can you tell me anything about that?"

"Sent by who?" The girl asked.

"The King," Toryn answered.

"Why are you polishing that?" She wasn't providing answers but the child was full of questions.

"Tomorrow I'm going to take Calgacus into the village and tell everyone I've been sent on a quest from Camelot to find their children," Toryn explained. "I'll tell them I am Sir Toryn, a knight of the Round Table. I don't know how they'll react but they need to know the King has sent me. It's important that I look like someone able to complete this quest. So tonight I'm going to polish my armor, so the people will see a champion they can trust. "

The girl nodded. Toryn let the silence stretch between them. When she finally did speak, her voice was much softer than he become accustomed to. "I don't like to think of it."

"I understand," Toryn said. "I've no wish to distress you. You know why I'm here. You know I'm a defender of the people and that includes children. Especially children. If there's anything you can tell me to aid my quest you will earn not only my thanks but the thanks of Camelot and the King."

The rest of the evening passed slowly and silently. Toryn polished his armor while the child lingered at the edge of the firelight. The knight spent part of his time wishing the child would tell him something, anything, but a larger part hoped she would head home to her parents. She did neither, nor did she eat the food he'd left for her. When he'd finished polishing his gear he turned to her and offered the child a slight bow. "I'm weary and I'm going to sleep in the cave. I do wish you'd go to your parents and take your rest there. The woods are not safe for children."

"I'm not a child," the girl said. "Not anymore."

"You mentioned that," Toryn said. "If I can help, call me. Your help is appreciated but, if you've someplace you need to be, I understand. We are friends, after all."

"Good night Sir Toryn," the girl said solemnly. Toryn wanted to say more but the words wouldn't come, so he gathered his gear and retreated into the cave's darkness. The meal still sat by the dying fire and Toryn hoped she would eat it, if nothing else. Lying in his blanket he found it difficult to let go of his frustration and concern for the child but eventually his weariness calmed him to sleep.

The next morning the food was gone and so was the girl. Toryn set about armoring himself and saddling Calgacus. He rode west into the village, the sun at his back, Calgacus making a slow but very loud trot. Lance in one hand, a banner of Camelot waving from its point, he pulled on the reins with his shield arm and brought Calgacus to a stop before the village's well in the center of town. The people gathered. There were, he noticed, no children among them. He thought he saw a woman whose golden hair reminded him of the ghost. Perhaps the child's mother? Before he could speak to her one of the people, a village elder by his beard, loudly asked his purpose. Where had he ridden from? What did he seek? Toryn answered. The people nodded, remarkably accepting. Arthur the King had heard of their troubles, Toryn announced he had been sent to render what aid could be had. None challenged his word. He asked the people for information. Who were the children? When had they disappeared? The elder answered, loud enough to be heard by all but none of those gathered argued with him. No one quibbled over his descriptions. No one added to the stated facts. The elder's voice was loud but, to Toryn's ears, the recitation sounded practiced. Without feeling. Without the hurt that must reside in those trapped in such a woeful tale.

And why shouldn't the words sound practiced, Toryn asked himself. Surely they had told this story over and over amongst themselves. If their misfortune reached the ears of Camelot, they must have told others. Perhaps the words, grievous as they were, had by now been worn smooth with use. Yet the compliance of the crowd, useful as it was, disturbed him. There was a harmony to the tale he was hearing but, in his experience, there were always voices seeking to agree or dispute whatever was being said.

Toryn considered this as the elder finished describing the last child. And then the elder spoke more.

He told who had taken the children. He told Toryn whose blood would make things right. None of those gathered disagreed. Toryn searched the faces gathered for some sign of dissent. Searched for an averted gaze or a shade of doubt in their eyes but he found none. Nodding then, he asked for the directions they so plainly wanted to give him. And the elder supplied them.

Calgacus snorted fiercely as Toryn gave the charger the freedom to follow the path ahead. The crowd parted before him, watching as he rode away. None followed. A satisfaction settled over the crowd as if they had done a difficult task well. Toryn sat proudly in the saddle. He was a knight in the service of a great king. His quest was clear and near its end. If he succeeded he was free to return to Camelot with glory. Why then did he not share the satisfaction of those he aided? Why did he frown beneath his helm?

When he traveled far enough along the road to be sure he was unobserved he dismounted. There was to be a battle. He should refresh himself and his stallion before undertaking the task. It wasn't a truth told by bards but amongst his fellows at the table preparation was counted high among the knightly virtues. Almost as high as truth.

Having fed and checked Calgacus, Toryn looked towards the woods and saw amongst the shadows the child. Removing his helm he strode over to her, offered greetings.

"What did they tell you?" The child asked.

"By the bend in the river there lives a troll," Toryn said. "A monster who consumes their children."

"And you believe them?"

Toryn frowned. "Such things are spoken of. Rumors. I do not know enough of trolls to say one way or the other. They are said to be monstrous, frightful. It may be true. The village says it is so, with one voice. Should I discard the word of those who have been wronged?"

"I know a troll," the child said. "He is fierce in appearance but gentle in appetite. He cannot abide the presence of men or women but the children know him. He sings with us, his voice like stones rubbing against each other but kind for all that. I think he was once a man but somehow he was changed. He is frightening but he means no harm."

"You think him blameless in this?" Toryn needed to hear her say it.

"He would not harm a single one of us," the child said. "Much less so many."

Toryn frowned, wanting to argue. His simple path had become fraught. "Come with me," he asked the child. "Talk to him with me. I must learn the truth here. I cannot be a child and if he will not speak to me how can I balance your truth against that of your neighbors?"

"I don't know if he'll be able to see me," the uncertain girl complained.

"If I knew another way," Toryn said. "I would take it. I must speak to him. Alone, if necessary. If what you say is true, if he will not speak with me—"

"I will come," the solemn child agreed. Refusing Toryn's offer to ride with him, she walked in front of the charger and led the knight to a steep riverbank. Motioning to him to stop, she walked to the edge and began to sing a cheery tune without words. The high, playful notes floated on the wind like dandelion seeds. The sound emerging from the girl shocked Toryn, so bright a sound from such a sombre child. More surprising was the low, rumbling notes rising up from the river. Very much, Toryn had to admit, like stones grinding against each other. Despite the roughness of the voice the singer's joy and amusement was unmistakable.

Abruptly, the troll's misshapen head emerged over the edge of the riverbank's slope. Huge, misshapen but with a large smile. From what he could see the troll was covered with hard, thick flesh, as if a man had grown outward like a tree, but there was nothing hard or fearsome in the creature's open face. Its eyes fixed on the child and a giant hand rose as the creature was about to climb up and join the girl on the grass.

The troll looked past the child. Saw Toryn astride his horse, armored and with lance in hand. The open smile disappeared and the singing stopped. The creature's expression collapsed into a scowl. The flesh of its face shifted under the skin, assuming a brooding countenance that hid the open, joyful expression it had an instant before.

"No! No!" The child called. "I've come to save you!" Turning, the child yelled commands at Toryn. "You're frightening him! Put down that silly stick! Let him see your face! Tell him you've come to help him!"

Beyond the riverbank a dull, angry face peeked over the edge. Toryn cast aside his lance and dismounted. On the ground he removed his helmet. Not knowing what else to do, Toryn knelt on one knee before the child.

The troll rose up, watching with interest.

The child, her scolding successful, turned back to the troll. "This is Toryn," she explained. "He's a knight and my friend."

"My friends," the troll rumbled. "All gone. All but you."

"I know." The child walked over and sat by the monster. How big was the troll? It was impossible to tell without seeing the rest of the creature. The face relaxed as the child laid her hand softly against its cheek. The child had no fear of the troll but it was obvious the creature was capable of inspiring fright. Had Toryn sought the creature alone, without the child, what would have happened?

"In the village they are saying you hurt them," the child explained. The troll's face flexed again its, scowl deepening. "I know it's not true," the girl continued. "Toryn has come all the way from Camelot to find our missing friends. He needs to hear you tell him you didn't do our friends any harm."

"Never!" The creature spat. "They lie!"

The child looked over her shoulder, her eyes seeking Toryn's. He nodded at her. Still kneeling, he spoke softly so as not to alarm the troll. "I've no wish to harm the innocent but I must be certain. I need to see your friend."

"Move slowly," the child said. "Don't do anything to frighten him. If you must ask him questions, whisper them to me and I'll ask him. The voices of the old hurt his ears."

Toryn rose and holding his hands out to his side, he walked slowly towards the unlikely pair. He looked down. The troll was over six feet tall, with long, strong arms and short legs. It wore nothing but river mud although it appeared to Toryn that the creature was sexless. It carried no tools, had no claws. The child obviously trusted it and, just as plainly, the troll trusted the girl.

Kneeling by the child, Toryn whispered in her ear. "I don't believe he is guilty of this crime but if everyone in the village does, then I fear for his safety. Explain the danger to him. I have some rope and a shield with my crest on it. Tell him if anyone comes to harm him, he should pretend to be my prisoner. That way he is under my protection, do you understand? I am honor-bound to defend my prisoner."

"You're not going to tie him up." It was almost a question but somehow not.

"No," Toryn answered. "But if someone comes he should pretend to be tied. And the shield should stay with him so they can see the crest and know he is my prisoner. I'm going to go back to my horse, get the rope and shield. You explain everything to him. I'll wait by Calgacus until you wave to me, then bring the rope and shield to you and you can give them to him. Yes?"

"Yes," the child agreed.

"Then I'll ride back to the village," Toryn said. "I'll wait for you, if you want to come too."

"I'll stay with him," the child said. "He's upset. And a friend."

Once he had given the rope and shield to the child, donned his helm and recovered his lance, Toryn mounted Calgacus and started back down the road. Thankful for the time to think, Toryn understood something remained unseen in all of this. If the troll had taken the children, why hadn't the villagers attacked the creature? Its form was misshapen but had born no scars. For that matter, the villagers had shown no signs of combat either. Why had they waited for a knight when the creature had no armor, no defense against the tools he had seen in the village? It was as if the village left the troll unharmed so they could accuse it should someone like Toryn arrive with questions. What were they hiding? What would they do if they discovered Toryn had seen through the ruse, through no virtue of his own? It frightened him how differently his encounter with the troll might have gone had the child not been there to help him.

The child...

"I have defeated the troll," Toryn announced when Calgacus stood beside the well again. "It is my prisoner and will be punished for the evil it has done. However the King has instructed his knights to bring creatures such as the troll back to Camelot. His enchanter, Merlin, wishes to study such beings. For this reason, I have not killed the creature. I have come to ask for your aid. I require a wagon with harness for two horses. This wagon must be large enough to contain the troll and it sides must be woven tightly and strongly so that none can see the frightful beast within. Will you help me?"

The village elder nodded. "It will be done, Sir knight, just as you ask."

"Remember, this cage must hold the beast's fury all the way to Camelot," Toryn said. "It is better done well than done quickly."

The village elder nodded. Spurring Calgacus forward, Toryn refused the offers of accommodation and rode back to the cave. Once there he carefully stowed his armor, tended to Calgacus and checked on the other horses. After a quick, cold meal he donned his plainest clothing, found Lune and rode her to the village.

Dressed in humble clothes with Luna he doubted any of the villagers would recognize him as the knight who had ridden into town but strangers, especially mounted strangers, were always noticed. He was careful but it was frustrating seeking for he knew not what. He circled the village, marking the paths leading to and from the settlement. As he rode he spied the golden haired woman he'd seen that morning, the one he'd thought might be the ghost child's mother. Completing her chores, the woman retreated from the late afternoon sun into a dwelling. Leaving Lune in the forest Toryn followed her. Knocking on the door, he realized he had no knowledge of what he would say to the woman when she answered. He didn't know what it was he sought here. Would he tell her of the mysterious child he had encountered? Ask for the child's name? He wasn't sure this was the child's family. Was he even certain the child was not what she claimed? Though the child's assistance was appreciated, there was an element of the unnatural to her aid.

The door opened and Toryn's doubts regarding the woman were banished. Whatever the state of the child who helped him, he had no doubt this was her mother. Opening the door the woman's grief was plain on her features, as was the underlying courage even sorrow could not diminish. Her eyes, the set of her chin and the fall of her golden hair left no doubt in Toryn's mind. And with that foundation, Toryn knew what to say.

"I am Sir Toryn of Camelot," he told her. "I've come to learn what happened to your daughter."

The response was tears. How could it be otherwise? Toryn stepped into the humble home and eased the woman into a seat. He brought her a blanket, fetched her a drink, allowed the wave of grief to pass through the woman and waited for the tide to recede. He meant her no harm, respected the grief rendering her mute, but did not retreat in the face of her raw hurt. There were things he must learn.

When her weeping slowed and the woman had composed herself, Toryn asked about the child's father.

"He lives still," the woman admitted. "Like me, he does his work. We follow the steps of our old life like shadows, hoping to remember the joy we once found there. He has taken to drink to ease his sorrow. I cannot blame him for I seek such respite myself."

"Why was I told the lie about the troll?" Toryn asked.

"Because they are ashamed," the woman admitted. "They wish to be done with it. The troll seemed an easy enough tale. Who would defend so deformed a creature? No one would believe a troll's cries of innocence. Everyone expected you to kill the beast and ride away. They still expect that. Better a simple lie than a shameful truth."

"I will learn this truth," Toryn said determinedly.

"Even if there is nothing you can do to change it?" The woman asked. "Even if knowing will only make everything so much worse? You'll find no glory in this quest. Knowing our shame will only insure both of us misery. Better you ride back to your King and your table with the troll's head for a trophy. Better they raise glasses to Camelot's returning hero than curse us for our weakness."

"The glory of Camelot is not based on lies," Toryn said sternly. "The knights of Camelot do not quest for glory. We seek only to help. Tell me. "

"There is an abbey..."

Toryn frowned, no one had described such a place to him. Recalling the roads he had crossed circling the village he remembered a worn path not on the map given him.

"Which Order oversees the abbey?"

"None you've heard of," the woman answered in a bitter voice.

"A sanctuary to the old gods?" Toryn asked. Such things were not unheard of, nor did the King persecute those who knelt before them provided their rituals did not bring murder and suffering. The King was nothing if not a man of conscience and such a man couldn't hate the old ways while keeping one such as Merlin at his side.

"No," the woman insisted. "Maybe," she allowed after a moment of silence. "There is but one who calls the abbey home. It is a voice speaking to you, a voice you cannot help but desire but know you should not heed. When the one arrived, some brought food and soon they promised to rebuild the abbey. There were offerings gladly given but soon the abbey demanded more. Offerings we knew to be shameful but which, against that voice, we were eager to give. Then the one asked for still more, asked for our very children. And we gave them..."

"It is magic then," Toryn concluded. "Who is this one? A man or a woman? Are there talismans?"

"I do not know," the woman admitted. "To some he appears as a man, glorious in form. To others a woman, to some it has appeared different each time. The voice ensnares and the one who appears matches the voice. None here know the ways of magic, not like this, but we are cursed all the same. We are slaves to the abbey. Bound by shame. We have given away our children. Knowing we will never see them again. Knowing it was evil yet too weak to resist. You asked about my husband and I told you he was a drunkard but that was another simple lie. He is there tonight, I know he is, lying with the one who took our child. The shame drains us of our ability to speak truth or to take joy in anything save the debauchery of the abbey."

Toryn nodded. "You have spoken bravely," he told the woman.

"You think to confront the abbey," the woman said. "Don't do it. You will fail as each of us has failed. And the abbey will gain not just a follower but a sword. A seat at the King's table to use as it sees fit. Take your troll back to Camelot. Be welcomed as a hero, not a spy. Save yourself and let the damned be damned. There is no shame in such a course."

"I don't—"

"Believe me," the woman warned. The pain in her eyes could not be denied. "You know nothing of shame. You've been offered a trophy. Take it and know that by doing so you save your King, his Table and their better world. Do not imagine your virtue will protect you. We are damned now but once we were as pure as any. Leave us to our damnation."

"I thank you for your warning," Toryn said. "I understand you are under a curse but, if you are able, I would ask you to speak to no one of our talk until I've returned to Camelot. Farewell. Know that a Knight of the table aspires to match your courage."

Lune waited for him in the darkening woods. The mare carried him slowly back to the cave while Toryn pondered the situation he found himself in. Lune made her way back to the meadow where Avis and Calgacus grazed. Toryn tended to the horse then made his way back to the cave. He was wearied and troubled but his day was not yet done.

The child emerged from the cave's darkness as he approached. Gone was her customary solemness, replaced by a fury which made the child seem older. Kneeling, Toryn started to relight the fire.

"You should not have gone to see her," the child hissed at him.

"I am a knight on a quest," Toryn answered. "I had no choice."

"You made her weep!"

"Her tears were not for me," Toryn answered. "Nor did I cause them."

"You did!" The child insisted. "And what are you going to do now? Pray that your armor can block a whisper? Run a lance through something you cannot see? Tell me, are all the King's men so stupid or are you special?"

"All the King's knights are special," Toryn replied to the child's scorn. Standing from the fire, he walked over to his provisions and gathered enough for two meals. "Each in their own ways. I am proud to know them all but, I must admit, we are not chosen for our cleverness. How is your friend?"

"He's fine," the child answered. "They are building a wagon in the village."

"The only delay I could think of," Toryn replied, preparing the meals over the fire. "He will not be a prisoner in the wagon, I promise you that." After a moment, he added, "I don't know what I should do but I am frightened to leave him by his riverbank."

"You think they'll hurt him," the child said. "Maybe you should take him and go."

She looked so much like her mother in that moment, Toryn could only nod. "That seems to be the wisest course. How long until they finish the wagon, do you think?"

"Day after tomorrow," the child answered. Toryn handed her a metal plate with food. To his surprise she took it and ate a mouthful before adding. "Enough time for you to put on your shiny armor and ride your fancy horse to the abbey. That's what you're thinking of doing, isn't it?"

"Exactly that," Toryn admitted. "Though not tomorrow. And not, I hope, alone."

— «» —

Toryn arrived at the abbey mounted on Calgacus, armored with his lance in hand. Behind him his mares, Avis and Lune, pulled the cage of woven willow. Toryn had not known what to expect but it wasn't children digging in a vegetable garden. Other children tended livestock while the older children climbed in the scaffolding over the stone abbey, adding to the structure. As he rode in one of the children, a small girl, stood directly in front of his stallion. By gender and age, the children he saw matched the missing but their hair and mannerisms did not. Their hair was long and white and their faces were strange. The girl child stood before the restless stallion without fear or any expression on her nondescript face. He stared down at her as the child spoke, examining her countenance for a sign of something familiar. He found he could not focus on her face. There was an enchantment on the child, on all the children.

The girl had stopped talking and stood looking up at the armored knight. Toryn hadn't heard what she'd said but it was obvious the child was waiting for a response. "I am Sir Toryn of Camelot," Toryn announced loudly. "A knight of the Round Table questing by order of the good King Arthur. I would speak with the master of this place."

Standing directly before Calgacus the child didn't seem to speak but the wooden doors of the abbey opened and more children emerged. That was, Toryn noted, thirteen. Fourteen children had been reported missing and thirteen of them stood before him, watching him through whatever magic obscured their features. Behind the children a woman, clad in white, emerged from the shadowed entrance.

Toryn drew in a deep breath. The abbess was lovely, her long auburn hair cascaded down her back. Her simple robe sheathed a slim, provocative figure but her eyes and the innocence of her smooth face captivated the knight. He'd been warned but, even after seeing the spells laid on the children, he'd doubted the magic's ability to bewitch him.

"You seek me, Sir Knight?" Despite the rags he stuffed in his ears her voice echoed in his thoughts, bathing them in warm honey. The sound of it surprised him. The voice stirred memories of all the women who had ever bewitched him. The Queen's voice echoed in the voice, as did Lady Isolde when she spoke of love, the laughter Enid shared with Sir Geraint, all blended into a single voice speaking only to him.

Panicked, Toryn knew the enchantment would claim him as it had claimed those in the village. With his knees he urged Calgacus to the right but the children moved to stand before him. Lowering his lance, Toryn stared through his visor at the feet of the abbess but the children moved quickly to stand between him and their captor.

"I had hoped you would come to me." The abbess' voice sounded in his ear, as though she sat behind him in the saddle, as if he had not stuffed his ears. "Long have I wished to see Camelot and desired a bold knight to introduce me to the great and powerful there."

Pulling with his shield arm, Toryn jerked Calgacus' reins further in the circle he was drawing about the abbey. The stallion darted forward but Toryn pulled up as the children hurried to block his charge. He could not ride through the children, nor could he surrender to this magic. Urging his mount further right, completing a quarter circle from the abbey's entrance, Toryn contemplated the necessity of charging through the children clustered before him.

"You struggle so sweetly," the abbess spoke from behind her battlements of children. "Do you not want me? I thought I heard you call yet it seems now you are struck dumb. Tell me, how may I serve you brave knight? What would you ask of me?"

Calgacus darted forward but again Toryn pulled back on the reins. The stallion reared, causing Toryn to drop his lance. Before closing his eyes he saw the banner of Camelot in the dirt. He urged Calgacus again to the right, knowing the barricade of children would follow, knowing the abbess would not let him go. Her voice was a whisper then, a series of soft gasps and low, private sounds that tormented him.

Toryn, eyes clenched shut, dropped his shield and raised both hands to either side of his helm. They did no more to block the sound than the rags in is ears. When he felt he could resist the siren's call no more, Toryn screamed as loud as he could.

The abbess chuckled at the sound of his agony. "Did you think you were different?" The abbess mocked him. "Did you think armor and vows could—"

Her voice stopped suddenly. Pulling the helm from his head, Toryn looked over the sudden confusion of the children and saw the troll — free from his hiding place in the wagon — knock an indistinct, gray figure across the yard. Beside the wagon a golden haired girl — his ghost child — waved and appeared to yell to the other children. Urging them to run. To come with her.

The children, dazed, nevertheless heeded their companion's call. The troll stomped at the gray figure on the ground but it managed to roll away. The gray figure rose and Toryn saw the flash of a metal blade catching the sun. Calling a battle cry, Toryn dug his heels into his stallion's side. Children no longer stood between him and his foe. Toryn drew his sword.

Before she could strike the innocent, she heard Toryn's cry and turned. The gray figure blurred, cladding herself in white and beauty once more. A woman's voice screamed in terror as the voices of a thousand desires cried for mercy in his ears. Closing his eyes he swung his sword, felt the sickening impact of the blade as it sliced into flesh and bone. His mouth filled with the taste of ashes. Flashes of sickening lightening streaked behind his clenched eyelids. Terror filled his ears with a shriek not his own. Blinking, he struggled to turn in his saddle, barely gripping the bloodied sword in his hand. As his head swam he struggled to see which figure he had struck, his love or the monster.

With a relief, he saw the troll standing unharmed over a bloodied gray shadow.

Toryn fell forward, gripping the stallion's mane, uncertain where the reins had fallen. He drew breath in preparation of speaking but the world tilted before him and he knew nothing more for a time.

— 《》 —

He woke in the cave once more. His armor was gone. He was wrapped in a blanket. The ghost was there, watching him with her customary solemn expression.

"How do you feel?"

Toryn considered the question before answering. His head felt like a blacksmith's anvil still ringing from the day's labour but otherwise he felt well.

"Did I fall from my horse?" Toryn asked, hoping he didn't sound as embarrassed as he felt.

"No," the child answered. "You dropped your sword but Calgacus would never let you fall. He brought you back here on his own. We couldn't catch him."

"Your friend, "Toryn asked."The troll, was he hurt?"

"No, you saved him before that … enchantress could strike him. You saved him, saved the children. We took them back to the village. With the enchantress dead, their parents could see them again. They were, well, they were hurt and ashamed but happy. I needed help. I had to get Avis and Lune free of the wagon. Had to get back to the cave before Calgacus dropped you. Had to find your sword and carry your lance—"

"And did you find help?" Toryn asked.

"I did," the child answered. Then she smiled, a radiant expression on her face. Looking past the child, Toryn saw a familiar, golden haired woman offer him a grateful smile.

"Your mother can see you?" Toryn asked.

"Now she can," the child answered, smiling.

"I'm glad of it," Toryn said. "Though I am sorry you had to see me draw my sword."

"If you hadn't," the child smiled. "I would be a ghost still."

The child leaned in, offering him a hug. Toryn returned the embrace. "If it hadn't been for you, your courage and your aid, I fear I would have made a mess of things. You have my deepest thanks and I intend to tell the king so when I return to Camelot. That is, if I ever learn your name."

And still holding him, she whispered the name of a living girl into his ear. In the nights to come he would hear the voice of the enchantress in his dreams. He would hear her beckoning him, his will melting as her words caressed him, feel the shackles as he yielded to shame, desire and enchantment. Yet even in the midst of the nightmare, the memory of a child's whispered name made the darkness bearable.

— «» —

JR Campbell is a Calgary based writer and editor. His stories have appeared in Tesseracts, Rigor Amortis, The MX Book of New Sherlock Holmes Stories and Fantastical Visions IV.

Along with his brother in arms, Charles Prepolec, he has edited the anthologies Gaslight Grimoire: Fantastical Tales of Sherlock Holmes, Gaslight Grotesque: Nightmare Tales of Sherlock Holmes, Gaslight Arcanum: Uncanny Tales of Sherlock Holmes, Professor Challenger: New Worlds, Lost Places and the forthcoming Gaslight Gothic: Erie Tales of Sherlock Homes.

The Prisoner of Shalott

Lawrence Watt-Evans

Elaine stood defiantly before her father and looked him in the eye. "I have done nothing wrong," she said.

"You have brought shame upon our house," Sir Bernard replied, meeting her gaze.

"What have I done that would shame us?" she demanded.

"Must you ask? Throwing yourself at Sir Lancelot, begging him to bear your token into the lists..."

"I love him!"

"You are a child," her father replied. "You know nothing of love — and apparently, despite my best efforts and those of your late mother, you understand nothing of the laws of hospitality, and the duty a host owes his guest. Lancelot was here to compete in a tourney, not to court you, yet you would not leave him alone."

"I love him!" Elaine repeated. "And would he not be a suitable husband for me? Lancelot is a worthy knight — indeed, one of the greatest in the land, the king's favorite..."

"And the queen's favorite, as well, yet you insisted he show your favor, rather than hers. Do you not see how poorly this reflects upon my hospitality?"

"But I would marry him, which the queen cannot!"

Sir Bernard sighed. "Oh, my foolish daughter — have you seen any sign that *he* would marry *you*? He did not approach me to seek your hand; indeed, he gave no hint, either directly or through his servants, that he had any interest in you."

"He bore my token in the lists!"

"He is too gallant a knight to refuse a lady such a favor to her face — and when the tourney was over, and he fell wounded, did he keep your favor and display it? Did he kiss it, as he returned it to you? No, daughter, he did not. When I saw you look at him, I bade your brothers to speak with him, to see whether he had anything to say of your charms, your wit — and he did not. Not a word said he of you, not one word. Cannot you see that he is accustomed to women, both high-born and low, desiring his attention? Though you are of noble birth and fairy blood, he thought no more of you than he would of some milkmaid or tavern wench."

"You lie!"

Sir Bernard rose from his chair. "You *dare* address your father so?"

Elaine realized she had gone too far, and bowed her head. "I... I know you are wrong, Father. You do not lie, I know, but you are mistaken. My heart spoke before my senses could stop it, and for that I am sorry, but I know that Lancelot must surely love me as I love him. God could not be so cruel as to have it otherwise."

"I tell you he does not," her father said, still standing.

"And I say you must be mistaken. Let me go to Camelot and speak with him, and you will see—"

"Go to Camelot? Where you would force Sir Lancelot to deny you before the court, and shame us before the King himself? Nonsense! I forbid it. You shall not set foot beyond our lands until you have come to your senses."

Elaine stared at him, struggling to find the words that would make him understand, but before she could say a thing he turned. "I have said enough for tonight," he said. "I will retire, as will you, and perhaps in the morning our passions will have cooled, and we can discuss this more calmly."

She stood on the carpet before his seat and watched him go, certain that *her* passions would not cool until she had felt Lancelot's hands upon her. At last, though, she turned as well, and under the watchful gaze of her father's guards and her own maidens she made her way to her chamber.

Alone in her room, though, she did not undress; instead she crossed to the window and looked out at her father's lands, extending for miles in all directions.

Far to the west, she knew, lay the lands of Faerie, whence her long-lost mother had come, but to the northeast, little more than a day's ride away, lay Camelot, where dwelt her beloved. She stared in that direction, wishing that she had some magic that could transport her across that distance unseen.

She did possess some small share of her mother's magic, as did her brothers, but not enough to cross so many miles before sunrise, and none of her enchantments could withstand the light of day. Her father's mortal blood limited her; by day she was merely human, her gifts lost.

But perhaps, if she gathered all her skills, she could climb upon the moonlight to escape her tower room and descend safely across the castle walls. Even without magic beyond that, she could be halfway to Camelot by dawn.

She opened the casement, then closed her eyes and gathered herself, drawing in the night's power, pressing aside her mortal weight and letting herself be as light as thistledown, as light as a dandelion seed upon the wind. She floated up upon the windowsill. Taking a deep breath, she stepped off into the night—

And the alarm went up upon an instant, men shouting, a bell ringing, startling her so that the spell broke, and she barely caught herself upon the sill, clambering awkwardly back into her room.

She had scarcely gotten back to her feet when the door burst open and two guards rushed in, followed by her uncle Kailen. Elaine stared at her mother's brother, astonished; her fairy uncle rarely involved himself with human affairs, preferring to spend his time alone, doing no one knew what.

"Child," he said, "that was rash. Did you think your father could be so easily deceived?"

"I..." Elaine hesitated, then admitted, "I did not think at all." She had never been able to lie to her uncle; she guessed that was an aspect *of his* magic, so much stronger than her own.

"I fear that will cost you dearly," Kailen said. "Though perhaps it will prove best for us all in the long run."

Then her father appeared in the door behind her uncle.

"Oh, Elaine," he said sorrowfully. "I had hoped that it would not come to this; I have no desire to lock my daughter up as if she were an unbroken horse, to be kept imprisoned until its spirit is tamed. You leave me no alternative, though."

"Then will you cast me into the dungeons?" Elaine asked, her voice wild. She was not entirely sure whether she feared or welcomed such a fate; it would certainly prove to her, if to no one else, that her father was in the wrong.

"No," Sir Bernard said, with a shake of his head. "You are still my daughter, and the daughter of a noble of Faerie, neither a traitor nor a common criminal. I will confine you in the tower on the island of Shalott, in the river seven miles hence, amid the gardens there, and I have asked my late wife's brother, your uncle Lord Kailen, to place enchantments upon you that will bind you, to keep you in that place."

"Is that why you are here, Uncle?" Elaine asked.

"I had been on my way to your chamber in hopes that I could sway you from your path in time to spare you this," Kailen replied. "Alas, that you were so quick to display your defiance!"

"I know the island of which you speak," she said. "And I will accept confinement there, until such time as you shall repent your cruelty — for shall I not be there seven miles closer to my beloved's home in Camelot?"

"Oh, daughter, you vex me sorely!"

"And you are blind to the truth of my love!"

At that, her father let out a wordless bellow of frustrated rage and turned away. "See to her confinement, as I have commanded!" he said, as he stormed away.

When he had gone, her fairy uncle said, "He does love you, you know, and seeks only what is best for you."

"But he will not *see* what is best for me — to be joined with my true love!"

Lord Kailen sighed. "In the morning I will see to your imprisonment, as your father has ordained." Then he, too, turned and left.

The guards, though, stayed.

— «» —

In the morning a party was assembled, and Elaine the White was escorted to her new home.

The island lay in the center of the stream, between banks lined with willows, and beyond the trees fields of barley and rye stretched far and wide, covering the land in rippling gold from one horizon to the other.

On the island itself stood a single structure, an old watchtower that had not been manned since the bad old days before Arthur took the crown and brought the warlords to heel beneath his banner. There was no need for such a defense now that Camelot's peace reigned over England. Four gray stone walls, a turret at each corner, stood in baleful contrast to the bright lilies and graceful willows that surrounded the little fortress.

This was to be Elaine's home, and her prison, until such time as she and her father were reconciled. Although her maidens did not accompany her, and the servants were under strict instructions not to speak to her nor obey her orders, it was arranged that her meals and other necessities were to be provided.

To occupy her hand and mind, a loom was set up in her chamber, and to ensure that she did not slip away, her uncle placed a geas, a curse, upon her — she was to work upon this loom, weaving a tapestry, during all her waking hours, save only when her meals were brought to her. If she turned away, and left the shuttle unmoved for too long, then the full force of the curse would fall upon her.

"And what is this dire fate that will befall me?" she asked.

"I will not tell you that," her uncle replied, his voice little more than a whisper.

"Will I die, then?"

"So it would seem," Kailen answered, and then he fell silent and would say no more.

Her belongings were stowed, her bedding prepared, brightly-dyed threads for the loom set out for her, and then finally her father's party prepared to take its leave and return to the castle of Astolat. She said nothing to her father, and for his part he several times seemed about to speak, but never did.

When the others had gone, though, her uncle waited behind, and drew forth something from beneath his cloak.

"You will be lonely," he said. "Trapped at that loom, you will weary of the same four walls. I cannot give you your freedom; I have sworn to your father that I would not. I can give you this, though, to lighten your days." With that, he handed her a gleaming disk — a mirror of the finest glass, perfectly silvered, utterly without flaw. "This can show you whatever you might see from anywhere in this tower," he said. "Hang it above the loom, and so long as you obey the geas and continue to weave, you need not leave your labors to see the view from each window, or from any of the four turrets, or the parapets between. The mirror will show you whichever you please."

"Thank you, Uncle," she said, accepting the glass.

And then she was alone in her island bower. She placed the mirror above the loom as her uncle had suggested, and began her weaving.

In truth, she found it was not so very terrible; no one troubled her, and the tapestry gave her distraction when she wanted it, as she planned out her design and chose the colors, but it did not require her full attention when she preferred to think of other things. Knotting the threads, working the treadle, and sending the shuttle back and forth was familiar, comforting work that she could carry on while her attention was elsewhere — on dreams of escape, or on fantasies of what it might feel like to rest in Sir Lancelot's arms, her head pressed against his mighty chest.

She could also continue her work when she watched her marvelous glass, for the mirror performed as her uncle had promised; with a word, a gesture, or even a thought she could direct it to show her whatever view she chose. What's more, she found that in some regards it was even better than peering from the actual window, for she could instruct it to show only a portion of an image, whereupon that portion would expand to fill the entire glass, as if she stood much closer than the tower truly was.

She watched barges pass by her island, heavy-laden with grain and treasure bound for the king's court at Camelot. She watched the drooping branches of the willows on the banks brush against the stacked bundles as they passed through the narrows that surrounded Shalott. Branches that had dangled into the river drew dark lines of water upon canvas and wood, and then the barges emerged again into sunlight and moved on toward their destination, and the streaks dried swiftly.

There were small, light boats that passed as well, driven by vividly-painted sails that bore the arms of their owners, or for those that belonged to none of the great houses, fanciful creatures and intricate designs. These flashed brightly in the sun, then dimmed beneath the shade of the trees only to blossom forth anew when they had passed the island. Elaine realized these were carrying messages from town to town, and sometimes also held passengers who preferred the smooth water to the jostling of riding horseback.

She would have waved to these as they passed, but she dared not leave the loom, for fear of her uncle's curse.

Beyond the willows she saw the farmers in the fields, reaping the grain with sickles, or with scythe and cradle. She saw them loading their carts, and wiping the sweat from their brows, and through the open window behind her she could sometimes faintly hear them singing as they worked, songs that celebrated their labors and helped them keep a smooth rhythm as they swung their blades. On occasion, when she knew the songs of old or had heard enough to learn them anew, she sang along, and more than once she saw a reaper raise his head and turn to look toward the island tower, showing that her voice could be heard.

None ever dared approach, though; they would pause, listen, and then return to their work.

The singing helped to lighten her heart, though, and lift the weight of her captivity, so she continued to sing, whether the farmers sang or not.

A road ran beside the stream, and she could see those who passed along it — peasant children in brown homespun, friars in their dark robes, pages and couriers hurrying to bring their masters news of other places, women in colorful gowns fetching goods to market. Most, she knew, were traveling to or from Camelot, which lay but a dozen miles downstream.

Indeed, if she set the mirror in just the right way, she could see the distant towers of Arthur's castle — a reminder that her beloved was not so very far away, and that if she were free of this place, of her father's walls and her uncle's curse, she could go to him. She even saw the means by which that might be achieved — whether by accident or design she did not know, but she found that a small boat, without sail or tow-rope, lay abandoned upon the rocks at the northern end of her little island. If she dared to leave her tower she need only drag that boat into the stream, and the current would deliver her to Camelot.

There were times when that knowledge cheered her, and she sang songs of love and happiness; there were other times when seeing the boat only reminded her of the walls and the curse that bound her, and all thought of music or gaiety left her.

At first she had thought her stay on the island would be brief, that her father would reconsider, or that she would find a means of escape, or that Lancelot would seek her out and rescue her, but the days passed, and the weeks, and finally months. The golden fields were stripped bare by the harvesters, the rye and barley hauled away to barns or to market; the leaves of the willows yellowed and fell, the flowers withered and vanished. The travelers on the road were now wrapped in woolen cloaks, hoods pulled forward to shield their faces from the bitter wind. Her unseen servants kept fires going in the rooms below, so that winter's chill did not penetrate too deeply, and her fingers remained nimble enough to continue her weaving.

The tapestry upon which she worked had become a grand panoply of the king and his knights, woven from her memories of the tourney at her father's castle, but where most would have put Arthur at the center, she had instead placed Lancelot there, and had arranged everything else around him, like children around a hearth's fire. She wove his tabard of the purest white she could find, adorned with a cross of the brightest red her dyes could produce, and the face she gave him was worthy of the gods of old and seemed to shine of its own light. His armor gleamed like silver. The other knights were mere shadows by comparison; even Arthur himself was only a man among men, far less than his chief servant.

As the winter wore on, though, she sought more color to counter the drab grays and whites of the outside world, and the stands on either side of the lists were woven of red and gold, adorned with flowers in every color of the rainbow.

At last the days again grew longer, the sun brighter, and the snows melted away, revealing fresh black earth and sprouting green. The mirror showed her travelers' faces once again, and more of them; the farmers, too, returned, to plant the seeds of the new year's crops. The windows were opened, and although she could not easily turn to look out through the casements she could feel the fresh breeze finding its way to her chamber.

She had by now despaired of her father's love; it was clear that he would not relent, that if he had his way she would spend the rest of her life here unless she foreswore her love — and that, she could not do.

At that, she sometimes doubted that her father even recalled her existence. Did he remember that he had a daughter, almost twenty years of age, locked away in this tower? Had he forgotten her and moved on with his life, as if she had died? What of her two brothers — had they, too, forgotten that they once had a sister, a childhood playmate? Neither of them had made any contact with her in all her long months of imprisonment.

Nor had her uncle, but that was less surprising; he was, after all, a lord of Faerie, with the cold and whimsical nature of his race, prone to forget how brief mortal lives might be.

And Lancelot had not come. Did he even know where she was? Might he be searching the kingdom for her, seeking her in every village and field, unaware that her own father had imprisoned her here, within sight of Camelot's spires? But surely someone would have told him; it was no secret in her father's castle, surely. Did he think she did not want him? Had her father lied to Lancelot, told him she was no longer interested? Or had her father forbidden Lancelot to come here, and he, noble knight that he was, respected that imperative, though it pained him?

Her moods varied from day to day; sometimes she worked at the loom gladly, singing as she wove, certain that in time her love would come for her. On other days she despaired of life, and passed the shuttle from side to side from simple habit, looking nowhere, ignoring both her tapestry's design and the world the mirror showed her.

On one such day she looked up at the glass and saw the farmers standing respectfully still as a column of knights rode by, their chargers churning the damp soil of the springtime road. Their banners whipped in the breeze — golden lions, and blue saltires, and green dragons, but nowhere a red cross on white. These were knights riding out from Camelot, but Lancelot was not among them, and none turned to look at her island prison as they passed.

Still, they were knights, Lancelot's companions, and she turned, as if to see what was reflected in the mirror, to see only the bare stone wall of her chamber.

"Shadows," she said, turning back to the mirror and the loom. "Only shadows. I am half-*sick* of shadows!" She grabbed the shuttle and flung it furiously across the warp threads.

The days passed, and her tapestry grew; she had completed the central scene of knights at tourney and was now extending it outward, to the lands beyond the castle walls, where magical beasts gamboled amidst bright flowers.

As the spring advanced more knights came and went; she guessed that the king had set the Round Table some new quest, and these men were traveling upon this business, whatsoever it might be. The fields grew green, the plants shooting up, stretching for the sun as the farmers tended to their crops. Flowers blossomed anew on the island outside the tower walls.

And then one day, when summer was almost upon her, she looked up from warp and weft and saw the image of a lone knight on horseback, riding down the road toward Camelot. He had already come alongside the island; the mirror had been directed elsewhere and had missed his approach. She could not see the front of his tabard, to see what sigil might be embroidered there, and he bore his shield on the far side of his mount, so she could not see his arms; his face was turned away, as well.

But she knew him. She had thought of him every day of her imprisonment, had dreamed of him every night. There could be no possibility of error. This was Sir Lancelot, greatest of the Knights of the Round Table.

And then he turned to look at the little tower, and there could be no mistake. It was he.

He wore no helm, as he was returning home, not facing any possibility of combat; his broad clear brow gleamed in the sun, and his black curls swept back from his face on either side, while his helmet rode upon the saddle behind him, a bright red plume waving from its crest as he rode. His greaves glittered like gold, and the steel that guarded his broad shoulders shone like silver. He rode upright, straight and strong. A cross as red as blood emblazoned his chest, vivid on a tunic as white as a summer cloud.

"He has come for me at last!" cried Elaine. She wanted to leap up, to run to the window call to him, but the shuttle in her hand reminded her of the curse; she could not leave the loom.

She would remain here until he had entered the stronghold, she told herself. He would find an entrance and come for her, and then she would fling the shuttle aside and throw her arms around him, and together they would find a way to escape the curse.

She tied off a thread, then unspooled another length and wound it on the shuttle; that done, she looked up at the mirror, to see whether Lancelot had yet found his way across the channel to the island.

He had not; instead he was still upon the road, and almost past the line of willows, close against the burgeoning green barley. He was no longer looking at her prison, but ahead, at the distant towers of Camelot, and she thought she could hear, ever so faintly through the open casement, his deep voice raised in happy song at the sight of home.

He had not stopped. He had not come for her. He would not be singing thus while he sought to breach the fortress that held her, so that was not what had brought him at all. He did not know she was here, she realized; he had not come searching for her, but merely chanced to be passing on some other business.

"No!" she cried, dropping the shuttle. "*No!*" She leapt to her feet and turned, trying to get her bearings — which way to a window where she might call to him? She had for so long seen the outside world only as reflections in her glass that she had lost all sense of how her prison was oriented.

She ran through a passage and found only an empty room, and windows that looked out upon barley fields and willows; there was no road, no passing knight, below her vantage point, but only water lilies upon the sun-dappled stream. She whirled and ran back the other way, flung open a pair of shutters, and again saw field and garden and river and tree.

But now, with two references, she knew where she needed to go. She turned once again and rushed up a short stair to yet a third window. Here she leaned out and saw the river between two rows of willows, and the road and green barley beyond. She let her gaze follow the road, and saw Lancelot riding away, the red cross upon his back as bright as the one upon his chest, the red plume of his helmet dancing upon his saddle as if to taunt her.

"No," she called again. "*No!*"

Wind rippled through the willows below, cool on her face. "Beloved!" she cried, "I am here! Come for me! Save me! *Lancelot!*"

But her voice did not carry over the wind, and over the growing distance between them. He could not hear her, shout as she might. Had it been night, when her mother's magic stirred within her, she might perhaps have reached him, have somehow gotten his attention, but in the warm afternoon sun she had only a mortal's throat to call his name, and it was not enough. He rode on, never looking back.

She watched him go, hoping that he might turn and see her, that he might casually glance back and catch sight of her, but no such miracle occurred; his horse carried him down the road away from her, his gaze fixed on the towers of Camelot.

And then she heard a noise behind her, a sound of strings snapping and wood straining. She turned.

Something twanged.

"Oh, no," she said. Then she leapt down from the casement and ran back to her chamber, to the room that had been her prison and her refuge for the past several months.

The loom had splintered, threads broken and tangled; her unfinished tapestry had unrolled and lay spread upon the wreckage. And above the stool where she had sat for so long hung the mirror that had shown her shadows of the world outside, but as she watched the glass shuddered and rippled, and the mirror cracked from side to side, the magical images vanishing so that the two pieces now reflected only the gray stone of the walls enclosing her.

"The curse," she wailed. "The curse is come upon me!"

And now, she knew, she was to die. That was what her father and uncle had agreed upon, should she abandon her labors, and she had left the loom too long as she sought to see her lover.

She was to die — but she did not know what form her death would take, nor how long she had before it befell her.

Even as these thoughts ran through her head, though, she felt a twinge in her belly, a tightening in her chest, and she knew her doom was upon her. She paused for a moment to snatch up a pot of dye and a scrap of cloth, so that she might perhaps leave a final message — she had neither paper nor ink, but the dye, she thought, would serve. It was the color of midnight, a deep, deep blue, and very beautiful.

She found the stairs and staggered down, the breath growing weak in her lungs. She wondered whether the servants were near, and whether they would speak to her in this final extremity, perhaps give a final message to her father, but she saw no sign of them.

She flung open the great oaken door at the base of the tower and stumbled out onto the graveled path, looking for that long-abandoned boat she knew lay on the island's shore.

She did not want to die on this island; if it took her death to set her free, then she would *be* free, no longer trapped in her stone walls, but out in the spring air and sunshine. And that boat — she could set herself adrift, let the boat carry her corpse past Camelot and out to sea, so that everyone would see what had become of her. Lancelot need not seek forever after his lost love; he would know she was gone, and could go on.

She swayed unsteadily as she walked, hoping she had time enough; it would be so … so *plain* to fall dead here, without leaving the island.

And though she could feel the strength leaving her limbs, she found the boat and righted it, setting it on the island's verge. Then she took her pot of dye and dipped the cloth in it, trying to think what message she might write, what her parting words might be, so that the world would understand the tragedy that was happening here.

"Here lies Elaine of Astolat," perhaps, "betrayed by those she loved."

But no, she was Elaine of Astolat no longer; she had been cast out of Astolat, her name taken from her. She took the stained rag and wrote upon the prow of the boat, as neatly as she could with her trembling hand, "The Lady of Shalott."

She had hoped to say more, but she could sense she had no time to spare, and her wits were fading, as well, so that she could not decide upon anything more. She tossed aside the dye and rag, and pushed the boat down into the river. As carefully as she could, she clambered aboard and felt her little craft drift free. As it found the current she lay down upon her back and folded her hands across her chest, waiting to die.

Clouds were gathering in the sky above, she saw — perhaps a spring shower was coming.

She would feel nothing of it, though. She closed her eyes.

She could no longer feel her legs or arms, but somehow her throat was still clear, and upon a whim she began to sing, composing her own dirge as she drifted down the river. How she found the strength, she did not know; why she still lived at all, she did not understand. Still, she sang, so that what little breath remained to her might not be wasted.

She sang as long as she could, but she had lost all sense of time, and did not know whether that was only a moment, or an hour. When at last she paused for a moment, she heard voices muttering.

Startled, she opened her eyes and found that her boat had already found its way as far downstream as the outermost houses of Camelot, where frightened people lined the riverbanks, watching her pass. There were merchants in rich velvet, peasants in drab wool, knights in gleaming armor, dames in shining silks, staring out at her. She saw townsfolk cross themselves in fear as she drifted by, and she wanted to call out to them, to let them there was no cause for concern, but now her voice was gone — she could not move at all, not even her eyes, any longer.

Her uncle's curse was stranger than she had anticipated. She knew, from the words she heard from the banks and bridges: They thought her dead, a corpse laid out as though for burial, but she could still hear them, could still see them gesture, not just the making the sign of the cross but also the devil's horns, to ward off the evil eye.

Was this death, then? Surely not. This was some spell that her uncle had placed upon her, some enchantment.

"The Lady of Shalott," someone said. "What is Shalott?"

"An island up the river," another voice replied. "It's said a fairy lives in the tower there, and the farmers can sometimes hear her singing."

"We heard singing," a new voice joined in. "Perhaps this is she, then — the fairy who dwelt there."

"But what is she doing here? Why is she dead? There is no mark upon her of either blade or fever."

"Someone tell the king, or his wizard! Let him tell us what must be done."

"Tell the king!"

"A messenger has gone to the castle, since first the boat was seen."

Elaine could not move her eyes, so she could not see who spoke; she could see only the sky above, the undersides of bridges, and the faces of those who lined the nearer bank of the river.

But then she heard a voice that she did not need eyesight to identify. It was the deep, rich voice of Sir Lancelot, calling orders.

A moment later, at his direction, boat-hooks grappled with her little vessel, pulling it toward the shore. A moment after that Lancelot's face came into Elaine's field of vision, dark against the sky, his black curls framing his strong features as he looked down at her.

Elaine thrilled at the sight, and a thought filled her. Perhaps a kiss from this, her true love, would break the curse her uncle had laid upon her, as might happen in an old tale. Perhaps if Lancelot were to lean down and press his lips to hers she would be freed of this enchantment and would return to life, ready to live with him for the rest of her life.

She waited as he knelt down over her boat.

"The Lady of Shalott," he said. "She has a lovely face, a rare beauty; it is sad that we should only see it now, when she is dead. God in his mercy granted her this grace; I hope that it served her well while she yet lived, and brought pleasure to her and those around her."

Elaine waited for him to stoop down, to give her a farewell kiss, a kiss that would restore her to life, but he did not; indeed, he straightened and got back to his feet, still looking down at her.

"What a shame," he said, "that I did not meet her while she yet lived. Perhaps I might have found the means to save her from whatever fate has befallen her."

Then he turned, and signaled to the men with the boat-hooks to release the little craft.

Elaine was almost too shocked to notice when the boat drifted away from the dock.

"What a shame that I did not meet her while she yet lived," he had said. *"What a shame that I did not meet her."*

He did not love her. He did not even *remember* her.

Her father had been right all along. She had been a silly girl, caught up in a romantic fantasy. Sir Lancelot had never really noticed her; she had just been one more foolish child drawn to his handsome face and manly form, and to the tales of his strength and goodness.

The boat drifted on, past the castle towers, the stone bridges, the soaring spires, the staring crowds, until Camelot was past and she was again in open country, beneath gathering clouds. She lay unmoving, trapped by her uncle's spell, unable to weep, unable to curse, wondering what was to become of her.

Then the clouds burst, and rain fell, and where the drops touched her she felt strength and sensation return. She could blink again, and flex her fingers; then she could turn her head and raise her hands to shield herself from the gentle storm. Her legs bent, and she was able to sit up and look around at the fields slipping past.

A willow dangled above the stream, and she reached up to grab its branches, pulling herself and her little boat to the shore. Still somewhat unsteady, she used the willow's limbs to pull herself upright, and to heave herself over the boat's side and onto the bank. There she let herself fall back, and sat upon the riverside, looking out at the intricate patterns formed by the willow's leaves and the expanding, interlocking ripples each fat raindrop made as it pierced the river's surface.

And then her uncle was there, standing on the shore a few yards away, watching her silently. She blinked and stared at him.

"I would not kill you," he said. "You and your brothers are all that I have left of the sister I loved. You should have known that, were you not so blinded by your infatuation."

"You *said* I would die."

"No," he replied. "I said it would *seem* that you died, and is that not what occurred?"

"Did you *know* that all this would happen as it has? Did you know Lancelot would not recognize me?"

"Not precisely," Kailen said. "I knew that he did not love you, and I knew you would not believe that until you saw it for yourself — not merely heard the good knight say it, for then you could say that he was denying the truth for some reason of your invention, but *saw* it, in a way you could not reject. I bent my spell to encourage the fates to arrange for such an encounter, but I did not know how that might be accomplished, nor how long it might take. The fates were kind, and found a way in less than a year. I am glad it took no longer; you mortals live such brief lives that it would be a shame to waste more than necessary."

Elaine stared at him, then said, "I know you have done me a great favor, Uncle, but I cannot yet bring myself to thank you. The pain is still too great."

"Of course. But *my* life is not brief, and I can wait." He glanced upstream. "And now, dear child, what will you do? Your death has been reported far and wide, but I am certain your family will gladly receive you back, should you return to Astolat."

Elaine shook her head before she had consciously made her decision. "No," she said. "I am a grown woman now, and I cannot yet forgive my father any more than I can thank you. I will find my own way in the world for a time; if I am careful I think I have enough magic and common sense to get by."

"I am sure you do," Kailen said with a nod. "Go, then, and find your path. In time it may bring you back to your father's halls, or perhaps to your mother's home in Faerie, or to the king's court in Camelot. If you ever feel you need help, always remember you have two brothers who love you, and a father who cares for you whether you believe it or not — and of course, you have an uncle you can call upon."

"I will remember," Elaine said. Then she turned and walked up the riverbank to the road, where she turned toward the sea, her back to many-towered Camelot. She glanced back, and as she had expected, her uncle was gone. He was a fairy lord, and did not need to go as mortal men did.

She managed a crooked smile, then walked on alone, eastward into the warm spring rain.

— «» —

Lawrence Watt-Evans is the author of some fifty novels and well over a hundred short stories, including the Hugo-winning "Why I Left Harry's All-Night Hamburgers." He has been a full-time writer since 1979, which makes for a quiet life and a dull bio. Although best known for fantasy, particularly the Legends of Ethshar series, he also writes science fiction and horror, and has served as treasurer of SFWA and president of the Horror Writers Association. He lives in Maryland, just outside Washington DC, with his wife of forty years.

The Root of All Things

William Meikle

"Sire? Why are we looking for the Grail in this place?"

Sir Breunor sighed, not for the first time in the week since they'd made land in Argoat and began this endless ride through the dark forest of Broceliande. His squire, Cormac, was industrious and keen, both of which were fine qualities in a lad, but they were offset by an almost insatiable need to ask questions; his young mind was full of stories of chivalry and magic, many of which had been embellished by time. Breunor knew the truth — and the lies — of most of the tales, but explaining that difference to a squire who had not yet been born when the events took place was proving to be tiring in the extreme. Indeed, another question came before he had even considered answering the first.

"Sire? Is it true that you knew the Queen — before the Betrayal — before she was even Queen, and that you saved her from a foul beast? And is it true you were friend to Lancelot, but chose to stay with the King when the Queen was taken from the stake?"

Three questions then — yet all of them linked — all, and none of them being the reason he was here, in this forest, and none of them easily answered. It was a thing he had never spoken of to any man — he was not about to begin by telling an inquisitive squire. He answered only the first question.

"We are not here in search of the Grail," he said as he rode his mount carefully down a narrow trail beside a rocky brook. "We are here to find someone who might help set us on the correct path on which to find it."

The squire — a red-haired youth of fourteen summers who until this journey had never been further than ten miles from Camelot — was not impressed.

"This is not at all what I had expected from a Grail quest," he said.

On that, at least, Breunor was able to agree. Six days riding had brought them nothing but more trees, they had not passed a dwelling for the last four, and had run out of any food but what they could forage this past morning. The possibility that they may have to retire and go back had crossed his mind more than once since a breakfast of rabbit so wiry and tough as to be almost inedible. But he was on the King's business — his Lord's health — indeed the future he'd been fighting for all of his adult life — was in peril. The Grail must be found — the table knights were all dispatched on the singular purpose.

When given the task Breunor had not known where to start — then he had remembered the Enchanter, and the tale of his imprisonment by Nimue in this Breton forest. If anyone could lead him to the Grail, Merlin could.

But first I have to find him.

And that was proving to be the difficult part. They must, by his reckoning, be half way through to Rennes by now, but the forest was getting thicker if anything, and several trails had already led them only to stagnant ponds or in circles back to where they'd already been.

It is almost as if there is some enchantment preventing me from making any headway.

As soon as the thought itself struck, there was a new thing on the trail ahead of him — something that wasn't tree or stone. It seemed to be a jet-black tear in the fabric of space, no bigger than a sliver of fingernail. Initially Breunor thought he had a hair near his eye and tried to brush it away before he realized he was looking at something several yards away, hanging below the canopy at his eye level. He urged his mount closer to get a better view of the thing, but looking at it straight on hurt his eyes — they struggled to focus, never quite managing it.

The only way he could really see the thing was by turning side on so that it was just on the edge of his vision.

It appeared to be spinning slowly in a clockwise direction. As he watched, it quivered and changed shape, settling into a new configuration, becoming a black, somewhat oily in appearance, droplet little more than an inch across at the thickest point. It hung there, its very impossibility taunting him to go over and look for the strings that had to be holding it in place.

It swelled, and now looked like an egg more than anything else — a black, oily egg from some creature whose nature could only be guessed at. As he drew his sword a rainbow aura thickened around the egg, casting the whole of the trail in dancing washes of soft colors as it continued to spin.

His sword hummed, suddenly hot in his hand as he had to kick the horse to get it to move closer still. The egg quivered and pulsed. And now it was more than obvious — it was most definitely growing. The sword sent a new flash of heat, like a searing burn in his palm as he lifted the weapon to strike, but before he made the blow the throb became a rapid thumping; the whole of the forest shook and trembled. The vibration rattled his teeth and set his guts roiling.

The aura around the egg wavered and trembled — and now there was a large tree there — an impossible tree, with an oak door embedded in it, hanging in space, right there, right ahead of him — a door that was swinging open.

"Merlin!" he called out. "It is I, Breunor. I need your help — the King needs your help."

The door was already starting to fade and disappear. He urged the horse closer but it had taken fright and reared, so much so that he had to fight hard to avoid being tumbled to the hard ground beneath. When he recovered enough to look there was nothing to be seen hanging there but empty space. The black egg — and the door it had created — was gone as quickly as it had come. But he now knew something he had not known before.

I was close. I was really close. Merlin is here — and there is a way for me to get to him.

— 《》 —

"Are you quite well, sire?" Cormac asked as Breunor turned away from what was now just another patch of forest. He saw no fear or wonder in the lad's eyes — only puzzlement.

"Tell me, lad — what did you see?"

"I saw you raise your sword, and call out for the Enchanter — only that."

"Then, if there is indeed enchantment here, it is for me alone," the knight replied. "We shall make camp here — it is as good a spot as any."

While the squire went to set snares and fetch water, Breunor sat on a rock by the side of the trail. He was still not sure himself that seeking out the Enchanter was the best course of action, for Merlin knew Breunor's heart —knew that his duty to the King had fought, long and hard, with his friendship for Lancelot — and his love for the Queen. In the end, duty had won out — but it had been a close thing, and the knight felt the weight of the decision every day as he watched the King grow older — frailer — more tired. Merlin had never spoken of it in the years before he too fell under a woman's spell — but both of them knew what others only merely suspected. And it was that thorn in Breunor's side — the feeling that, despite staying by the King's side, he had also, somehow, failed as a knight, that had brought him on this quest.

He was still lost in memories of past disappointments when the squire returned with water and three more stringy rabbits that were almost gone to nothing by the time they were cooked.

"Sire?" the squire asked as they sucked on the last of the bones. "Why do we tarry here?"

"Because we are as close as we are ever going to be allowed to get —now hush — this is a time for patience. I know it tries you sorely — but at least attempt to hold your peace. There is enchantment here — if we allow ourselves to see it."

The lad had the sense, for once, to obey his directive and they sat, each lost in thought, on opposite sides of the fire.

At first, when the enchantment returned, the effect was so subtle that Breunor again suspected a problem with his own sight. He saw a rainbow aurora ahead of him in the fire. He gripped his sword and moved forward quickly, hoping for another door, readying himself to react more quickly than he had on the first encounter.

Two eggs hung in the air at eye level above the flames, side by side, just touching, each as black as the other, twin bubbles only held in check by the dancing rainbow colors. The whole forest throbbed like a heartbeat. The eggs pulsed in synchronized agreement and calved.

Four eggs now hung in a tight group, all now pulsing in time with the still rising thumping that seemed to come up out of the ground itself. Colors danced and flowed across the sheer black surface; blues and greens and shimmering silvers that filled the trees above with washes of color. The beat got louder. The eggs throbbed, beating time like a giant drum. Soon there were eight, then sixteen.

Breunor's head pounded with the rhythm, and nausea rose as his gut roiled and rolled. He started to back away, back toward the trees, hoping for some respite.

Thirty-two now, and the canopy above shimmered with dancing aurora of shimmering lights that pulsed and beat in time as the eggs calved again, and again, everything careening along in a big happy dance.

He couldn't take much more. He stepped forward. The sword screamed as he struck at the growing mass of eggs. The rainbow aura seemed to breathe in, breathe out, twice. There was a sudden burst of color; red, blue and shimmering silver filled his head with a glare brighter than the brightest sun.

When he blinked, he was still in the forest — or rather, a forest, for there was no sign of the camp, his squire or their mounts. Instead the trail on which he stood crossed what had once been a river here, over a stone bridge so ancient that it too had taken on a dark, almost burnt aspect, as if the old rocks were themselves turning to ash. He stood on the near bank to inspect the structure — he didn't want to get part way over and have the thing collapse under his weight — it was a long way down with no sign of any way back up, even if he miraculously survived the fall.

He took a firmer grip of the sword and, tapping it hard on the surface of the bridge ahead of him to test for weakness, began to make his way slowly across. The bridge was narrow — only five feet at the widest, and if it ever had a wall guarding against a fall, it too had long since crumbled away. He felt exposed to the height — a drop of fifty feet or more to the black, dry rock below that used to be a riverbed — and was thankful that the wind was not any stronger than a stiff breeze from his right.

The old decaying stone settled alarmingly in several places under his weight, and he went across slowly, inch by inch, tap-tapping the sword all the way. He kept his head down, eyes on the bridge, ready to run should any cracks appear, so he heard the voice before he saw anything — it was soft, almost sibilant.

"This is not your path, Sir Breunor of the badly-fitting coat," it said.

Breunor looked up. Another knight stood at the far end of the bridge, his armor gleaming silver, his feet planted firmly on solid ground. The air seemed to shimmer — and beyond that, up a small rise in the ground, stood a great shining tree with a partially open oak door.

"You have me at a disadvantage, good knight," Breunor replied. "How is it that you know my name and I do not know yours?" he said, at the same time inching forward — it wasn't worth attempting to go back — he was past halfway, and every little bit toward the far side was less far to drop.

"I have many names," the silver knight replied "Dweller on the threshold, keeper of the way — gatekeeper if you like. You could even call me Janus, and you would not be too far wrong. It is my place to offer you options, to see if you are decided on one course — or many?"

One of the black eggs rose up from the chasm under the bridge and popped. An image formed in the air and Breunor saw himself as an old man, in a comfortable chair by a roaring fire, with a dog at his feet, a flagon of ale in his hand and an air of such contentment that he could scarcely imagine it.

"What is this place?" he asked.

The silver knight laughed.

"Everywhere — nowhere — the dreams of a sleeping enchanter — or of the Grail itself? Who really knows? All I know is that I am here — and I can go somewhere, anywhere, else, taking you with me or leaving you behind depending on the result of your choice. This is the Threshold — a gateway to the beyond and all that it holds. You will only pass this way once — and it is a choice only given to those of the Table. You may come with me into an infinity of possibilities and all the wonders that lie there — or fight me. If you prevail, you may go to meet your Enchanter — a man who has so far forgotten himself that he will not know you and cannot help you."

"I do not know what I am being offered, and I will not be swayed from my duty. Let me pass."

The knight sighed.

"Why would you wish to go that way?" he said. "There is nothing there for you but sorrow and loss — nothing to find but what you already know, nothing to see but what you have already seen."

"Nevertheless — you will allow me passage — or you will die here on this spot."

The silver knight sighed again.

"It is always thus. Remember — you had a choice here. And remember what you have refused, for you will never see it again."

The silver knight drew out its sword and said no more.

With that Breunor took a bigger step forward. The sword sent a burst of heat in his palm as the bridge swayed slightly. A lump of rock the size of his head fell away and tumbled into the gorge. It seemed to take an awful long time to fall.

He was less than ten feet from the silver figure, but now that the bridge had started to move its final decay accelerated. Rubble and dirt tumbled away underfoot, and he felt his balance threatened as the whole structure swayed.

The silver knight laughed as Breunor tried to stay upright. Being on firm ground, he was in no hurry whatsoever. The bridge was steadily collapsing away under Breunor's feet — he had no way back, no way down — the only option was forward. He braced himself — and leapt into attack.

He had moved just in time, for even as their swords met in a clash of sparks and steel, the bridge fell away completely behind him, and he only just found his footing in time — right on the edge of the precipice. The silver knight's sword flowed, fast and fluid, seemingly effortlessly, and it took all of Breunor's skill to keep him at bay and prevent himself being forced backward into the chasm.

And yet, for all the silver knight's masterly swordplay, Breunor gave as good as he took, and the fight ebbed and flowed, one way and the other, but with neither ever gaining enough of an upper hand to land a telling blow. Time seemed to have halted and there was nothing but swordplay and movement, cut and thrust, defense and attack. They might have been at it for hours — days even — had Breunor not seen the shining tree start to fade from view, the oak door start to close.

"No!" Breunor shouted, and pressed hard in an attack with a risky blow that left his left side open to a killing thrust should his own blow falter. But luck was with him — his blade struck the silver knight full on the crown of his helm and kept going — through into a visor empty of anything save more of the black, pulsing, eggs. Before Breunor could call back the stroke the edge of the sword caught one of the eggs and there was a blinding flash

Everything went black as a pit of hell, and a thunderous blast rocked the forest, driving Breunor down into a place where he dreamed of empty spaces filled with oily, glistening bubbles. They popped and spawned yet more bubbles, then even more, until he swam in a swirling sea of colors.

He drifted in a blanket of darkness, alone, in a cathedral of emptiness where nothing existed save the dark and the pounding. He saw more stars — vast swathes of gold and blue and silver, all dancing in great purple and red clouds that spun webs of grandeur across unending vistas. Shapes moved in and among the nebulae; dark, wispy shadows casting a pallor over whole galaxies at a time, shadows that capered and whirled as the dance grew ever more frenetic. He was buffeted, as if by a strong, surging tide, but as the pounding beat grew ever stronger he cared little. He gave himself to it, lost in the dance, lost in the stars.

He didn't know how long he wandered in the space between. He forgot himself, forgot his quest, forgot his duty, lost, dancing in the vastness where only rhythm mattered.

Lost.

— «» —

"Sire! Sire!"

It was duty — the realization that he would be leaving the lad alone in a wild forest — that called him up and out of the dark dance, and when he saw the relief in the squire's eyes, he knew he had made the right choice, for once.

"I am here, boy — there is no need to shout."

Once again, Cormac professed to have seen nothing.

"You fell into a faint, sire," he said. "I thought you stricken by some poison in the rabbit, or by some invisible spell. I could not rouse you for the longest time — and then you smiled — and I knew you still lived."

"Aye," Breunor said softly. "I still live. And the third time is a charm. Get some sleep now, lad — I will watch — and wait."

He did not have to wait long — just long enough for Cormac to start to snore quietly. A faint, far off, throbbing joined the sound, and then the first egg appeared.

It quickly calved, and calved again.

Four eggs hung in a tight group, pulsing in time with the beat of the throb from the ground. Colors danced and flowed across the sheer black surfaces; blues and greens and shimmering silvers on the eggs.

In the blink of an eye there were eight.

Breunor had no thought of escape, lost in contemplation of the beauty, remembering the dance in the dark.

Sixteen now, all perfect, all dancing.

The throbbing grew louder still.

Thirty two now, and they had started to fill the arched canopy with dancing aurora of shimmering lights that pulsed and capered in time with the throb of magic, everything careening along in a big happy dance.

Sixty-four, each a shimmering pearl of black light.

The colors spilled out over him, crept around his feet, danced in his eyes, in his head, all though his body.

A hundred and twenty eight now, and already calving into two hundred and fifty-six.

As if right at his ear, he heard the silver knight's voice.

"If you prevail, you may go to an Enchanter who has so far forgotten himself that he will not know you and cannot help you."

"And yet, I must go," Breunor said. "It is my duty."

"As you will," the knight said.

Five hundred and twelve black eggs swarmed forward and engulfed him. One touched him at the forehead, he saw a door, and he stepped through it to elsewhere.

— «» —

At first it was so bright he could not see anything at all, then he realized he was inside some kind of great tree. But what a tree, one whose trunk was all of crystal ingrained with greens and gold and yellow and blue and red, flecks of mineral, all shimmering as if lit by small, internal suns. The crystal — he soon was able to see enough to realize it was a chamber, of sorts — filled the whole internal bole of the tree, high up above his head and way down below his feet, root and branch and twig. And right in the center of the chamber, more crystal — a shard as tall as a man, opaque and milky at first, but clearing as Breunor stepped forward.

There was a man inside — one that he knew, or had known — the enchanter himself, hunched over clutching to his tall quarterstaff, his beard, thicker and grayer than Breunor remembered — almost reaching his waist. He stood, completely encased inside a hollow, and surrounded by more — hundreds, perhaps thousands more, of the dancing, glistening eggs. Every so often one would pop, and Breunor would see what Merlin saw. His heart sank when he realized what so preoccupied the enchanter here in his imprisonment — for it was the same thing that was forever in his own thoughts.

Guinevere and Lancelot, in her chamber, caught betraying the King — Lancelot saving the Queen from the stake — Arthur, alone, on a throne as dull as old ash — Lancelot, in his cups, Guinevere, in the habits of a follower of the White Christ — a land, barren and cold. It was the same sights, over and over, with no respite and never a sight of the Grail, never a hint of hope.

"Merlin!" Breunor shouted, and rapped hard at the crystal with his fist.

An egg popped inside. Guinevere again, smiling, forever young.

Breunor only noticed he had his sword in his hand when he raised it for another strike at the crystal. He rapped the hilt, hard. The tall shard rang a high note, sending it reverberating through the whole chamber. Did Merlin twitch? Breunor thought so, and hit the crystal again, harder this time. The resulting sound — and accompanying vibration — threatened to knock him off his feet. But the enchanter had definitely moved, his head turning so that he looked straight at the knight.

Breunor raised the sword again, but never got to make the blow.

"Stop," a voice said at his ear — not the silver knight, but a tone of command he knew of old, and one that had never brooked any argument.

"I can free you," Breunor said. "The King has need of you."

"You cannot. He does not," Merlin said. Another egg popped. Arthur, alone, not on the throne, but at the head of the Table, holding a court where all the other seats were empty.

"He needs the Grail," Breunor said.

"Then let him find it for himself," Merlin replied. "It is not something someone else can do for you."

The crystal started to go opaque again. Another egg popped; a sword, rusted and pitted, sat, plunged deep in a stone in the middle of a field of ice.

"Merlin! At least tell me how to find the Grail!"

The voice came from a great distance, as if shouted in the wind.

"Find the silver knight, and take his offer."

The crystal went dim but Breunor scarcely saw, scarcely noticed when the tree faded around him and disappeared, the campsite drifting into sharp focus in its place. The wide-eyed face of his squire looked into his.

"You found him?" Cormac said. "You found the Enchanter?"

"Found him — and lost," Breunor said, suddenly as tired as he had ever been. "Ready the horses — we are going home."

"We are not questing for the Grail?"

"No, lad," he said, almost too softly to be heard. "We are not. Not any more — a man might yet find his own silver knight and takes his offer — but that man will not be me. I let my duty lead me where I should have followed my heart. But at least we can tell the King that we were close — at least we can tell him that much."

Cormac had clearly not understood.

I wish that I did not — for my own sake.

As they broke camp and rode off, it wasn't Merlin's visions he saw, not the Enchanter's voice he heard, but one, last, whisper in his ear. He had ignored it the first time, but now it would haunt him forever more.

"Remember — you had a choice here. And remember what you have refused, for you will never see it again."

— «» —

William Meikle is a Scottish writer, now living in Canada, with twenty novels published in the genre press and over 300 short story credits in thirteen countries. He has books available from a variety of publishers including Dark Regions Press, DarkFuse and Dark Renaissance, and his work has appeared in many professional venues including five previous EDGE anthologies. He lives in Newfoundland with whales, bald eagles and icebergs for company. When he's not writing he drinks beer, plays guitar, and dreams of fortune and glory.

The Hive of Fair Women

M. K. Hume

Arthur's face was a study in concentration as he kneed his destrier in the ribs to urge the beast onward. The day was dying, and a long line of bats were rising into the darkening sky that threw the orchids of Glastonbury into shadow. The horse snorted its anger but obeyed his master without hesitation.

As he scouted the land ahead of him and searched for a suitable place to make his overnight camp, Arthur realized that he had been on the road for almost two days and his mount was feeling tired from the distance it had covered.

The landscape in the vicinity of The Isle of Apples was rich from nature's bounty, so the underground springs and fertile soil ensured that the farms were heavy with apples that were ready for the cider presses. Arthur's pack still contained a heel of bread, half a wheel of cheese and several servings of nuts, so the King of the Britons would never go hungry.

If Arthur regretted his decision to make an unannounced departure from his fortress at Cadbury, then his relaxed face and easy seat in the saddle belied any concerns.

Arthur knew that Targo, his bodyguard, would be concerned over his absence, and he could expect a tongue-lashing from Gruffyd, his sword bearer, for failing to keep this admirable servant aware of his movements. But the sheer pleasure of riding towards a distant goal without the hindrance of well-meaning friends and assorted hangers-on outweighed any guilt he felt over this harmless escapade.

There were few times when the high king could escape the many eyes and ears that were permanently attuned to his every action. The responsibilities of his royal duties hung over his person like a lead weight that even surpassed his hatred for his long-dead and never-lamented father, Uther Pendragon. His sense of boredom was such that he decided to escape from the prying eyes and never-ending, ineffectual tasks that filled his days.

He cast off his role as the Warrior of the West as if he was divesting himself from a heavy robe.

Fortunately, he felt justification for his absence from his court in Cadbury. He could still see the face of the ragged boy who had run past the outer defenses of the Cadbury fortress. The lad's clothes were blood-stained and he was stumbling along in complete exhaustion when one of the king's guards picked him up by the scruff of the neck and carried him bodily to the stairs outside the King's Hall.

This ancient fortress was reputedly designed by Merlin, the king's sorcerer, but Arthur had been moved to laughter whenever such superstitious nonsense was uttered in his hearing. The Tor at Glastonbury had attracted religious fanatics from the beginnings of time, and any number of religious sites had been constructed by the Britons in the shadows thrown out by the defensive monolith. These people pre-dated the Roman invasion.

That a young lad should have wanted to penetrate Cadbury's defenses at the run seemed crazed, so Arthur had stirred himself to question the youth. As it happened, the elderly Targo, Arthur's bodyguard and minder, had brought the lad to a halt.

"What do you think you're doing, you young lump? If the guards had been doing their duty, you'd have been killed by our warriors before you'd taken three strides."

Targo voice had been thick with sarcasm, but the youth tried to gabble out an explanation.

"I didn't mean any disrespect to you, Highness, but Selwyn will die if you can't help me to save him. I couldn't think of any other way to help him."

The boy's tears slipped down his face and fell onto the dust of the roadway.

"Your feet are a mess, boy," Arthur mused. "You've been running fast and hard."

The boy's feet and legs were showing signs of blisters, scratches and numerous cuts from the flint-stones that could be clearly seen on the uneven ground. His swollen toes bore mute witness to how desperate his need must be, for even old Targo recognized the pain that was evident on the boy's face. The old soldier motioned to one of the nearby warriors to carry the lad to a place in the hall where his wounds could be treated.

"You'd best call for Merlin," Arthur ordered. "You can also arrange for some food and water for him as well. He must be famished!"

Targo strode off to obey Arthur's orders, and the boy found himself seated at a bench in Cadbury's hall with a mug of cider and a piece of cheese in front of him.

"Speak truly, boy, and no one will hurt you. Who is this Selwyn, and who'd want to harm him?"

The boy looked from one stern face to another and shivered in fear, but the King demanded that the boy speak out bravely.

"My name is Lorcha. Selwyn and I live with me Ma in the lands of the Atrebates King. I ain't been anywhere else until the lady come to our village. She saw Selwyn had pale hair, yer see, so she tried to buy him from me Ma. The lady made an awful fuss when Ma threatened to call out the head-man, so the woman went away."

Wise to the eating habits of boys, Arthur could see that Lorcha was staring fixedly at the food. It was obvious that this lad hadn't eaten for some time.

"Get to it then," Arthur nodded, so Lorcha fell on the food like a starving animal.

After the lad demolished the bread and cheese, he looked up to see that Arthur's eyes were full of humor and compassion, so a lump formed in the boy's throat. He had tried his best to reach Cadbury and save his brother, but he was bright enough to know that everything rested on the High King's willingness to assist him.

"Who was the woman and what did she do to your Selwyn that has upset you?"

Arthur's eyes were keen with intelligence and Lorcha shivered as if he were cold.

"I don't know much about what was happening, Highness. I don't know what she took, but our old dog barked and barked until Selwyn went out to see what the fuss was all about. My brother screamed, and I reached the door in time to see someone in a long cloak drag my brother off on his horse. Selwyn screamed and screamed, but I couldn't keep up with them. I'm the oldest boy, Lord, so my Ma told me that I have to look after Selwyn. But I've failed him!"

Lorcha wept amid the crumbs of his meal. His dirty face was twisted in despair, but Arthur noted that this lad possessed a rugged beauty, for he possessed long dark curls that were almost as tight as Arthur's own. Although the king longed to comfort him, he knew that he must extract every possible item of information that could be gleaned if his warriors were to help Selwyn in his quest.

"Where did the attack take place, Lorcha? Was it near to the religious mission at Glastonbury?"

Lorcha shook his dark curls.

"No sir! We live on a farmstead that lies on the far side of Glastonbury Tor. I could show you if you had a mind to help me."

"This boy's wounds must be cleaned and rested before he goes anywhere," Merlin interrupted from his kneeling position beside Lorcha's feet. The healer used his long, gentle fingers to raise the boy's foot to eye level and began to clean the collection of cuts and scratches that afflicted him.

"He can still show us the way!" Merlin responded. "If he's familiar with the landscape near his home, I could draw up a map that might serve our purposes."

Lorcha's eyes grew very wide indeed, for he had never heard of such a thing. Arthur used a lump of charcoal from the fire-pit to draw a long line that represented the Roman road. At the very center, he drew a large cross that noted the position of Glastonbury and the tor.

"This line on the table shows the road that passes through Glastonbury, and the cross shows the position of Glastonbury adjacent to the road. The morning sun rises on the left side and the setting sun sinks on the right side. Have a look at the marks I've made on the table and see if you can show me where your mother's house lies."

Lorcha's eyes grew rounder still as he pondered over the shapes that had been made on the table before him. Fortunately, he was a clever boy who learned quickly despite never been given any tuition with his letters. After a few minutes of deep thought, he stabbed his finger down on the table to show his audience that his family lived to the north of Glastonbury.

"There, sir! That's where the woman went when she captured Selwyn. I've been running for so long that anything..." The boy's voice trailed away.

"You've been very brave." Arthur said in a kindly voice. "This is all I need for the moment, so you can rest now and regain your strength. I'll do my best to help you."

Lorcha barely felt the muscular arm of the warrior who lifted him as he was born away into the heart of Cadbury's great hall. He slept like a dead man, so he missed the discussion that took place between Arthur and his servants; an argument that sent Arthur on his lone quest to find a missing boy.

"Surely there's something that we can do to help the boy?" Gruffyd asserted in his usual brusque manner. "But there could be unseen dangers in travelling into unknown terrain to solve a problem about which we have very little information."

Arthur's sword bearer closed his lips to indicate his displeasure, but Arthur knew Gruffyd too well. Where Arthur led, Gruffyd would always follow.

"I've heard recent rumors of children being taken captive in the north," Merlin said quietly. His voice sounded hollow, as if his cautious remarks had been dropped into a deep, dry well. "Rumor has it that some of the old gods have returned to lay claim to their adherents in Britannia. The farming folk and poor people in the villages are saying that She whose name must not be spoken has returned to bedevil us and collect her blood price."

Arthur stared incredulously at Merlin. His healer always knew everything, but Arthur found it difficult to believe that pagan worship had returned to these peaceful fields in the west of Britannia. He said as much to his mentor.

"It's true that the Christ-child has held sway over men of learning in recent years, but there are still pockets of religious zealots where the old ways still hold sway. I have heard that the Wicker Man has made a reappearance in parts of the North and it is not impossible that the Mother Goddess is still worshiped in some of the dark places."

"But this boy is telling us of occurrences that have taken place adjacent to holy Glastonbury," Gruffyd snapped. His bluff, red-bearded face was taut with alarm.

"I'm not afraid of a coven of silly women," Arthur said and laughed.

"You should be!" Merlin said softly. "Such a woman fought a major revolt against the Roman legions and she damn near won. You're quite aware of Boudicca because I've spoken to you of her exploits on many occasions. The easternmost parts of Britannia ran red with Roman blood, and Boudicca cast out the Romans after defeating them soundly in a number of major confrontations. They learned to treat her with respect."

"But Boudicca died centuries ago. Any woman playing at being a goddess in our modern world would have few warriors at her back, so it's unlikely that she could cause me any harm."

"You've fought in many battles, Arthur, and you've faced many hurdles that would have crushed a lesser man. But Fortuna warns us that we should always be on our guard. If we decide to seek out this woman and rescue young Selwyn, you should exercise extreme caution. We know little about this matter, apart from what the lad has told us, so there would be no harm in waiting a day or two while we make solid preparations for whatever action is required. There would be no harm in taking a small troop of warriors with you if you undertake a mission to rescue this boy, for your warriors grow fat through inactivity," Merlin explained with all of his persuasive powers.

Arthur agreed readily enough, but Merlin realized immediately that the king's response was far too easily given. The healer wasn't the least surprised to discover that Arthur had ridden away in the dead of night without a single warrior to protect his back.

"It's a pity I love that boy so," Gruffyd declared sadly, before releasing a string of profanities that showed his true feelings. "He'll have ridden hard and fast throughout the night on that black horse of his. The stable boy has also told me that he took a spare beast with him, so he'll be far away by now. Methinks he'll go straight to Glastonbury."

"Then you'd best hurry off after him." Merlin snapped as his lack of composure indicated his concern for the king. "Drat the boy! You'll have no end of trouble picking up his trail."

"I'm hoping we can find him before he lands in too much shite," Gruffyd added.

"We can only hope! In any event, a show of strength won't hurt and your presence might prevent this cult from gaining momentum."

— 《》 —

A line of women moved silently down the uneven path that led towards a rocky knoll and their naked feet were almost silent on the uneven, shale-strewn ground. Had there been eyes to see, their silence and fixity of purpose would have seemed threatening. Above, a nacreous moon turned their faces and forms into a series of shadows that seemed like wights or creatures of the Underworld, so their black robes and the occasional glint of metal hinted at ritual and sacrifice.

At the head of the column, a slightly-taller shape could be seen through the flashes of scarlet. Any casual onlooker would have been surprised at the number of devotees, all female, who were marching in unison to unheard music.

The ground was littered with shards of flint and shale, so the women's tender feet were bruised and cut during the journey. Yet they made no complaint. No sound could be heard to interrupt this day of the winter solstice. Even the Christians were familiar with the importance of the sacred rituals practiced by the old religion. These same women could also be counted among the congregation in the Christian services, but the solstice promised wild abandonment and the promises that must be offered to She Who must be Obeyed during her sacred rites. The worship of the old religion had been absolutely forbidden by the Christian church, but women who needed love potions, charms that caused death or assistance with long-sought pregnancies were still prepared to meet secretly in places where they could honor the old goddess in the ancient ways.

At the top of a hill, the land slid away to reveal a path that had been cut through the brambles and gorse that thrived on the inhospitable earth. As the ground became softer and wetter, the women moved steadfastly towards a rift in the earth where the fabric of the hill slid precipitously into darkness. The woman at the head of the column of worshipers braced herself before crossing what appeared to be a yarning chasm. Then, after lifting her torch, she stepped across the threshold and vanished from sight.

One by one, the other women followed her into the blackness.

Behind the rough gorse and slope of the hillside, the path led downwards via rough-hewn steps into a fantasy world of light and brilliance. The torches of the worshipers were caught by the light of many sharp pinnacles and shards of stone that had been created by nature's processes into a display of rainbow-colored crystals. The stairs led downwards until the women reached a flat area that had been carved by long usage into the shape of a seat or throne. The women moved on silent feet to form a rough circle around this stone as the worshipers became clearly visible in the reflected light from the many torches that lit the room.

"Mother of all things - bless us on this sacred day with your indefinable presence. We call on She Who Must be Obeyed to look kindly on loyal petitioners and to accept our sacrifice for the bounty you will give us."

The woman, who spoke in the harsh tones of middle age, stood just below the ominous stone throne and bowed her head in obeisance in the direction of the empty seat. With a soft rustle of cloth, the other women followed suit, until all heads were bent in obeisance to their god. Somewhere, a reed pipe began to play a thready melody that was more suited to a funeral than a celebration of worship. The women began to sway in time to the music and their shadows began to dance along the walls of the meeting place like waves of darkness.

A huge man, threatening and mute, joined the worshipers like some gross growth that had grown upon the Earth. The man's ruined mouth gaped wide so that any watcher could see that his tongue had been torn out at its roots. Purposefully, he moved forward into the light so that the gold chain he carried was clearly visible. There, at the end of the chain, two boys cowered in abject terror.

Both boys were no more than ten or eleven years. Neither had reached puberty, so their bodies were smooth and hairless except for their heads. What little body hair they possessed had been shaved away, leaving each boy oiled into smooth perfection. Each lad had fair hair hanging unbound almost to their waists. One lad, in particular, had locks so blonde that they were almost white and, because of his extreme beauty, the women pinched and poked at him as he and his fellow sufferer were dragged forward by their bindings.

The priestess moved forward, until she was almost touching the beautiful boy.

"Oh, Mother who sees and knows all things, we bring these sacrifices to demonstrate our fealty to you. Look upon these fine young boys, my lady, and bless us with your favour."

She paused and gazed around the assembled audience.

"Bring forth the cup!" she declared in a firm voice as she turned to face the worshipers.

The large man-servant stepped forward and handed a goblet to the priestess. Roughly-carved from the crystals that lined the walls of this ancient and beautiful temple, the audience members were always amazed that an artisan could create such a beautiful object from a large piece of rock crystal. The servant removed a number of objects from his capacious robe and filled the cup with a red, blood-like liquid that seemed to cause the shadows on the walls to bleed in mute sympathy.

The priestess took the goblet and raised it high above her head.

"All hail to the Mother of all Things. Bless us with your tears."

Any cynical observer would have decided that wine filled the goblet, and they would have been mostly correct, for berries from the mistletoe vine had been added to the liquid as a gift to the goddess. Every member of the audience was fully aware that the fruit of the mistletoe was poisonous to humans and its progress was swift once it was ingested.

But the priestess had no intention of allowing her followers to die. After the cup was passed from woman to woman and each took a mouthful, the priestess poured a generous amount of a vile smelling antidote into the drinking vessel. The priestess smiled with foreknowledge as she swallowed a mouthful of the paste and daubed a small amount of the mixture onto her brows and breasts.

The other women did as the priestess directed.

Then, as the boys watched in sick horror, the reed music rose in volume until it became a shrill, piping staccato. As the notes rose and fell, the women began to sway, at first gracefully then with greater and greater speed. They began to spin, swirl and turn like marionettes moved by unseen hand until, with the exhausted women bathed in sweat, the ugly music stopped and the final part of the ceremony began.

The mute manservant moved forward and took the slender arm of the beautiful boy so he could move him towards the stone throne. The servant's eyes were totally lacking in emotion, for he had seen this ugly ceremony many times before. Behind him, the remaining child cowered at the end of his chain and tried to make his body as small as possible.

The priestess shrieked in a high-pitched crescendo of sound. She turned towards the throne and raised a short length of black cloth which she held high for the audience to see. Then she pulled aside the strip of material and exposed a ceremonial knife made from rough-cut stone. The women howled as the priestess lifted the blade high. For his part, the beautiful boy would have screamed and flinched away from the priestess, but the mute held him tightly.

The blade fell and the victim screamed. But this blade had been blunted by years of ill-use and the priestess was forced to hack and stab at the boy's flesh while he tried to pull away from her. The crowd screamed wildly and called out to the goddess, their eyes blank with madness as the terrified boy struggled to maintain his fragile grip on life.

But this lad was far stronger than the priestess expected and she eventually lost her grip on his blood-slick arm. One on one, he might have forced his body off the stone altar in an attempt to save his life, but the mute man-servant gripped him firmly.

With a frenzied shriek, the priestess redoubled her efforts and bludgeoned his body with the hilt of the knife until he ceased to move. The mutilated boy was dead.

In the silence that followed, the maddened women slowly ceased their ululating cries.

But the mute servant remained unmoved. He lifted the second boy carefully as if he was a mother and tried to speak, but only guttural sounds came from his ruined vocal cords. But any comfort he might have given was lost on the remaining child, Selwyn, who was fortunate to remain in that distant time and place where Fortuna protects some boys while sentencing others to death.

"By all that remains holy, take this child away and then come back and clean up this mess."

The priestess pointed towards the blood-stained stone and the women who were smearing their bodies with the child's blood. Now that the ritual was over, the woman seemed to have shrunken in size until she was just another middle-aged woman in a black, ill-fitting robe. Her face was expressionless as she watched the wild dancing of the worshipers, for she realized that she and Gad, the mute servant, were the only persons to have their wits about them in this ancient and blood-stained place of worship.

The servant secured the surviving boy near the entrance of the subterranean cavern. Fearful of punishment from the priestess, he made certain that the boy could not harm himself before returning to the cavern to complete his ugly duties. Only the priestess noticed that the dead boy's head lolled strangely, as if from a broken neck. If she wondered that Gad had spared the boy from the last ugliness of his impending death. She made no sign of her suspicions.

Outside in the cold night air a fox coughed in the darkness and a dog howled as midnight came and went.

— «» —

Ignorant of the murder of the first child and the imprisonment of the second, Arthur had camped beside a pleasant stream and eaten the last of his rations. Then, before dark had fallen, he had found a croft and learned that an ancient fortress lay just beyond the river where a colony of women lived and worked. The place had a vile reputation, and the king realized that the country folk believed that these women were responsible for the disappearance of several children.

"A family of women live there! They seem harmless enough when they bring their goods to market, but we suspect that they're too nice to us by far. Colonies of ladies don't usually mix with the common folk, but these ladies are extremely friendly to everyone.

"For who would go to their homes in the dark of the night," the good wife murmured, and Arthur noticed she surreptitiously made the sign of the cross.

"Shut your mouth, woman! The master doesn't want your bellyaching when he's looking for directions," the farmer said bluntly.

He turned back to Arthur.

"That place is odd, master. The women might be polite and friendly, but no one would willingly go there. I can only ask that you remember my warnings if they try to seduce you. Those women are not God's creatures!"

The farmer refused to speak further, but his wife gave Arthur a piece of her treasured cheese and a glossy red apple to help him on his journey. She also whispered to the young king that the women were often seen on the pathways, although their destinations were a mystery. Arthur accepted that these women might have earned an evil reputation through spite and jealousy, so he decided to wait and make his own assessment of their activities.

"Be careful, Highness, for them that go into that fortress never seem to come out," she whispered as she stood at the entrance to a croft and made her goodbyes.

That night, Arthur dreamed of serpentine women who tried to lure him into deep water ponds. In the dream, he had lost his sword and the women of the colony had wound their arms and floating hair around his body until he was powerless to resist their inducements. When he woke, he was drenched in sweat.

— «» —

Shortly after dawn, Arthur set out to cover the short distance to the House of Women. As he followed the uninviting track that would take him to his destination, he was forced to cross several fords that offered a semblance of safety through the fast-flowing rivulets that impeded his progress. Eventually, after topping the brow of a small rise in the terrain, he saw a stone fortress of sorts that rose out from the side of a hillock. Constructed from local stone, its walls appeared as gray sheets of rock in the morning sun.

The building itself was un-prepossessing, but its construction was similar to that of Tintagel, the fortress in Cornwall where the king had been sired. Tintagel always filled Arthur with disquiet, for this was the place where his birth-mother, the fair Ygerne, had been raped and impregnated by his villainous sire, Uther Pendragon.

Now in the early-morning sunshine, this fortress seemed old and worn, and Arthur could see tree branches growing outwards from gaps in the stone walls. Nature was having its revenge on the builders, and she was tearing the fortress apart with tree roots.

Snorting sharply, Arthur's horse shied away from an unseen reptile in the grass, but the king pulled at the animal's reins and the war horse quickly settled.

The king followed the contours of the hill as he rode toward the castle gates that yawned widely like a set of badly-formed teeth. He noted the obvious signs of decay and he began to form an opinion that this once-fine castle was being allowed to fall into disrepair. Ropes had been strung across what had been a water-filled moat, but several of them swung limply where the heavy hemp had rotted away. In fact, the moat itself was almost dry, except for large patches of muddy water and green slime that were no impediment to a trained warrior. The king completed the crossing with ease and rode up to the gate.

His pulse quickened as he felt the first frisson of danger. To ensure that the inhabitants of the castle had been alerted to his presence, he pounded on the wood of the open gate with his sword hilt. Despite this courtesy, his common sense told him that he should enter the castle unannounced.

"This place is derelict, so I cannot understand why I'm bothering to knock," Arthur said aloud in a bid to break the overwhelming silence of the place.

But nothing stirred! It was almost as if the castle had been abandoned and no humans remained in attendance. Unafraid, Arthur forced his charger to move between the sagging gates, so the horse picked its way delicately over broken masonry and fallen rock. Then, just when Arthur was convinced that the castle had been abandoned, a flash of yellow material susurrated along the castle walls and a peel of girlish laugher shattered the unnatural stillness.

"Come out! Come out, whoever you are," Arthur shouted. "I wish no discourtesy by entering unannounced. I am Arthur, King of the Britons, and I come to your castle in search of information."

A rustle of clothing stirred the quiet of the ruined stairs that rose above the area where he was waiting and, once again, the gurgle of female laughter came to regale him. It was eerily childish, as if very young girls had been disturbed at their play.

Then, in the blinking of an eye, the courtyard was filled with flower-like girls that were clad in all the colors that a master dyer could create. One girl wore primrose, while another wore an expensive shade of azure. Still another damsel in a saffron gown came down the stairs in a rush to stand beside an older maiden in a gown of sanguine red.

Finally twelve girls were standing in the courtyard to bid him welcome.

The lady in red was the first to bid the girls to be silent and she strode fearlessly up to the still mounted king.

"I am Sanguine, the eldest of the many daughters of Lord Leonides. My father died before he could see us wed, so we have determined to remain in his castle. You can easily tell, my lord, that our home is falling to pieces."

"I've never heard of your father, but I'd be the first to admit that these lands are foreign to me," Arthur countered carefully, but his eyes never left the faces of the brightly-plumed young ladies who had been paraded before him.

Strangely, the air was stinking, and Arthur's ever-cautious mind told him that something, animal or human, had died between the castle walls. Every part of his being told him that this place was dangerous.

Despite the doubting expression on Arthur's face, Sanguine simpered and spread her skirts wide in a simple curtsy. "Had we know that you were about to join us, your highness, we would have made some provision for your hospitality."

She smiled again, and Arthur imagined that the glistening white teeth that filled her mouth had been sharpened into points. He shook his head to clear his vision and Sanguine's features returned to those of an attractive young lady who had recently passed her youth.

"I need very little in the way of hospitality, my lady, but I would appreciate some hay for Coal and a bed for the night. In fact, I am part of a group of searchers who are trying to find traces of a missing child, Selwyn, who disappeared from his home near Glastonbury. He was believed to be in the company of an unknown female. Do you know anything of this missing lad?"

"Come, your highness, dismount and rest. I'd be surprised if the lad isn't already in the bosom of his family by now. Children are renowned for disappearing like wights for the simplest of reasons that are totally unimportant to older citizens. Meanwhile, we have very little in the way of luxuries at our castle, but what we do have is yours to command. My father did lay down some goodly wines before he met his death, so perhaps you could taste them for us."

Arthur felt his hackles rise at Sanguine's casual response to his query, but this strange place held many secrets and a veneer of friendship to the ladies might lead him to the lost boy. He felt equal to the task of dealing with these fair women so he dismounted and watched his horse led away in the direction of ram-shackled stables. Suddenly aware that he was surrounded by a large group of lissom females whose hands plucked at his armor and his weapons, Arthur decided it was time to exercise extreme caution.

Two more of the girls made themselves known to him. "I am Violet," one girl said sweetly as she smiled and led him into a dusty hall.

"And I am Primrose," another girl added as she removed his breast plate. Arthur discovered that the names of the other girls included Peony, Pansy, Buttercup and Rose. Then, with a welter of female forms clustered around him, Arthur was maneuvered into the dimly-lit hall where the last of his armor was removed from his body.

With a sudden feeling of nakedness, the king refused to relinquish his knife and sword, although the girls made little noises of disappointment. "What is this place called," he asked, as he swept one hand out to encompass the castle and its surroundings.

"Our home is called The Castle of Fair Maidens," Sanguine replied with a tight little smile. "We are all alone and vulnerable, except for some common women who scrub and clean for us. I am the eldest, so it has been agreed that I would look after my sisters after our father passed into the shades."

"She always talks too much," Primrose replied and stuck her tongue out at her older sister. "She never allows the rest of us to have any fun."

Somehow, Arthur found himself seated at a long table with roasted chicken, sliced ham, bread and new butter laid out before him. Two large flagons of wine were also placed on the table, reminders that he must beware of the guile displayed by these strange women. Arthur was encouraged to eat and drink. As he dined, a small group of the maidens played tuneful melodies on reeds, harps and drums. The sounds were strangely hypnotic to Arthur's ears and he found the music relaxed him. With a sudden jolt, the king realized that he could be in grave and imminent danger in this strange castle.

Somehow, in the brief time that he had broken bread with these beautiful young women, the day had slid away and dusk was beginning to fall.

"I've enjoyed your hospitality for far too long," Arthur said as he leapt to his feet. "I've allowed myself to forget my quest and my reasons for visiting your home. My question is simple, Sanguine. Have you seen the boy who is the object of my search?"

The girls tittered behind open hands while Sanguine gripped his arm with surprising strength and slowly drew him back to the table. "The day grows long, my lord, and you are very weary after your travels," she said in a soft-seductive voice. "Pansy and Primrose will take you to our father's bedchamber were you can rest for the night in comfort."

With nerveless fingers, Arthur realized that his strength had dissipated. Weary to the core, he was led across the hall by the two girls and taken into a dusty bedroom which had the faint stench of mildew, must and something unclean. Then, although he tried to pierce the fog that filled his brain, his legs began to weaken until one of the girls pushed him back onto the bed. Giggling, they moved to the doorway and looked back to his muscular form as his heavy eyelids began to close.

Was it his imagination or did the faces of the girls alter as his eyes began to close in the dim light. The last image he had of the two erstwhile maidens was of two elderly crones whose ancient skin and scrawny arms belied their names and the aura of love.

Sleep enveloped him in a black shroud.

— «» —

Despite his confusion and anger, Arthur returned to consciousness slowly. The steadfast spirit that had served him so well against his murderous father, Uther Pendragon, was protecting him from incautious action until he was fully aware of the situation in which he had found himself. His stomach roiled from the after-effects of the drugs that had been secreted into his food and drink, but he forced himself to remain still and silent until he ascertained the dangers of activity. He realized he was moving, and was being carried over huge shoulders as if he was a small child. Through hooded eyes, he could make out the figure of Gad who was bearing his weight with consummate ease. His sword was loosely held in the servant's free hand.

Gad was descending a series of steps now and a kaleidoscope of colors that reverberated from the lighting swirled above Arthur and nauseated him. He knew he was in a precarious position inside this coven of miscreants and any sudden movement of Gad's shoulders could cement his fate. But he forced himself to remain still, for his continued silence was the only path to freedom.

The servant reached the bottom of the stairway and Arthur was placed on the ground with more care than he would otherwise have expected. The surface was hard and cold, and was slick with moisture from the huge stalactites of stone that hung down from the ceiling above them. Surprisingly, Gad straightened Arthur's clothing with inexplicable tenderness, so Arthur took a dangerous risk. He began to move sluggishly as if he was slowly returning to consciousness, and then groaned softly so that the man above him could hear the slurred words he was about to utter.

"Is the king returning to consciousness, Gad?" the woman in the thick black cloak demanded. Arthur realized it was Sanguine's voice.

The king felt Gad's hand press on his shoulder in warning.

The man made a guttural sound in response to Sanguine's request, but he also shook his head so strongly that Arthur felt that the mute had made a sympathetic response to his dire predicament.

"It seems I have an ally in this dastardly place," Arthur thought to himself with a sudden surge of hope. He had slowly rolled onto one side by this time, a movement which gave him a better view of the women who had assembled at the base of the stairs. As his shoulder hid his eyes, he was able to obtain a partial view of the worshipers.

A small boy with pale hair had been dragged forward from his place of confinement and forced to sit in chains beside the prone body of the King. Arthur's mind was as clear as crystal now, so he knew that these women intended to undertake a religious ritual.

His sword lay upon the stone at his feet but, even if he could reach it, some thirty women would be more than enough to capture him. No! He needed a reliable ally and the mute Gad was the only possibility. Could this mute servant be persuaded to help his king and risk the fury of these misbegotten women?

Sanguine stood over him and kicked him hard in the ribs, and it was only through his strength of will that Arthur was able to remain prone. Although he groaned, the king had rolled slightly closer to the chained boy and the sword that remained on the stone floor.

With great determination, he forced himself to peer through his eyelashes as the ritual began.

This is nonsense, he thought to himself. This capering and play-acting is like no heathen worship I've ever seen, but it seems that these women use it as the font for their power.

The ritual was filled with strange rantings to Don, the mother goddess whose mystique had been cobbled together from Roman religions and the superstitions of the old British faiths. Snippets of women's magic had also been interwoven into the ceremony to energize the participants.

Then, once the women had anointed themselves with the paste of the antidote and drank further from Sanguine's goblet, Arthur deduced that they were imbibing in some form of hallucinogenic drug. This decision was borne out by the increasing frenzy of their dancing and the heightened expressions on their faces.

As the intensity of the dance increased, Arthur realized that the women had almost forgotten his presence.

Meanwhile, Gad had brought the terrified boy to sit beside the King. He placed his hands upon the boy's lips to hush any noise, and Arthur watched as the servant retrieved the King's long knife from his filthy cloak.

He placed the weapon beside Arthur's prone body with a look that seemed to plead for the king's understanding.

"Be assured that I will remember you for helping us," he whispered in a voice so soft that only Gad could hear him. The huge man nodded his head immediately, and Arthur was appalled to discover that the mute's eyes filled with tears.

God only knows what have these bitches done to you, the young king thought.

Gad's large brown eyes looked down at him, but he remained silent and Arthur was heartened by the mute's grim expression.

Suddenly, Sanguine approached the boy. She howled hysterically and the other women repeated the cry. "This sacrificial child is Don's payment for the power he has given to our coven," she shrieked above the noise of the other women who began to chant the goddess's name in unison.

Even Arthur felt the increasing threads of fear, for he had been raised in a household where the goddess's name would never be spoken.

Sanguine leaned over the boy's body now and gripped his chained wrist savagely.

"See, Mother? We've brought you a boy who will serve you in the underworld. And we have also been given another rich prize. The erstwhile King of the Britons will also die by your knife and his blood will enrich our coven. Hail to the Mother, the font of all being."

The women chanted out their responses as Sanguine lifted up the stone knife, so Arthur permitted his eyes to snap open. Let them think that I'm awake — and that I'm very frightened!

Selwyn screamed at Sanguine's and tried to squirm as far from her as his bonds permitted. At the same time, Sanguine laughed at Arthur's pretense of fear and placed the stone knife on the ground.

"Perhaps the King of all the Britons should die by his own sword, a weapon which deserves to be dedicated to the goddess."

The women howled their approval.

Sanguine lifted the heavy sword above her head. The weapon was a dull gray color, and an ugly thing when its reputation as Excalibur was considered. Gifted to Arthur by the Lady of the Lake, it rose above Sanguine's head like base lead — a thing of no consequence!

"Gad, raise the King to his feet and make him kneel before me. In his case, the Mother wants more than blood, and men will do anything to prolong their grip on life."

Gad shook his head in response and Sanguine approached him and slapped him with full force.

"Obey me, you lump! If you are tardy, you will receive your own punishments."

With surprising resolution, Gad continued to shake his head, even when the priestess struck him again and drew blood from his ruined mouth. The mute manservant slumped, as if in acquiescence.

Sanguine smiled. "Perhaps we'll let you live for a little longer, Gad."

Then Hades broke loose. Selwyn reached for Arthur's concealed knife with a little cry, and Arthur surged to his feet. Although his head was swimming, Arthur forced down the last effects of the drug-induced weakness and moved swiftly towards Sanguine. He snapped her neck before she had time to utter a sound.

The cavern was suddenly filled with angry women, all with talons outstretched and hungry to tear at his flesh. Meanwhile, Gad snapped the golden chain that had bound Selwyn and lifted the boy to his chest. Before any of the women could grasp him, the servant ran up the stairway and deposited the boy outside the darkness of the entry.

Grossly outnumbered, Arthur reached out and grasped Excalibur, the singing sword. Those women who survived the melee would swear later that they heard the blade singing a tune with a single note. In the hands of its master, the weapon shed off its dull gray coloring and became a glittering, flaming brand that set the stalactites in the ceiling to come to life and dance.

But the women, armed with improvised weapons, were quickly upon him.

Knives and even fingernails scored his flesh as they ripped at his body. Excalibur hummed and sang as it carved its way through the flesh and bones of the maidens and completed movements that covered the surrounding earth with hot, red blood.

The air was thick with the sounds and howls of the women as they died.

But Arthur would still have been defeated by their sheer numbers if it wasn't for the persistence and courage of Gad. After years of suffering, he had finally decided to cast off the yoke of his servitude. Captured as a child, his formidable strength had been used and abused by these women in abject slavery. When he eventually found the courage to complain, the women tore out his tongue to silence him. He had come to realize that he was a possession and was at their mercy. Then, for years, he had hidden the bodies of beautiful boys who had been taken from their homes by stealth. Ultimately, he had been forced to swallow his rage while he carried out unspeakable duties in the service of these witches.

Tonight, he had seized on an opportunity to free himself from the chains that bound him. The High King of the Britons had come to this hideous place and Gad saw an opportunity to end his suffering. Armed only with Arthur's knife, he was determined to protect the High King's back.

The momentum of Gad's charge drove the women back, but there was still ten women intent on killing the High King and his protector. Arthur's sword had cut a swathe through them until his hands were slick with blood, but there still seemed to be too many of them. At the top of the stairs, back to back and with Selwyn at their feet, Gad and the King readied themselves to face a final charge from the maddened women.

Then, as all hope began to fade, male forms appeared on the slopes leading to the cavern. Their long swords glittered in the moonlight and Selwyn screamed out that their livery that was decorated with the Red Dragon.

— «» —

"You finally made it," Arthur gasped as Gruffyd blocked the arms of a demented woman who was intent on tearing out his throat. The warrior dispatched her with a single stroke of his battle-axe.

"I've left some of the witches for your entertainment, although you have arrived on the scene at a later time than I would have expected. I must ask that you don't harm my huge friend who cannot speak for himself. I'd be long dead if it wasn't for his fine efforts."

Gruffyd's warriors forced them to retreat away from the steps and the last of them were died against the stone walls. If the warriors felt any guilt at killing unarmed women, the cursing of the harridans and the eventual discovery of the skeletal remains of a number of children eased their consciences.

Gad showed them a smaller cave beyond the main chamber where a huge throne had been constructed from the bones of dead boys. Tears came to the faces of grown men when they found that the skin of these children had been tanned to make a soft seat for the priestess's comfort. Even the strongest of warriors were sickened by evidence that evil still lived in the peaceful isles of Britannia.

Arthur refused to either eat or drink in the castle of Fair Women.

"Everything that the members of this coven have touched is tainted and deadly," he explained to his warriors. Even Merlin was repulsed by the specimens found in the castle's interior and the pair agreed that the accursed structure should be burned to the ground.

As they rode away, a new dawn was breaking. As they topped the hillock, Arthur suddenly pulled up his horse and Merlin saw that his face was pale beneath his helmet.

"What ails you, lord? You've had a great victory, and the populace has been freed from the cruelty of these women."

Arthur turned in the saddle and stared at his magician with flinty eyes.

"I saw the bodies of the women before we set the castle afire. I also know that Sanguine is dead, for I killed her myself. But most of the women who died there seemed to be servants. Several of the sisters might well have escaped."

"But Lord, Merlin replied. "What are one or two vicious women? How much damage could they do?"

"I suppose you are talking sense," Arthur replied, but Merlin could see the shadows in his eyes.

"I doubt that we will ever hear from them again, he murmured he looked back at the burning castle.

Meanwhile, two blackened figures struggled to cross the damaged moat and limp away into the forest.

"Don't fret, sister! We're still alive — and we have someone new to hate."

As the two women disappeared into the shadows, the end of daylight scoured all traces of the castle away.

Only the broken gate still smoldering as a memory of the Castle of Fair Women, for only sunshine can clean out the vestiges of evil. In the years to come, no one would dare to disturb its fearsome ashes. Only the two sisters who limped from shadow to shadow would want to find those items of value that survived the destruction of their home.

The withered forms of the two sisters searched for a dark haven where they could secrete themselves for the night. There, in the shadows, their forms could shift and change. Pansy and Primrose hugged each other, and then walked off to find some willing men who would take them in their arms and offer them comfort.

There are always more men.

— «» —

M. K. Hume is based in Brisbane, Queensland, where she has put her PhD in Arthurian literature to good use, writing the three books comprising the King Arthur Trilogy (Dragon's Child, Warrior of the West & The Bloody Cup), the three novels of the Merlin books (Clash of Kings, Death of an Empire & Web of Deceit), three novels in her Twilight of the Celts series (The Last Dragon, The Storm Lord & The Ice King) and two novels in the Tintagel Cycle (The Blood of Kings & The Poisoned Throne).

The Song of the Star

Renee Bennett

We are called to Camelot, my lady sister and I, riding in under the great gate, listening to the banners snap in the breeze off the fields. The air smells green with young barley, and the sun is warm on our shoulders. Too warm, on mine; I have chosen to wear my armor to greet my lord. The weight of leather and iron is familiar, though, so I don't mind.

My horse huffs in relief as I get off and I laugh, patting his neck, before a stablehand arrives to take him away. Eirean smiles, too. I help her from the saddle. I have a vague thought that trouble is why we are here in Camelot, but I cannot hold it; the day is too bright and too full of the promise of summer. So I bow over her hand and lead her into the cool darkness of Arthur's hall.

It soars four stories over our heads, not even counting the battlements. Great beams hold up the roof, and tapestries layer the walls, though none so fine as Eirean's in their making, of course. My hold of Talfryn could fit within that hall.

The Round Table is pushed against the walls just now. When the pieces are together, it looks much like the henge at Glastonbury. I suppose that is Merlin's doing.

The space is still full. There are near a hundred people crowded before the throne dais, and at least that many more scattered about the hall, all of them deep in conversation. Most are women, though — I see few of my fellow knights. Arthur's herald proceeds us down the center of the room, shouting, "Make way for the Lord of Talfryn and his lady sister!"

People step aside and give us curious looks as we fill the space behind him. Some frown, and one, Sir Habren, looks furious. Then we are at the foot of the throne and the herald announces, "My king, I present to you your knight, Lord Eilian of Talfryn, and his sister, the Lady Eirean."

"At last!" Arthur replies. "Rise, Lord Talfryn, Lady Eirean. How was your harvest?"

We talk, about last year and this year, and the increase of Talfryn's herds. We are doing well enough. Wolves are taking lambs, though.

He nods. "We will send hunters to see to the wolves," he says. "But it would seem to us that your holdings will do without you for a while."

"I imagine so, my lord," I say. "But may I ask why they will need to?" I don't tell him that I would rather be back there now, chasing the wolves and dickering with stonecutters for the blocks that will become the new watchtower.

"Lady Mairwen!" he calls, and a rustle in the crowd answers. I turn and the most beautiful woman I have ever seen steps out from the throng.

She is near as slim as I or Eirean, and tall enough to look me in the eye, though she does not; she wears a veil of white silk, only her eyes visible, and her attention is on the king. This gives me opportunity to admire her, from the dark, shining hair that falls to her waist to the jewelled slippers that peep from beneath the hem of her dark green gown. Slim hands with long fingers. The shadow of her face beneath the veil is narrow with a proud blade of a nose. Silver pins fasten the veil in place, set with green and red jewels, as if someone has crowned her with blossoms as May Queen. "Your Majesty," she says to Arthur, and dips a curtsy to him so deep and smooth she might be floating.

"Lady," he replies. "Allow us to introduce to you the Lord of Talfryn and his sister, the Lady Eirean, who will escort you to your lord husband in Ergyng."

He gives her no time to reply. "Lord Talfryn, the Lady Mairwen of Caer Baddan is promised to King Ercwlff of Ergyng. He requests she arrive for the nuptials by Midsummer."

Ah.

Lady Mairwen turns to me. Her eyes are dark and deep, drinking in the light. I am struck dumb, thinking of holy wells and the marvels that spring from them. Then I see lines tighten around them; I think that she thinks I am witless, to stare at her so.

Perhaps I am, but I can turn to my king and tell him, "My lord does me great honor to entrust me with this task, for I have heard, even in humble Talfryn, of the recent strife between those two fair holdings, and your work in ending it."

"Work not yet done, we fear," Arthur says. "Ercwlff has said that if his new lady is not at his side by Midsummer, he will rise against Caer Baddan the day after.

"This war does not please us," he says, leaning back into his throne. "It wastes good men's lives. Our lands are at peace, but we have enemies outside our borders who would take any chance we give them to create strife. Such strife serves them, not us. We are not minded to make their ends easier than we make our own."

"Yes, sire." I bow again.

"Sire." Eirean speaks up. "What is your will of me?"

"The Lady Mairwen has been ... unfortunate in her handmaidens," Arthur says, and I raise my head, because there is something in his voice that is not right. The look he gives us is a warning. "Midsummer is nigh. You will leave tonight, my Lord, my Ladies. The horses and equipment you will require are being readied as we speak. We regret that you will not grace our court longer, Lady Eirean. Please, come back to us so that you..."

"Sire!" Sir Habren pushes through the crowd toward the throne like a horse breasting water, people rippling aside from the disturbance. "My king, I have cried for this task!"

"You have, Sir Habren, and we have listened." Arthur's voice changes again to a different kind of warning. "We repeat, we have need of you elsewhere in the realm, most urgently—"

"I am every bit the knight Sir Eilian is! He may take my place!"

"Sir Eilian is more suited to this task than you, Sir Habren." Arthur raises a hand to silence Habren's protests. "We have decided."

"Tell me what Eilian has that I do not, then!"

"An unmarried sister, gentle and good, a suitable handmaiden to a Lady who will be a queen come Midsummer's Day."

Habren stops beside us, glaring up at the throne, his hands in fists. The room is hushed. I can see in the tension of his jaw, he wishes to argue further, but all know that Habren has no sisters, unmarried or otherwise.

Arthur turns back to me. "You have our leave, Lord Talfryn. Godspeed."

I bow. Habren turns to me, but I give him my shoulder. My king has spoken. "Lady Mairwen, well met. I shall see about the preparations for leaving. If you require anything, pray allow my lady sister or myself provide it."

I think I hear Habren begin arguing again as I leave, and wonder. He is not a knight known for his tempers. Habren is steady. Not the kindest man, but not unkind, either; he has a reputation with the ladies of the court that implies courtesy and discretion. This insistence seems unlike him.

But the Lady Mairwen is astonishingly beautiful. Perhaps it is that.

I find a dozen horses — mounts and remounts — gathered in the forecourt, mine and Eirean's among them, plus two guardsmen and a priest. Three pack horses are being readied as well. A serving man will ride the lead pack horse and tend us at camp. It seems a very small retinue for a queen-to-be. I mention that to the seneschal.

"Merlin's choices, every one," says the seneschal, ticking items off on a list. "You, too." Then he goes off to speak to the servants packing victuals, while I stare at his back and wonder what he meant.

Eirean and Mairwen come out of the hall, a trail of admirers in their wake. Within the hour, we are ahorse and on the road for Ergyng. Mairwen has put on a long gray cloak and a thicker veil to keep the dust of the road from her face. I am grateful; she is not so distracting, though truth be told, I like the way she distracts me. I order the guardsmen to follow the ladies, one to each, with the priest and the pack ponies and our remounts as our train. I ride on ahead.

Have I fallen in love with Mairwen? I hope not. I know what such love did to Tristan.

We ride until dusk and camp in a fair copse by the side of a river. I leave the priest and the servant to set up camp while I ride for the nearest village. Arthur gave me a purse; I buy a jug of beer and a loaf of good bread, and as many early apples as fit in my pockets. Travel rations are good, but not this good.

By the time I get back, Habren is riding into the camp. "Hail, Talfryn! Well met!"

I have my doubts. "Hail, Sir Habren. How unexpected." There is no polite way to ask him if he has defied Arthur, not and avoid a fight I would rather not have. "Would you take supper with us? I have fresh bread."

"I will!" he replies, his face so tense and his voice so jovial that I think he was expecting the fight. He swings down from his lathered horse and drops the reins to stride toward the fire. I hear him greeting Mairwen and, belatedly, Eirean.

Safe, steady Habren, riding a horse hard, then letting it stand wet? I call the servant over and give the steed into his care, and lead my own horse after. The priest bustles up with a "Did I hear fresh bread?" and I give the food into his delighted care. It is several minutes to remove my horse's tack and rub him down, give him grain and the little rubs on his jaw and behind his ears that he likes so much. Beside me, Habren's mount is so tired it dozes off, nose to grain.

I wash my hands and face in the river before approaching the fire. Habren is frowning. "You bought beer!"

"Good beer," I say, refusing to rise to the tone in his voice. The priest gives me a cup and I thank him for it.

"You bought beer for the Lady Mairwen!"

Perhaps he thinks a queen-to-be should only have wine? Eirean rescues the matter, saying, "My Lady has been sharing my wine. My brother has always preferred beer, and the beer near Camelot is very good. Please don't deny him the pleasure of it!"

Habren looks like he very much wants to do just that, but Eirean is being winsome, and he is a good enough knight

that he declares that she is right. The beer near Camelot is
very good.

Then he declares that he will make sure to provide
proper wine for tomorrow night, and every night after, which
is what I need to ask, "Are you to come to Ergyng, then? Have
you finished your other task for Arthur so soon?"

You can see the thunderclouds in Habren's face. "I have,"
he says, and there is no one present, not even Habren, who
cannot hear the lie in his voice.

Eirean, still winsome, smiles and says, "Is it a deed
worthy of a song? Will you sing it for us?"

I think he might strike her. I raise the beer as if to
drink, but plan to throw it if Habren moves wrong. But he
only stands. "I have a wine flask in my saddlebags, Lady
Mairwen. Let me gift it to you." He leaves the fireside,
stomping.

Mairwen is silent this entire time, still hidden behind her
veil. She murmurs something to Eirean, who nods. "Please
tender our regards to Sir Habren, brother. My Lady Mairwen
would retire to sleep."

I stand and bow. "Of course, my Lady. Thank you, sister,
and rest well. I think," and I look toward the horses, who are
snorting as Habren moves among them, "I think that I shall
sleep across the threshold of your tent tonight. The night is
fair, but I would not have you disturbed."

"Thank you, brother." Eirean winds her arm around
Mairwen's. "Until morning, then."

I finish my beer — truly, the beer near Camelot is
excellent — and set the servant to preparing my pallet. The
priest blesses us all and retires to his own rest. The guards
will share the night watch. By the time Habren returns, we
are all well into our preparations for night.

He stops by the fire, staring at the spot where Mairwen
sat. I cannot decide if he looks bereft at her absence or
incensed by it. "Where—"

"Hush," I say. "The ladies are resting. Please, Sir Habren.
It has been a long day for all of us. Let us sleep."

He turns that odd, ambiguous stare on me. "You are
sleeping across her doorway."

"I am guarding the Lady and my lady sister, yes, as Arthur bid me. From brigands, bandits, or even spiders." I lay my sword to hand. "Good night, Sir Habren. Sleep well."

Habren mutters something that might be a good night, but which sounds rather coarser. He wheels and stomps off into the dark, declaring, "I shall scout the perimeter before resting, that the Lady Mairwen will be assured of perfect rest."

I cannot but think that the Lady Mairwen would rest more perfectly if Habren were not prowling about in the dark. I tell the guards to stand picket on the rear of her tent while I watch the front.

Sleep does not come easily, despite my weariness. The Lady Mairwen is uncommonly pretty, yes, but is that enough for Habren to behave so recklessly? He has thrown over his duty to Arthur for her, and inserted himself into mine — if I were a less peaceable knight, I would be dueling him on the matter even now. I may yet have to.

Troubled thoughts slip into troubled dreams. I come awake, my sword in my hand, and find Habren at the point of it, caught halfway to stepping over me, hand reaching for the ties on the tent.

"Good sir," I say. The deepest part of the night surrounds us, the stars painting him in shades of black and silver. The air almost shivers with the way he yet leans forward, though the sharp tip of my weapon rests against his throat. "It is not dawn, good sir. I hardly think the ladies would appreciate your interruption of their sleep."

"I... wanted to test your ward," he says, and I can hear the lie in his voice again. More, he has insulted me.

"Habren of Heil," I say, very low. "Return to your blankets. Please."

He is older than I, and has been in Arthur's service longer. I should not be dictating to him, but he is in the wrong, and I am the one with bared steel. The 'Please' is a sop for his honor, if he has any left.

He does — barely. "Good night, Eilian of Talfryn," and he melts back into the dark.

I spend the rest of the night sitting with my back to the tent and my sword across my knees. Habren stays away, which makes me hate him a little. But only a very little.

Eirean raises a brow to see me sitting there when she emerges into the first light of day, but she only says, "Will we breakfast here, brother?"

Breakfast. The long night makes my thoughts slow, but breakfast will speed them. "Yes. I will ask the priest to warm the last of the bread and to make a tea."

"Let me, brother. You look comfortable there." She slips past me to the fire, where the priest is poking it to life. I watch her go and catch a movement in the corner of my eye.

When I turn to it, Habren turns away. I slept little, but from his haggard look, I think he slept not at all. I decide in that moment to visit the old Roman fort today. It is out of our way, and tomorrow's camp will be less comfortable than this one, but I need to send a message to Arthur. This cannot be allowed to continue.

Habren argues with the decision, his voice rising, but I will not be moved, and as we turn onto the track leading to the fort, he retreats to the rear of our little company. By midday, when we arrive at the fort, he has disappeared altogether.

Eirean and I share a look. When we leave, we will cut across country. The trek will be harder, but something tells me it will be less hard than dealing with Habren's presence.

He might have bared steel, himself, the next time he tried to sneak into Mairwen's tent.

The men of the fort are curious to see us and happy enough for news of Camelot, though they are only a day away from the castle and get news regularly. I pen a note to Arthur and give it to the fort sergeant to be carried back to Camelot, as swift as he might send it.

He asks to see the Lady Mairwen, who is still veiled. "They say she is as fair as spring after long winter, or heart's desire after deprivation." He leans in and whispers, "Is it true?"

"She is most beautiful," I say carefully.

"More beautiful than Guenivere?"

I want to say yes, but only say, "All queens are beautiful. The Lady Mairwen will be queen in Ergyng."

He is not satisfied, but we have no time to spar with words. Within the hour, we are ahorse again. With luck, Habren will wait for us at the main road until past nightfall, when we are sure to be long gone. With better luck, he will not find us again before we have reached the ferry across the Severn. With the best of luck, we will lose him there.

Gambling is not one of my skills. Swift passage, however, is.

Mairwen says nothing about our change of course, and nothing when we make cold camp that night, sharing the provisions from our saddlebags. I think she is watching me, but the veil prevents me from knowing for certain. So I pretend she is not, pay her the proper courtesies, and sit watch again that night. We do not put up the tent, for it slows us and I have left it at the fort, along with the pack pony which bore it. We spread a pair of cloaks over bent willows as a lady bower, and Eirean declares it enough.

Morning finds me exhausted. The priest is in fine fettle, chattering about what an adventure this is, and trading couplets with the servant as he writes a song about it. The guards are yawning, too, but they have spelled each other in the night, so they have some sleep. I envy them and think longingly of the beer from, what? Just a day ago?

The ferry is still days away.

I catch a little sleep in the saddle, and when we stop for the night, Eirean makes me nap, promising to wake me after an hour. It is nearer two before she rouses me, which is kind of her, but I tell her not to wait so long again. She only smiles and kisses my forehead.

I hear her talking to Mairwen in this night's lady bower, built between two tall stones thrusting out of the turf. Twins, she says, and I hear surprise in Mairwen's reply.

Yes, I think. We are. Is that why Merlin chose us for this task?

I ask the priest and one of the guards; neither is a twin. So no, it is not that.

Eirean makes me nap in the morning for half an hour as camp is packed. I do, and am grateful for it. We go on. Habren is nowhere to be seen.

We fall into a pattern, that day and the next and the ones after. One of the pack ponies goes lame and, after consideration, I leave both at the nearest village. The priest's mule becomes the slowest mount, but I cannot bear to leave him behind. He is a merry man and excellent company, and even Mairwen is flowering under the influence of his good humor. I hear her laugh at his joking and clap along as he presents us with a first pass at his song, wherein a tale of Theseus pursued through the labyrinth by the minotaur somehow becomes transported to the British woodlands we travel through. "It needs jocularity!" he declares, and the second pass is full of Theseus turning corners and coming upon absurd scenes, such as upside-down cows and drunken crows. He seems very pleased with our laughter.

We reach the Severn at mid-morning the next day and hire the ferry. As we file on, Habren crests the last slope on the road and rides for us, shouting.

"Cast off," I tell the ferryman. "Double fare if you do."

Habren screams at us from the bank, his sword waving in the air, but though he tries to force his horse off the end of the pier it shies and dumps him instead, then runs back to dry land. I lean on the aft rail of the ferry and watch as watermen swarm to rescue my fellow knight. He would drown without their aid, but he shrieks and fights them even so, trying to follow. At least he has lost the sword to the river. One enterprising fellow smacks him over the ear with a fist and he goes limp.

I make a note of the man's face. I can use a fellow like him in Talfryn, practical and unafraid.

The men of our party, even the ferryman, have crowded the rail with me to watch the show. The ladies have retired to the prow of the vessel, however, and I see them sitting, heads together over their clasped hands. I think the Lady Mairwen is weeping.

I give the ferryman triple his fee when we reach the far bank. "So you have no need to return tonight, nor perhaps even tomorrow," I say, and he nods knowingly. We leave him happy and ride for Ergyng, now only three days away.

At camp that night, as the priest and the servant are entertaining each other with song and the guards are sorting out their night pickets, I say, "Lady. Tell me why Habren pursues you, past all reason. I see you do not encourage him."

Mairwen looks to Eirean, who nods. Then Mairwen puts her veil up.

It is like looking on the face of a star. The bones in my body go liquid and I go to my knees. "Lady," I say, and stop, because words are such small things before one such as she.

"Ask," says Eirean.

The Lady's voice trembles. "Am I beautiful, Sir Knight?"

"Beyond all description, Lady." My throat is dry. The words scrape their way out and drop like stones before her.

"And if you could, would you possess me?"

Tears fill my eyes. "If you were free, I would lay my sword and my soul at your doorstep and call my life yours forever."

She pauses. I see her hands tremble, and even her eyes widen, though I could not describe her beauty beyond its own overwhelming existence. How do you describe a light like the sun, but greater? "You acknowledge that I am not free."

"Your lord husband is fortunate above all other men. Were I he."

Mairwen lets her veil fall and I blink, bereft. Eirean smiles and takes her shaking hands in her own. "You see, heart's sister. You are safe from him."

To me, she says, "The Lady Mairwen is under a spell, dear brother, set by a faithless handmaiden to stir the trouble between Ergyng and Caer Badden to a froth again. Any man who looks upon her shall fall in love with her and try to possess her. The spell will break only if her own lawfully betrothed weds her by nightfall of Midsummer's Day."

I am breathing as if after a race. "Habren."

"He saw her face when she came to Camelot. There was ... an incident. Merlin determined the cause and its correction."

"Merlin gave only those to the task who would not fall to the spell…" I catch my breath. "But the guards are men. The priest. The servant…"

"Have you not noticed how they cleave to each other, those guards? And the priest and the servant?"

I had not. "I know the priest sings with the servant," I say stupidly, and Eirean laughs at me, though not unkindly.

"He does more than sing." She retreats. "Lady, I must speak with my brother. Have no fear. I will join you in a very few moments."

Mairwen vanishes into the latest bower. "I should go away," I whisper. "The spell…"

"This is not the spell," she says, taking my face in her hands. "It affects men."

"I am…"

"You are. In thought and word and deed, in name and title, and even, it seems, in love. But not in birth. I think," her smile is crooked, "that your malady is the regular sort, God given to mortals to confound their senses."

"As you say, sister, I am not a man."

"An accident of body, my brother." She kisses me on the forehead. "Now, sleep. Habren will not catch us tonight, because he cannot cross the Severn yet. He might tomorrow, or the day after, because he knows where we must go. You need your rest."

My thoughts are whirling. "Does she…"

"No, she knows not. And if you do not tell her, she never will. Sleep." Another kiss and she leaves me, slipping into the bower. I hear her murmur to Mairwen, and a reply, softer yet. I rise and stumble into the dark, where I find a tree to lean my forehead against.

We were raised as sisters, Eirean and I, put out to foster when our lady mother died in our birthing. But when we were ten our lord father died. Talfryn needed a strong hand, so I took a boy's name and boy's breeches and returned to give it the hand it needed, defending the place against all claimants for years. Arthur took notice, and, after a particularly harrowing season defending Talfryn and the road to Camelot from bandits, he gave me the honor of knight in his service. I have striven ever since to prove his choice wise.

Just now, however, I fear I have reached the limit of both my ability and my wits. Arthur will be disappointed. Worse, Mairwen will be.

I did not know I loved women. Perhaps Eirean is right. She has said before that shape alone does not make a man. I have thought that she was speaking of honor, and courage, and leadership, of prowess in war and the hunt. I have those, never having felt anything but a man in their doing, and now I have a man's love, besides.

My breathing settles. I hear the guards preparing to swap shifts and turn my head. They are silhouetted against the fire. A few words, a touch, and they part, the one to his pallet and the other to his post, but it is there, the love they feel for each other. Why have I not noticed before?

Perhaps because my own love has been blinding me. Or perhaps the spell has some hold on me, despite my birth.

I return to my own pallet. Eirean is right; Habren may come upon us tomorrow.

The next day passes peacefully enough. We are hurrying now, speeding along the road to Ergyng. How closely Habren follows, only the One above knows, but knowing what I now know, I do not want to meet him. That can only end in bloodshed. So we push, dropping exhausted to sleep each night and rising near as exhausted each morning.

The third day is Midsummer. We are half a day from Ergyng. "One last race," I tell our little band, and am met with faint smiles and tired hope.

By noon we are trotting our horses out of the endless wood and the hold of Ercwlff of Ergyng lies before us, nestled in a loop of the Afon Mynwy. It is a comely castle, the wooden palisade striped in bright colors and its banners bravely flying. I tell a guard to run up Mairwen's pennant on his spear and to take the lead. I swear I can hear the cheering from a mile away.

Of course that is when Habren attacks.

The first I know of it is the searing pain of an arrow through my thigh, pinning it to the saddle. My horse squeals and jumps sideways, which saves me from the second arrow, though the jump tears at the wound so that I cannot see for pain.

Pain does not matter. "Eirean! Get the Lady to the castle and get her wed! Go!"

She does not argue. My vision clears enough so I see her horse leap toward Mairwen's. My sister leans over and catches the bridle, and the both of them are pounding down the road toward the castle. A stray thought crosses my mind — what if Habren is between them and the castle? But another thought chases it: no, we can see all the way to the castle. There is no cover.

Knees squeeze and my horse spins. An arrow thumps into my shield — when did I take it off the hook on my saddle? When did I draw my sword? Idle thoughts, useless things, as I scan the treeline. Beside me a guard is ripping Mairwen's pennant off his spear. Then an arrow seems to push him out of his saddle and his horse pirouettes in place, once, twice, before speeding after the ladies.

"Habren!" I roar, putting pain and anger into it, every ounce. "Coward! Face me like a knight if you dare, sir, or be ridden down like the base bandit you are!"

I cannot decide if my thigh feels fevered or cold. My horse crabs sideways and keeps trying to turn his head toward it; the arrow must have pierced the saddle and the cloth beneath to scratch him. The wound is annoying, but not more; he is bothered, but not so much that he cannot carry me. But it is one more thing to think about.

Habren appears from the trees, on foot, bow in hand. "Give me my Lady, foul Eilian, and I will make your death a short one!"

"She is neither yours to take nor mine to give." I point my sword at him. "Give over, Habren. If you surrender, I will see you to Arthur for justice."

For answer, he raises the bow.

I think he will shoot me, but he shoots my horse instead. I feel the beast gasp and the forelegs collapse, and fling my shield one way and myself the other. The arrow pinning me breaks in a burst of agony and I roll away from my poor mount as it dies.

My first attempt to stand fails. My second has me on my feet just as Habren rides past — where did his horse come from? But I can't think about that. With no other choice, I fling my sword at the animal's hocks and it screams as it goes down.

The guard's spear is lying near. I scoop it up and am braced by the time Habren faces me again. "You slew my horse!"

The creature is kicking and crying behind him. My own is still. "Give over, Habren of Heil. Justice can still be yours."

He spits. "Die like a dog." With a howl, he comes at me and gets the butt of the spear in his gut for his trouble. I miss the follow-up, spinning the head of the spear into the side of his helmet, because my leg won't push and he rolls away from the blow. But he is more cautious as he gains his feet.

"A spear," he snarls. "A peasant's weapon for a peasant!"

"You don't expect me to use a knight's weapon against a cowardly ambusher?" I bare my teeth in the best smile I can manage. "For shame."

He roars and starts a rush, reverses as the spear comes around, then slams his blade against the shaft. It's his strength against mine, getting the spear out of his way, so he can shove in close where he can use his weapon and I can't use mine.

Strength is a useful gift for fighting. But any man who fights with nothing but strength is a fool. I let him push the spear aside, spin on my good leg as fast as he shoves, letting his sword thrust skim past me, bringing the longer weapon around in a great arc around us both that slams it into his shoulders. He falls to his knees.

I try to pull the spear around to hit him again while he's down, but a step onto my bad leg has me flat on the ground, seeing stars. This will not do.

The spear is a decent crutch to get me back to my feet, at least. I stand as Habren does, and we stare at each other across a body's length of ground. "Sneak attack," he growls at me.

"I came at you from the front, Habren. That is more courtesy than you showed me."

He growls and his gaze slides past me. I am now between him and the castle, and seeing it has renewed his anxiety for Mairwen. I hope she and Eirean have made the gate.

A feint of the spear snaps his attention back to me. "Yes, you will have to go through me to follow her. Her lord husband awaits her. She is not yours, Habren of Heil. You are ensorcelled, under a spell! Fight it!"

He blinks and for a moment it seems as if he understands. But it is only a moment. "She is mine!"

Bloody sorcery. I swear I will suffer no witch in Talfryn ever again. But I will have to survive this fight to keep that promise.

And to do that, I must slow Habren down. There is only so much a wounded knight with a spear can do against an unwounded one with a sword.

He circles, trying to get past. I thrust, he parries, I rake the spear point across his knees. The armor saves him, but he jumps away, cursing. My sword is a dozen yards away and I shift toward it as I turn to keep Habren in front of me. He runs at me, yelling, then dodges aside to pass me in the road. I tangle the spear with his feet and he goes down again, his weight tearing the weapon from my grasp. I lunge for my sword and get it on the third staggering step, hear a step behind me and get my blade up in time to catch his with it.

"Got you," he crows, and he stabs me low in the belly with his dagger.

Oh, Eirean. I am sorry.

He relaxes. My vision is narrowing, focused on his face. As he steps out of the sword bind, I reverse grip and slam my pommel into his mouth. He goes down like a sack of grain. I go down on top of him.

— «» —

I spend a week in fever and more weeks recovering. But I live.

Eirean and Mairwen nurse me back to health, taking turns, though Eirean claims the portions involving the cleaning of my wounds and the changings of dressings. She claims I have vows of chastity and humility, and that while a sister might see me bare, a good gentlewoman, newly married, should not. It seems to suffice, for Mairwen never once treats me as other than a young knight wounded in her service.

Every moment spent in her presence is painful, for she is still radiantly beautiful. Worse, she has a particular smile she wears now, and that smile is given only to Ercwlff.

I inhabit Ercwlff's best guest chamber during my convalescence. He comes to see me several times, first with thanks, later with comradery, treating me the way one lord would treat another. We discuss husbandry and architecture and the techniques for fighting bandits, and profess friendship for one another. He is an excellent man.

Habren lives, too. Mairwen's wedding freed his mind, but Ercwlff will not have him within his walls. He removed to a nearby abbey, where he prayed with the monks, before returning to Camelot. The priest comes to me after he leaves, bringing the news and Habren's heartfelt apologies. Those moments are painful, too.

One day the priest sings for me the song he made about the journey, about fighting giants and bears and goblins, all in service to a lovely woman who appears in moonlight on water. She has had a cruel geas placed upon her that traps her beneath the surface. The king, her husband, calls his best knight to free her, but the knight falls in love with her himself, and...

"That isn't what happened at all," I complain, and he just laughs. I tell Eirean it is time to go home to Talfryn after he leaves.

We go to Camelot first, where Arthur hears my tale and judges what Habren owes me for the wounds he gave me. Eirean has quietly let it be known that those wounds, while not fatal, have permanently scarred me, and suggests a marriage between me and Habren's niece, the heir of his dead brother. The girl resists the match, because she spent time kidnapped by the lowest sort of bandits, but when she is told of my 'infirmity', and that she will never be expected to share a marriage bed with me, she is willing enough.

She introduces me to her sons, bastards of those same bandits. "They are beautiful!" I say, and I mean it. You have never seen three flowers bloom the way those three faces did that day.

As the years pass, I sometimes hear the song the priest wrote. It has changed. Now it has no bears nor goblins, but it still has the lady in the water and the knight who rescues her from the giant who trapped her. But, she is a star, and freed, she rejoins her lord in the sky above, leaving the faithful knight mourning her every night forever after.

I always weep, hearing it. I tell my wife and my sons that it is because I pity the poor knight, alone in the dark, without a family to love him the way they love me.

Thank God they believe it.

— «» —

Renée Bennett is an author and editor, with memberships in SFWA and CAFÉ, and is a six time Aurora Award nominee. Her fiction has appeared on CBC Radio, in the Enigma Front and Rigor Amortis anthologies, and in Year's Best Fantasy, edited by David Hartwell and Kathryn Kramer.

Shadow of the Wolf

Diana L. Paxson

The air is warm, weighted with the scents of new grass and thyme. The air echoes with birdsong, but I am the only four-footed being in this part of the forest. I want to leap and roll, forgetting all else in that rush of sensory ecstasy. I want to split the air with an exultant howl. But the mingled perfumes of growing things awaken a memory of the pink petals of the briar rose, and another memory that sets excitement and anguish pounding in my veins.

The human female walked this way. How long ago?

On the hillside the gorse blooms golden, and new trails of bramble have laced across the path. I push through, four paws finding the hollowed track where the tight fronds of bracken are beginning to unfurl.

The ground levels. I smell moss and damp stone, glimpse the rough gray of granite through the new leaves. With my muzzle I push aside the springing branches of a young pine. Before me, the stones of the old lair shoulder through the thicket — two great stones supporting a third, the back still closed by the earth that once covered the whole.

I poke my nose through the opening, smelling damp earth and old bones. My own scent remains, and another that makes my hackles rise, the odor of an unknown human male. There should be something else here, but the only cloth is a crumpled bit of linen. I crouch down, rubbing my muzzle against the fabric, nostrils flaring to suck it in.

And then I jerk back. The scent, *her* scent, has unlocked memory. My long jaws open in a howl of desolation as I remember that once I was a man.

The sound reverberates against the stones and the birds grow still. And then, a distant echo, comes the wail of a hunter's horn.

Fight, or flee? The horn is echoed by the war-cry of the hounds. *"We smell you!"* *"We'll find you!"* *"We'll kill you!"* come their cries. Too many. A full pack, they have heard my howl and now they are on my trail.

Reason flees. Rage and terror gallop through my veins. *"Run!"* they tell me, *"run!"* Unwilled, my legs carry me out of the stone trap and away.

This is *my* forest! How dare they hunt me here? Beyond the lair the land breaks into a moorland of hill and gully covered in gorse and sallow, studded with stunted pines. My feet know all the pathways where the forest is broken by outcrops of bronze-colored stone, the tangles of last summer's bramble, the place where the path is blocked by the branches of a fallen pine.

I race down a hillside, hoping to break the scent trail by running in the rivulet that flows through the red mud there. I leap the remains of a bronze helmet that still holds a few bits of broken skull. Humans have wandered here 'till they died, but I know the way.

The hounds catch my scent again and come after. They have only to follow, while I must choose a trail. I gather my strength, scramble up the bank. From the top I can see a rolling slope of gorse and heather and below it to the north, the intense green of the forest. I speed down the slope, racing for its shelter.

I can run faster beneath the trees, but swift as I go, the dogs are gaining, the cry of one hound giving way to the next as the leader tires and another takes his place. I leap to the top of a fallen log and see them behind me, white ghost-shapes flitting among the leaves. I gather myself to run and suddenly the first dog is upon me, a sleek rache-hound with flapping ears. He yammers defiance, but I am no deer to be so easily pulled down. I whirl, teeth closing on his foreleg.

He snaps at my side and with a shake I send him flying. The others hang back as he squeals in pain. I dart forward. From the forest the horn speaks again. Men shout. The dead stalks of last year's bracken crackle as horses push through the trees.

I savage the next hound, yelp as a third fastens his teeth in my haunch, shake him loose with a bound. A flurry of gaping maws and flapping ears surrounds me. Too many to fight, but I am bigger. Snarling, I barrel through them.

I race ahead, dogs and horsemen spreading out behind me. Now they have a blood trail to follow. Ahead there is comfort, though I cannot remember what or why. The fastest hounds are pacing me now, the boldest darting in to snap as I run.

"You are one and we are many, many, many!" they cry.

Ahead, the sound of water, but the dogs are louder. The ground levels. I leap among the tumbled stones where men once lived, reach the great oak tree. From its roots flows a spring. I whirl, my back against the rough trunk, half-crouched and bristling, curled lips snarling fury as the dogs close in.

"Blood, blood!" shriek the dogs. The sharp tang hangs in the air. The ground trembles as the riders gallop forward. Spear points glitter in the spring sun. A dog darts in, his fangs gashing my shoulder, a swift snap, I get him by the throat, shake, cast him aside. They draw back, but my own blood is flowing from haunch and shoulder and side. I lean against the rock, chest vibrating with a low growl.

"A wolf!" cries one of the men, "A royal beast indeed!" An arrow flashes by to splinter against the stone.

Sunlight shafts downward as leaves flutter in the breeze, flashing on weapons, glittering on the water that burbles from the spring. A man on a white horse pushes forward. The sun strikes fire from the gold band around his brow.

Recognition blinds awareness of all around me — I catch his scent and I *know* him, know, for a moment, that other life in which he was my friend and my king.

Marc'h... Conomor... Wor-tiern of Lesser Britain, and lord of Ker-haes....

"*My lord*!" Why does that come out as a whimper of appeal? In his presence, human words blossom in memory.

Dogs recoil in surprise as I surge forward. A strong hand reins down the rearing stallion as I reach the king's side. Instinct pushes me to cower, tail curled and head down, but memory sets me on my hind feet, clawing at his stirrup with paws that try to work as hands. Horsemen mill in confusion, spears swinging as they seek a target that will not also endanger their king.

"Spur away, my lord, and we'll get him!" comes the call, but the king shakes his head. I sense the shift when wonder begins to replace fear.

"No!" he speaks suddenly. "The beast is mine! Call off the hounds!"

I drop down, suppressing the instinct to present my throat in submission. Instead I bow before him, forelegs splayed, nose to ground, as the hunters wrench their horses' heads around, and the grooms, staves swinging, beat back the hounds.

"See, he makes obeisance before me! Is this not a wonder?"

"A noble quarry indeed," says one. *Drustan*... memory supplies the name. "A beast that knows to beg mercy like a man."

"May he set an example for your enemies!" cries another.

"We'll hunt no more today!" Marc'h says suddenly. "Leash the hounds." The white horse is still trembling, the acrid scent of his sweat strong in the cool air. But his master has him well in hand. As the clamor lessens, the burble of the spring seems suddenly loud. They say its waters heal madness. I have the wolf-sickness, the *bleiz claffet*, but those waters did not heal me.

The huntsmen begin to call in the hounds. Drustan and two men from Marc'h's own houseguard circle with lances poised in case the king is wrong.

"He will not hurt me..." says the king.

I should run now, bury myself in the wilderness until the wolf-mind consumes the human mind entirely, and with it my pain. But Marc'h is speaking.

"So, wolf — I give you your life. What will you give me?"

I lift my head. My eyes meet his. There is more silver than I remember in King Marc'h's dark hair, but the piercing gray gaze remains the same.

The faith I swore to you when I was Edern fil Trallon, Tiern of Lan Bleiz.... My wolf's throat will not form words, but perhaps he can read the answer in my amber gaze.

"Come, then," says the king.

Going with him, I condemn myself to constant awareness of what I have lost, but mindless, my life will have no meaning. Marc'h looses the rein, and as the stallion steps out, I heave myself to my feet and follow.

— «» —

The feast of Beltane is past, but today it is raining, a strong spring storm that drums on the roof tiles and drips from the eaves of the hall. Since I followed King Marc'h to Ker-haes, a year has passed.

At the king's hall in Ker-haes, the chieftains of Armorica gather around the braziers, playing fidchel and drinking ale. Once this was the hall of a Roman lord. Now, the white-washed walls are dark with smoke, and rushes, not rugs, lie across the floor. From the high window, light filters through triangular panes of greenish glass. The air is full of mingled scents of woodsmoke and wet wool, dog and horse and the sweat of men. I am glad of a place by the fire.

As the door opens, a rush of cold damp makes the flames swirl, bringing with it an intoxicating mix of green growing things and cooking food from the kitchen hall outside. Men call out greetings as another lord comes in, big, bluff, with stringy graying hair. He was my neighbor, when I was a man. Petroc fil Dunnorec is his name.

"And is this the wolf the peasants are all talking about? The one they call the king's shadow? A handsome fellow, isn't he?"

Perhaps that is true. My wife used to praise my looks when I was a black-haired man. Well-fed, with a glossy coat of black guard hairs growing over gray, I am a good-looking beast as well.

"We tracked him from the haunted valley!" exclaims young Hoel, dark eyes gleaming. He is a grandson of Marc'h by the son of the king's first marriage to the daughter of Budic of Dol. Father Jonas makes the sign of the cross and takes another sip of wine.

"That's just north of my lands," says Petroc. "An uncanny place, but even a wild beast, my lord, sits tamely in your hall!"

The hair of my ruff lifts slightly. His laugh is hearty, but I can smell his fear.

"Gnawing his bone like a good dog! Are you a good dog?"

The king has given me a golden neck-chain, but that does not make me a dog. In my chest at Lan Bleiz is the gold chain that he gave me when I was a man. As Petroc reaches to pat me I lift my head from the beef rib I have been stripping and stare. They say that a wolf cannot outstare a man, but this man's eyes shift before mine do.

The king is watching from his curule chair. I do not need to growl to give warning.

Do not trust this man. He hides his heart.

Petroc recoils and my powerful jaws clamp back down on the rib. There is a sharp crack as the bone breaks. He jumps, and now it is the other men who laugh. At the note of a harpstring they grow quiet. My ears twitch as the vibrations fade. Marc'h's nephew Drustan, dark of hair with tanned skin stretched tight over the good bones like a younger reflection of the king, has taken out his harp. He bends to listen to a string and turns the peg, then plucks a chord.

> *Before Gerontius, the enemy's dread.*
> *White horses rearing, and the red*
> *After war cries, bitter the home of the dead.*
>
> *In Portcaster, I saw them striking sore—*
> *The heroes of the great Artor—*
> *Our labor's lord, Imperator.*
>
> *In Portcaster, Gerontius was laid low,*
> *And heroes of Dumnonia also,*
> *But before they all were slain they slew.*

"An old song for an old enemy!" exclaims Fragan Tawr. "Childebert and his Franks are a kingdom, not a heathen rabble like the Saxons we fought in our fathers' time.

"A rabble?" the king shakes his head. "They did not seem so puny to Artor. He used to argue with my father when they sat over their wine. It is easy to discount a beaten enemy."

"If they will *stay* beaten," mutters Mevennus Maglos, newly come over from Dumnonia. "What good can come of defeating Franks in Armorica if the Saxons chase us out of Kernow?"

I echo the murmur from the men with a muttering growl.

"You see, even Master Shadow agrees—" says someone. At first they thought the sounds I make uncanny, but now they laugh.

Drustan sets down the harp. "That is why we must win here! If we unite, Greater and Lesser Britain can support each other. I have been among both the Franks and the Saxons. The fathers of their fathers all came from beyond the Rhenus, but these days they'd as soon kill each other as us. Half of you—" he gestures around the circle, "are lords both in Armorica and Britannia. We are still one people, speaking the same language, following the same law."

But their bodies are stiff when they look at him — he's no kin to them, they are thinking, for all he is the nephew of their king. How is it that Marc'h does not see it? But I did not either, when I was a man.

"Well then, if the Franks do march against us, who can you count on to come to your call?" says Mevennus Maglos. In Kernow he would have known the men and their families back three generations, but British Armorica is a patchwork series of alliances between the surviving families of old Roman Gauls and the British chieftains who repopulated the country after the Yellow Plague swept through.

I ease down before the fire and let my eyes close as Drustan begins to reply. I am half asleep when a name sets my ears twitching.

"A pity that Edern of Lan Bleiz was lost. He was a skilled warrior."

I lift my head from my paws.

"What happened to him?" asks Fragan Tawr.

"No one knows," says Petroc. "It has been more than a year now since he went hunting in Broceliande and never returned. They searched, but found no body, nor any of his gear."

"I heard that the Lady Rimoete, his widow, has married again," says one of the men.

Without thinking I am on my feet, ears flattening. I look around — no one has noticed my agitation. I force myself to sit again.

"She has indeed," Petroc confirms. "The groom is Lucian Rufio, from Venetia. His folk were ship-builders in the Roman days."

The hair lifts along my spine. Rimoete was from the old Veneti lands. I remember a young man with red hair who watched her at our wedding feast with eyes like a sick calf.

"Can he fight?" asks Mevennus. When the Picts began to raid Britannia the Romanized tribesmen called in the Saxons to do their fighting. We all knew how that had ended. He might be forgiven for wondering if the Roman Gauls were the same.

"If he cannot, the estate still owes me the service of his men," answers the king. "We will send for him."

Of the bone only a few fragments remain. I move to the king's side, lean against the solid wood of the bench as his long fingers smooth the fur over the top of my skull and dig into the thick tufts at the base of my ears. Surely to allow this does not make me more the wolf. I used to lay my head in Rimoete's lap and she would stroke my hair, in the days when I was a man.

"Shadow! You are trembling!" Marc'h exclaims. "Are you cold, or wanting your dinner? We will eat soon, and you shall have the bone from my share if they have saved none for you ."

Warmth... shelter... food.... That is all the wolf-mind desires.... But it is the man-mind that remembers a white face and beseeching dark eyes framed by a cloud of black hair.

Rimoete...

There is a stir at the other end of the hall. Men rise to their feet as the queen appears, her maid, Branwen, like a shadow at her heels. The two women are much alike, the maid a base-born cousin to the queen. Esseilte is brighter of hair and thinner — too thin, I think, but she walks like a woman who knows that she draws men's eyes.

The queen arrived in Armorica just before I joined the king's household, along with Drustan, who had been left as Marc'h's regent in Kernow. Some say the king sent for them because he needs Drustan's sword against his enemies, and some, because he did not trust him in Kernow. Others whisper that the king trusted his nephew with his kingdom, but not with his queen.

Marc'h reaches out to draw her down to a stool beside him. She does not look at Drustan, nor he at her. I am the only one who sees the sudden shimmer as his hand on the frame transmits a tremor to the harpstrings. And when Branwen looks from the harper to the queen there is trouble in her gaze.

"We will summon this Lord Lucian," says the king. "We will summon them all — every lord and landowner and clan chieftain, be they Briton or Gaul. Fragan Tawr, I want you to send word round the whole country for a meeting at Riedonum at midsummer. And Mevennus, you will help me to write to Odovicus, whom Childebert has set to hold the marchlands."

"Do you think him a threat?" asks Fragan Tawr. "The border has been quiet since St. Melaine negotiated that treaty in our fathers' time."

"And the word is that Childebert and his brothers are planning war against King Godomar in Burgundia," says another man.

"A good time for an ambitious man to strike out on his own," Mevennus Maglos comments then.

"Or to realize that he will get little support from Paris against whatever we may choose to do—"

It seems to me that there is something wolfish in Marc'h's smile.

— «» —

Night is falling and the rain has ceased. Beyond the palisaded wall, budding branches trace a lacy black edging against banners of golden cloud. As I trot toward the cookhouse, in the shadow of the porch I see Petroc's bulk and a smaller man.

"He is not making any secret of this meeting," says the other man. "King Riwal will hear of it soon...."

"As soon as you give him the word?" Petroc laughs. "Nay, what you want to be telling him are the names of those who are here and what they say."

"And where do you stand, Petroc?"

"For myself—" the big man laughs. "Only safe place to stand in times like these!'

I move, or perhaps my golden collar caught the light, for Petroc turns suddenly, peering through the dusk.

"What is it?" his companion's voice goes shrill.

"Nothing — only that damned wolf the king dragged home. I don't mind telling you that given half a chance I'd put an arrow through his mangy hide."

I snort my disdain for that and trot past him, tail high, to disappear into the shadows once more.

It is an evening for whispers. In the arbor by the kitchen garden my keen gaze picks out two more figures half-hidden by the unfurling leaves. I pause a moment to test the wind. It is Drustan ... and the queen. I take more care with my stalk this time, easing from shadow to shadow across the open ground until I crouch behind them.

"I do not know how much longer I can bear it here," says the queen. "To see you every day and pretend to care nothing, when I feel hollow with the need to have you in my arms."

"Do you think it is easier for me?" Drustan's voice grates with strain.

They are not touching, but their scent has changed.

Those scents wake memories of a woman's smooth flesh and a soft bed that still smells of our loving, the warmth, and her voice in my ear—" *My sweet Edern, you give me such joy. When you are gone, I grow afraid! When you disappear into the forest and are gone for days, where is it you go? Do you have a fairy lover in the woodlands who you prefer to me?"* I remember her soft arms around my neck and her soft lips on mine. I remember that I told her the secret behind the black wolf's head that is the emblem of Lan Bleiz. I told her about the ancient dolmen tomb, and the magic that let me change from man to wolf, seduced by the freedom of the forest beneath the moon, and how I changed back again.

When the next full moon laid its enchantment over Broceliande, I responded to its spell and sought the forest. When I returned to the tomb, the clothing whose scent would have enabled me to reclaim the shape of a man had disappeared.

Esseilte's voice grows louder. "You are a man. You have decisions to make, things to do. I look out of my window as the fields grow green, and think that soon the woods will be warm and fair. Take me away, Drustan! Your bow will feed us and the forest will give us shelter. Broceliande is a magic place. Surely we would be safe there!"

In the kitchen there is a woman whose nose was cut off to punish her for adultery. Would men still praise Esseilte if she suffered the same penalty?

"Until the Frankish army comes marching through," Drustan replies. "There is no safe place, Esseilte, unless it be the lands beyond the western sea. Marc'h needs me here, my love. I cannot leave him now!"

The growl fades in my throat as I understand. They are betraying him in thought, but not in deed.

"What was that?" she whispers. I move past them, a shadow from the shadows, and Esseilte flinches away.

"The wolf ... I can feel him watching me, judging." She sinks down on a bench. "I would ask Branwen for one of my mother's potions to poison the beast, but he loves the king."

"And so do we, " Drustan replies. "And so we suffer what we cannot change." His voice grows lighter. "The wolf knows, my horse knows, even the nightingale in the treetop knows how I love you. But none of them will say a word."

Two threats of death in one evening — should I be honored or afraid? My life is not so dear to me that either arrow or poison causes me to fear. Drustan is right. Trapped in this body, what honor remains to me? What deed, for good or for ill, have I the power to do?

The gates have not yet been closed. Drustan and Esseilte cannot seek the freedom of the forest, but I can. As I pass the stone where the women pour out milk for the fay folk, my trot lengthens to a loping run. The forest awaits me, a world of enticing scents released by the rain.

— «» —

The weather grows warmer. On the farms the wheat is already high. As Midsummer nears, the chieftains of Armorica begin to ride in. The meadow beside the aqueduct that fed the town when it was the Roman Vorgium sprouts an early crop of tents. The banners of Venetia and Cornovia, Domnonia and Poher and Léon ripple in the breeze. I wander among them, nose twitching at the mingled scents of dogs and horses and men. The dogs come out to challenge me, but I stand tall, tail gently wagging in mockery, and they go scuttling to the protection of their masters. I trade insults with their dogs, but I listen to the men. Marc'h is already *Wor-tiern* of Kernow. Can he claim that title in Lesser Britain as well? Some of the men, especially those near the border that stretches from Riedonum to Namnetum, see in him a worthy defender against Frankish land-lust. There is less enthusiasm from the lords in the coastal lands.

When I see Petroc making his way toward the tent of Budnouen of Kemper, I follow, at first because his discomfort in my presence amuses me, and then because I am wondering what business takes him there. With a last look he enters the tent. I continue on my way, but I do not go far. The trampled earth before the doorway holds the fresh scent of several men. A subliminal growl silences the dogs and I crouch in the shadow of a cart, ears twitching to pick up the murmur of conversation a few feet away.

"You are with us, then?" says Petroc.

"Aye," comes the answer. I recognize the voices of the chieftains from Léon and Poher.

"What about Venetia?" Lord Budnouen asks.

"Waroc is with us," Petroc replies. I remember that he married King Riwal's grand-daughter, so that is no surprise.

"And your own people?"

I tense, ears pricked to learn which of my neighbors have become Marc'h's enemies.

"Lucian has already given me his word," says Petroc. "He should be arriving soon."

I miss the other names. If Rimoete thought me dead, can I blame her for marrying again? Like the briar rose, she was sweet. I twitch, remembering how a howling wind or a strange sound in the forest would send her trembling to my arms. But now it is young Lucian to whom she clings.

"And they will join us?" Budnouen asks.

"With Frankish daggers honed and hidden—"

"Like the Night of the Long Knives," says someone. My neck-ruff bristles, for no man of British birth can forget how the Saxon Hengest shouted *"oute seaxes"* as his warriors sank their blades into the hearts of the British leaders who had come to swear peace in Vortigern's hall.

"But this time the Franks will fall as well. If the only weapons found among the dead are Frankish, who can deny that it was their treachery that killed Marc'h and his allies, and our valor that kept us alive?"

"And Childebert will not avenge his kinsman?"

"In public the Frankish king will rage. In private — he will thank King Riwal for delivering him from an ambitious cousin."

"And win us peace for another few years...." says one of the other men.

I suppress a growl. We would have peace if Riwal were willing to work with Marc'h instead of fighting him, but the bad blood between them goes back many years. I should not be surprised at the current treachery. If the princes of Britain had been willing to stand together, the Saxons would not hold half the land today. For one brief golden age Artor had united them, but though Marc'h's father Constantine was Artor's heir, he had not been able to keep the kingdom from disintegrating into a tangle of rivalries.

From the southern road come hoofbeats and a chorus of greetings. I sit up, ears swiveling, and glimpse above the heads of the men who are coming out of their tents a yellow banner. As a red-headed man pushes through the crowd the wind snaps the banner taut to reveal the black wolf's head of Lan Bleiz.

I rise, every nerve tensed and twanging, and the wind brings me the scent of the man. I breathe in, and memory matches it to that of the strange male whose scent was in the tomb. I take one step forward, then another. Along my back the hairs lift from ruff to tail, quivering as a deep growl shakes my chest. A boy points. Men begin to edge away.

Lucian... In that instant all is clear. *He* the one who took my clothing — as he has taken my wife and my land.

The wolf-mind overwhelms all awareness as snarling, I spring.

The next moments are a tumult of screams and shouting, the crunch and hot salt taste of blood as my jaws close on Lucian's shoulder, the impact of the ground as I bear him down. I snarl over my shoulder as some brave soul kicks me. Lucian tries to roll away as they recoil and I pin him, his terrified whimpering mingling with my growl. Focus narrows to the white throat beneath the jutting red beard. I lower my head, jaws opening.

A shock sends me sprawling. I try to rise, snapping at the blade whose point, deflected by my collar, has passed through the loose skin beneath my ruff, pinning me to the ground. Men are dragging away my prey.

"Kill him! Kill!" roars the crowd.

"Nay, 'tis the King's wolf!" cries someone. "See the gold?"

The spear is jerked loose, but my struggles are useless as the muffling weight of a net traps my limbs. I am battered by staves as they roll me over, tighten the net, drag me away. I am still howling in fury when a last blow strikes me down into the dark.

—— 《 》 ——

"She told me you were a black wolf. She was right to be afraid."

The voice is soft, wavering between triumph and fear. I stir, wincing at the throb of a hundred bruises and a sharper pain where my neck was pierced by the spear. My nostrils flare, identifying the scent that matches the blood I lick from my teeth. With an effort I open my eyes.

Twilight has fallen. The air is heavy with the scent of wood smoke and cooking food. I am in a cage. Through the stoutly woven withies I glimpse Lucian. His arm is in a sling. I lick my chops again.

"Lord Edern, good evening...." Lucian glances over his shoulder and steps closer. "They are still arguing about what to do with you. They can't understand why you attacked me, keep saying how you never threatened anyone before. We know better, don't we?" He manages a rather shrill laugh. "Rimoete would not listen to my vows of love, so dazzled was she by your name and your lands. But when she found out what you are, she was afraid to lie at your side. She did not scorn me then! She led me to your lair, told me how to keep you from reversing the spell." He pauses as if waiting for me to answer him. "In the morning we will be leaving for Broceliande, but this cage will hold you, wolf, until we return. King Marc'h won't be here to protect you then." He takes a deep breath. "He won't be here, but I will. And then I will go home to your hall and lie with your wife and stake your mangy hide to the wall!"

Perhaps, I think then, but I doubt he himself will have the courage to strike me down. He could come into the cage with me and be safe enough as I am now, but at the rumble deep in my chest he steps back. He turns then and walks away. I lift my head and find the strength to howl, hoping it sounds like defiance and not despair. It is enough to turn his saunter to a trot.

I would laugh, if I were still a man.

In the morning, the encampment begins to sort itself out and get into motion. I lie stretched on my side, listening as the clamor fades, with barely strength to drink from the wooden bowl they have pushed through the slot at the end of the cage. They say a wild animal can will itself to death. The spear did not pierce anything vital, but I have bled a great deal. I cannot tell how many bones are cracked or broken, but my body is a mass of pain. If I refuse to eat or drink can I deny them the pleasure of killing me?

On the second day, the scent of food awakens appetite. The magic that holds me in wolf-shape is healing me. The wound in my neck has scabbed over. Cracked ribs protest and there is still a weakness in my left foreleg, but I can stand.

And do what?

I am still caged, and yet I find myself examining my prison. The cage is made of tough willow poles, the gaps big enough for me to get my head through, but no more. The door is held by a padlock and an iron chain, but the posts themselves are bound by rawhide lashings. Once dried they will hold like iron, but the cage is new, and last night it rained. I move around, examining those lashings, exploring the knots with my tongue. These barriers baffle the mind of a beast and defeat the strength of a man. But can they hold *me*? The campsite is deserted, and it will be tomorrow morning before someone comes with food. I crouch against the back of the cage, and begin to gnaw.

The rest of that day I work at the bindings, and most of the night. If the boy who brings food the next morning thinks my exhausted sleep is weakness, so much the better. I allow myself a few hours rest and begin to work again. The corners are the weakest, and they did not think to reinforce them. Some time after midnight, I feel something give way. I push, stifling a yelp at the pressure on my wounded neck, feel one pole pull away from the floor and another from the end of the cage, push with an effort that awakens every inch of my battered hide to new agony, and wriggle through.

It's a moonless night, but my eyes are keen. I seek the place where the aqueduct runs through an open channel, drink deeply, then submerge myself, letting the cold water wash away filth and blood and soothe the spots where the poles scraped my hide.

When the pain eases, I seek the midden. They left in a hurry, and there are scraps enough to fill my belly. I turn eastward, breathing deeply to let the wind from the hilltops scour the stink of the camp from my lungs, then lope across the road and across the open fields. The scent of the wildlands beyond is like wine, league upon league of forest, barely touched by humankind.

Men held me captive for three days, but I imprisoned myself among them for a year. The townsfolk will tremble when they hear my howl, but I am singing for joy because I am free.

— «» —

Dawn finds me still moving eastward. The first ecstatic rush of freedom has faded. I am limping, and I feel my bruises once more. The scent of four-day-old cow-droppings startles me into full awareness. This close to midsummer the sun comes early. In the growing light I recognize the worn paving of the old Roman road.

I did not mean to follow the king. He is moving slowly, bound to the pace of the ox-carts that bear the food and tents of oiled wool with which they hope to impress the Frankish lords. For carts, the Vorgium/Riedonum road is the fastest way through the hills, even though in places young trees have rooted themselves among the stones, but they will have to follow a dirt track through deep forest when they head south to Broceliande. It will be several days yet before they can hope to reach the meadow where they plan to meet the Franks, by the fountain of Barenton.

I pause to lap water where an icy rivulet trickles from between mossy stones and sink down beside it, listening to the morning concert of the birds. As the sun rises, the nightingale has fallen silent, but I am surprised by the cheerful "tee", "tee", of a blue tit swinging upside down from a branch. From farther off comes the "weela-wee-oo" of an oriole, and the rat-a-tat of a woodpecker is more distant still. I sigh as the early morning peace seeps into my bones. This is where I belong. To live in the human world brings only pain. I will hunt when I hunger and sleep when I tire and forget the speech of men.

I leave the road. Beech and oak grow thickly along the road. It is easy to disappear beneath their deep shade. I should rest, but no place seems right to me. I only stop when a branch hooks my collar and I must pause to pull free.

My golden chain... A glance at the sun tells me that my feet have been carrying me southeast, taking the shortest route toward the place where King Marc'h will meet the Franks three days from now — the Franks, and the men who mean to betray him. But how can I warn him? The men of Armorica are noted archers. They will shoot me down like a mad dog if I appear.

And yet I keep moving. I escaped the cage, but I am still chained by love and loyalty.

I smell the camp before I see it — odors of roasting meat, of horses and oxen, the fresh earth of a privy trench mingled with human waste — but not the tang of blood. I hear no screams or battle cries. I am in time.

Shadow to shadow, I move through the hazel thickets that edge the meadow, dotted now with leather Roman army tents and pavilions of tightly-woven oiled wool. For the meeting they have set up a circular enclosure, unwalled but roofed with poles and thatched with boughs. In the center burns a fire. The men, Briton alternating with Frank, are sitting on sectioned logs, except for the two in the portable Roman curule chairs whose curving sides and legs can collapse flat when the seat and back are removed. The big, fair-haired man sitting in one of them must be Ordovicus. He wears a coral tunic whose neck opening is lapped over on one side in the Frankish style. His semi-circular cloak is a deep green, everything pinned with gaudy brooches set with garnet chips in gold. Both garments are edged with silk trim. Next to him, Marc'h's blue tunic is plain, but his cloak is of a fine wool whose dark red is just this side of purple. There is no doubting which of them is a king.

As I ease forward one of the dogs catches my scent, a little brown and white yappy thing, He begins to bark, but when I face him, ears pricked and tail flat out in threat, he falls silent. One of the hunting dogs tied among the tents takes up the cry, but a servant shouts him down.

Near the entry, I see the gleaming pile of swords and daggers, guarded by men from each side. They have disarmed to show good faith during the negotiations, but Petroc is sitting rather stiffly, as if he bears something more than a linen undertunic beneath his robe. Lucian, as a lesser lord, is not in the enclosure, though I am sure that once the fighting starts he will rush to Petroc's aid. Drustan, two men down, sits lithe and wary as a wolf. He watches the king and the Franks, but he and the British chieftains do not trade glances in the manner of allies.

At the moment, the conversation seems stuck on allegations of cattle-raiding. Every moment I wait increases the chances of discovery. When will the conspirators make their move?

Petroc shifts position uneasily. I have him pegged already as an impatient man. Can he be stampeded into showing his hand?

I ease closer and the little dog starts up again—" *Watch out, out, out!*"

"*Be still,*" says my growl, "*or die!*"

Petroc twitches, hand fumbling at his breast. The time is now! I am a black streak across the trampled ground, flashing between two men to leap, not for Petroc's throat, but for the hand that grasps a Frankish sword.

Petroc tries to jerk away, but I have him by the wrist, and no matter how he flails at me with his other hand my grip is sure.

"Mad wolf!" someone shouts. "Get a bow!"

"No, you'll hit the man!"

I go back on my haunches and pull Petroc down.

Swords flash — some of the other conspirators have been startled into drawing their hidden blades. "Treason!" someone cries. Drustan darts past me, grabs his sword from the pile and springs back to guard the king.

I crouch above Petroc, holding down both arm and sword, fighting the lust to lunge for the throat that flutters with each scream.

Now the enclosure is full of shouting men. A speartip pricks my ribs and I go still, but I do not let go.

"*Armas pone!*" across the tumult, Marc'h' voice snaps the order to ground weapons that warriors of both sides will know. For a moment, everyone is still.

"The Franks drew hidden blades—" babbles the *tiern* from Kemper, but everyone can see that he's the one holding a sword.

"Is Frankish blade," growls Odovicus, "in Briton's hand? It is dishonor — you bid us here to betray!"

"Not I," says Marc'h, his voice heavy with pain. He stretches out his arms, and the smooth line of the tunic over his broad chest is clear for all to see. "After they took you down, I think those swords were meant for me...."

Odovicus grunts, looking around him. One of his men has brought his commander's sword. The Frankish leader pulls the baldric over his head and settles the sheathed blade at his side.

"You say you can make pledges, but cannot make treaty if you do not rule your men."

Marc'h bows his head. "I too was betrayed ... but I will find out by whom!" his gaze grows keen once more.

"I leave you to clean your house," rumbles Odovicus. "This meeting is done!" He begins to shout orders in harsh Frankish and his warriors scatter to obey.

"What about the wolf?"

I release Petroc's wrist, and very carefully ease back onto my haunches as the spear is withdrawn. His wrist is somewhat mangled, but his fingers still move.

"The wolf," says Marc'h, "is clearly a better judge of men than the king." He looks at Petroc. "Was this all your own idea, or were you set on?"

Petroc turns his face away, cradling his injured arm. The king looks at me and snaps his fingers. I rise, plant my forefeet on Petroc's heaving chest. Tongue lolling, I open my jaws in a grin. My captive begins to moan.

"See how wide he gapes, Petroc, how sharp are his fangs. He could crush your skull like an egg, I have only to give the word. You have wasted a great deal of my effort. Tell me, Petroc."

I growl softly and lower my head. He twitches as a little drool drops onto his chin.

"Riwal," he whispers. "King Riwal," he repeats more loudly as I growl again.

The king sighs. "At least he is an enemy I already know. Who else, Petroc? Your allies in this council I know, but who else in secret is Riwal's man?"

Petroc begins to babble names. I snarl when he gets to Lucian.

"I should let my Shadow tear out your throat," says the king, "but I have better uses for my gold than paying out an honor price to your kin. You are banished, Petroc, you and all the other traitors here — forbidden to dwell in any land I rule. Go to King Riwal if you love him so well, and see how he rewards you!"

He gestures, and moving rather stiffly I get off Petroc's chest. That spear drew blood. I lie down by the king's chair and begin to lick my side. I am draggled and dusty, with wounds old and new marring my hide. It is no wonder that the others view me with awe mixed with fear.

Marc'h looks down at me. "And you, my poor friend, deserve a reward from me. We will start with water and something to eat—" His wave sends a lad running off to the cookfires.

But what I want most is rest. While King Marc'h puts his house in order, I lie in the shade. Even Lucian's voice barely rouses me. Some have accused him, but he was not in the meeting. His injured shoulder will be punishment enough for now. Spent, I sleep at last.

When I wake, it is evening, and the swallows are flitting back and forth above the trees. When I first try to rise I fall over, because in my dream I was a man. From the direction of the road comes the creak of a wagon. I tense, but the voices of the men on guard are raised in welcome.

"Where is he? Where is my husband?"

A new voice. Her voice.

Rimoete is here.

"They said a wolf attacked him, that he came here with you—"

For a moment I had thought she meant me.

I creak to my feet and pad toward the commotion. Her back is to me. She is trying to unwind the bandages that wrap Lucian's shoulder, chattering with the abandon that comes with relief. What silences her is the terror in his eyes.

Rimoete turns and sees me watching her. Staring, she stands, and then she screams, sways, falls. Stiff-legged, I pace toward her. Men reach for weapons, but the king stops them.

"The wolf was right before, when we were wrong. Let us see what he will do."

I stand over her. The luminous white skin is as I remember, and the tumbling black curls beneath her veil. I lower my head, feel her shudder as my tongue passes across the round of her breast above the low-cut neck of her gown. Her skin was always petal-smooth. I did not know about the thorns. She still tastes of briar rose, but the intoxicating woman-scent is soured by fear. She moans, her eyes white-rimmed. I think I could tear out her throat and the king would protect me. I want to laugh, but what comes out is a growl.

I cannot accuse her, but I can punish. My lips draw back, and very delicately, I bite off the tip of her nose.

She shrieks in shock and pain. I back away a few paces and sit, daring them to judge me, glaring at the shouting men until it is they who look away.

"Does he accuse her of adultery?" asks someone.

"Is it because she married Lucian with no proof that her husband was dead?"

"If he *is* dead…" Drustan eyes me uneasily.

Are you remembering all the times I have seen you with Esseilte? All the things I have heard? I look back at him. *Don't fear — so long as you stay loyal to your king you are safe from me.*

Now they are all staring at me.

"Perhaps he is under a spell," says Mevennus.

"Or he's a *garwal*…" says Fragan Tawr, offering the word for a man-wolf that the country folk use.

"Or he is shape-strong," Drustan replies. "When I traveled among the Saxons I met an old man who had been a bard at the court of Oesc of Cantiacum. He was a Burgund, and sang how the hero Sigmund and his son once found a pair of wolf-skins and ranged the woods in that form. But taking them off proved to be harder than getting them on."

"Is that it?" Marc'h stands over Rimoete, who is crouched with her veil over her face, hiding her shame. "Does he have the wolf-sickness, the *bleiz claffet*?"

"Please, my lord! Don't let him near me!" She gulps, sobs. "You do not understand! Edern would leave me sometimes, be gone for days. I grew up near the seacoast. Alone in these forests, I was afraid. I made him tell me where he went, and then I was terrified. How could I lie beside him, not knowing if he were beast or man?"

A beast, you can predict. He will answer attack with aggression, and love with loyalty. It is only men who need oaths to ensure their troth.

"Rimoete, be still!" Lucian reaches for her, but Marc'h 's men hold him.

"Lucian had always loved me," she goes on. "When I promised to give him all his desire, he came. We went to the dolmen and took away the clothes my husband had left there, the clothes that would change him back into a man...."

Yes... that is how it was.... In the shock of that betrayal I had taken refuge in the wolf-mind. Hearing her words, I remember it all.

The king is already ordering men to ride to Lan Bleiz. No one throws away good cloth. Some of my clothes must still be there.

Now it is Lucian who is a prisoner. If I could speak, I would have them build a cage, but it is enough that he is chained. Rimoete huddles beside him, weeping. Whatever happens to me, Marc'h will send them into exile, and she can tell whatever tale she wishes to explain her nipped nose.

I tear at the venison they put before me, and then I sleep once more.

— «» —

It is a day's ride to Lan Bleiz, south of the Haunted Valley, another day to return. My strength has returned to me. I pace back and forth, lifting my head to sniff the clean wind. I cannot sit still. As a wolf, my life is very simple. Do I hope I can be restored to manhood, or do I fear it?

I am the first to hear the hoofbeats when the messenger returns. He has brought an old wool tunic that I used to wear hunting — when I used to hunt with bow and spear as a man. The king unrolls the bundle and shakes out the garment, pauses as if wondering whether he should toss it over me, then lays it on the grass. Stiff-legged, I approach, ruff bristling as the familiar scent sends tremors rippling along each limb.

I nose at the wool. The scent releases a flood of memories. But the place is wrong. The ancestors are not here to guide me. Without them I do not know how to exchange fur for human hide, sinew for sinew, muscle, flesh and bone. I shake the fabric, whining in frustration, in agony as the magic sparks ungrounded along my nerves.

"Give him some privacy—" says someone. "He would not want us to see him half as wolf and half as naked man!"

He is right. I cannot do this here. With a snarl, I seize the tunic in my jaws and leap forward. Men scatter as I dash through the camp and settle into the ground-eating lope that will take me through the Haunted Valley to the tomb. I hear shouts behind me, then hoofbeats and the belling of hounds. They hunted me to the fountain a year ago. Let us see if they can hunt me back again.

As the ground rises, forest gives way to moorland. The sun, descending, sends long shadows reaching from knobs of ruddy rock and wind-tortured trees. The hunt is behind me, I splash through the stream that winds down the valley, through the gorse and down toward the gray stones sheltered by the pines. The capstone of the dolmen glows in the last sunlight, but the space beneath is shadow, a tomb in which the wolf will die, the womb from which a man may be reborn.

I pause, panting, and drop the tunic. A horn calls from behind me. They have followed faster than I expected. I seize the cloth once more and go in.

The other scents in the tomb have faded. I smell my own rank odor, intensified by fear. The tunic is muddied and torn by its swift passage, but it still holds the mingled smells of old sweat, horse and wood smoke, of cooked meat and wine. The smell of Man.

I look down at the tunic, remembering the day my father explained that the dreams that haunted me at night and the rages that tormented me by day were more than adolescent growing pains, the day he led me to the dolmen where the bones of my ancestors still hallowed the ground and told me the history of the black wolves of Lan Bleiz.

In Drustan's tale Sigmund became a wolf by putting on the skin. Perhaps the wolf is what I really am, and it is only by putting on the clothes that I become a man....

I thought I had made this choice already, but now it is truly upon me. If I emerge from the tomb as a wolf, they will believe the magic failed. I can return to Ker-Haes as Marc'h's hound, viewed askance by men who can never be sure whether I will find a way to tell him what I have heard. Or I can let the wolf-mind claim me, disappear into the shadows of the forest to become yet another legend of Broceliande. To the wolf-mind, everything is simple. Human life is a tangle of conflicting loyalties. Why would I want to return to it?

But I cannot go on as I am.

Rimoete saw only the shadow of the beast within. Marc'h saw my soul and did not care if it belonged to a beast or a man. Drustan sings of Artor and the heroes who served him. In the days to come, King Marc'h will need such warriors.

I take a step forward, nosing at the tunic, breathing in that scent and claiming it as my own. I crouch down and roll, stretching to my full length, grinding my body into the cloth, and howl as agony flashes along every limb.

Help me! I cry, and suddenly the ancestors are with me, each one claiming what his blood has given me, reshaping each bone and muscle to leave me spent and gasping upon the rocky floor.

—— «» ——

When my heartbeat ceased to race I struggled to sit up, stretching out my arms, curling my fingers, re-learning the movements of limbs pale-skinned and corded with muscle though still shadowed by dark hairs. Shivering, I pulled the tattered tunic over my head, abandoning the effort to tie the laces. Another push got me to my feet.

The entrance to the dolmen was a bright rectangle in the gloom. I felt my way to the opening, resisting the urge to drop to all fours. They were all waiting, fingers white on the leashes of the whining dogs. In the midst of them King Marc'h reined his stamping stallion down.

Men drew back, gaping, as I stepped from the shadows. A last ray of sun blazed from the king's diadem. I stumbled towards him, half blinded by a haze of gold. I set my two hands to his stirrup, let it take my weight, for it was still hard to stand. I took a deep breath, forced my mouth to shape human words.

"My lord, I am your man...."

Author's note:

"Shadow of the Wolf" is based on a tale in verse called "Bisclavret" written in the twelfth century by Marie de France, a noblewoman at the court of Henry II and Eleanor of Acquitaine who drew her material from the "Matter of Britain" popularized by the bards of Brittany. Marcus Cunomorus, the King Mark of Arthurian lore, was a historical person from the generation after Arthur who ruled lands in Cornwall and in Brittany. He was probably not as evil as he appears in the medieval tales. I first encountered him when I was writing *The White Raven*, my own version of the Tristan story. For those of you who have read that novel, this story would take place somewhere between chapters seventeen and nineteen.

—— «◇» ——

Diana L Paxson is the author of over ninety short stories and multiple novels, including the Westria novels and the later novels in the Avalon series. Following Bradley's death, she took over sole authorship of the series. She is also the author of several nonfiction works, including a book about the Norse god Odin. One of the founders of the Society for Creative Anachronism, she makes her home in Berkley, California.

Echoes

Shannon Allen

Clear blue skies fade into dusk's gentle embrace,
Horses graze in lush pasture,
Shield and sword lay in wistful slumber.

Moonlight's gentle fingers
Caress walls no longer grand.
Hearths stand cold and barren.

The breeze dances with the bard's tales,
Merriment sequestered in hallowed halls,
Guarded at the doors by memory.

To King and Land we pledged,
The brotherhood of the table round, our foundation.
The grace of Camelot, our light.

We were men of quests and honor,
Held fast by loyal oath,
Riding upon the fields of adventure.

Of maidens fair and beast foul,
Into forests dark we charged,
Where steadfast hearts prevailed.

Deceit and want wound her silver serpent,
Spreading whispers and half-truths,
Sowing seeds of discontent.

Hearts withered in sorrow.

Doubt and suspicion claimed seats at our table,
The lights dimmed as we faded into the summer sun.

The stones stand silent now.
Majestic sentinels
To the echoes of our past.

Let not our deeds recede into the featherings of memory
But live on in noble hearts
In a world overthrown with stars.

— «» —

Shannon Allen's short fiction has appeared in Enigma Front and Enigma Front: The Monster Within. A long time fan of all things Arthurian, Shannon lives with her husband Lloyd just south of Calgary, Alberta.

About the Editors

JR Campbell

JR Campbell is a Calgary based writer and the editor of the anthologies Gaslight Grimoire: Fantastic Tales of Sherlock Homes, Gaslight Grotesque: Nightmare Tales of Sherlock Holmes, Gaslight Arcanum: Uncanny Tales of Sherlock Homes and Professor Challenger: New Worlds, Lost Places. His short fiction can be found in Fantasical Visions IV, Rigor Amortis and Tesseracts 21.

Shannon Allen

Shannon Allen is a Calgary based writer who wrote for Calgary Community Publications before turning to fiction. Her first work, Confession, was published in Enigma Front: Now Everything Changes. By the Light of Camelot is her first editorial endeavor.

If you enjoyed this read

Please leave a review on Amazon, Facebook, Good Reads or Instagram.

It takes less than five minutes and it really does make a difference.

If you're not sure how to leave a review on Amazon:

1. *Go to amazon.com.*

2. *Type in By the Light of Camelot edited by JR Campbell and Shannon Allen and when you see it, click on it.*

3. *Scroll down to Customer Reviews. Nearby you'll see a box labeled Write a Review. Click it.*

4. *Now, if you've never written a review before on Amazon, they might ask you to create a name for yourself.*

5. *Reviews can be as simple as, "Loved the book! Can't wait for the Next!" (Please don't give the story away.)*

And that's it!

Brian Hades, publisher

Need something new to read?

If you liked By the Light of Camelot, you should also consider these other EDGE-Lite titles:

— 《》 —

The Black Chalice

by Marie Jakober

Award Winning Novel...

It's 1134. In a bleak monastery somewhere in Germany, Paul of Ardiun begins the chronicle he has been ordered by his religious superiors to write: the story of the knight Karelian Brandeis, for whom Paul once served as squire, who fell prey to the evil wiles of a seductive sorceress, thereby precipitating civil war and the downfall of a king.

But before Paul can set down more than a sentence or two of this cautionary tale, the sorceress herself magically appears to him. He is a liar, she tells him, and always has been. She lays a spell on him: from this moment, he will only be able to write the truth.

But what is the truth? All his life he has rearranged his memories to suit his faith. He has judged Karelian, judged the women, judged the world.

Now, against his will, an entirely different story begins to emerge.

Praise for The Black Chalice

"This is the finest fantasy novel I've read in a very long time; it's more powerful even than Mists of Avalon. Like everyone, I have demands on my time, but I was so intrigued by Jacober's approach to her tale that I read The Black Chalice three times in three weeks, and it was just as engaging the third time around! Her characterization of Pauli is unforgettable, and heart-rendingly credible. His final resolution of his personal conflict feels at the same time both surprising and inevitable — and the victory that it clears the way for is what makes the impact of this story such a magnificent feat of writer's sorcery."
— F E Anderson

"If I could, I would have given this book 6 stars. I haven't read such an absorbing fantasy for a long time. Excellent characterization, interesting approach to narrative, vivid magic, high drama, moral ambiguity ... It's a pity that the loose ends were tied up so well at the end, otherwise I would have liked to read a sequel. I hope that Edge Publishers in Canada follow up with more books of the same caliber."
— Paloma

For more on The Black Chalice visit:

tinyurl.com/edge2001

—— <> ——

Even the Stones

by Marie Jakober

A young queen must confront her destiny, and overcome the powerful forces arrayed against her.

When she is kidnapped by enemy invaders, Marwen of Kamilan must escape her oppressive foe and reclaim her throne. But it will be a fight that will test the very limits of her will, both in an ill-matched war against her former captors, and in the political intrigues that await her in her own land. It is only with the help of a battle hardened soldier, that Marwen finds the strength to face her greatest fears, and discovers that love may be the most dangerous weapon of all.

Praise for Even the Stones

"Even the Stones is a rare gem. Marie Jakober tells an artful and thoughtful story focused firmly in this book, not on plot threads for subsequent volumes. The result is a strong, frank and engaging tale with well developed characters clearly motivated through a theme as old as men and women, birth and inheritance - the pursuit of power. ... Marie Jakober is clear that her work focuses on power and how it shapes the world: the power of gender, wealth, religion or sex, of a queen, a king, or a slave-born soldier. She writes about the power of power to create and destroy through indifference and ignorance. Marie is also honest;

Even the Stones reminds us that nothing is as powerful or ceaseless as the pendulum that gives and takes power from us all."
— Terry Baker, The The Alien Online

"… a stunning tale of adventure and romance … a spellbinding epic of courage and passion … It is an amazingly incisive probe of the psychological and political dynamics of partnership and domination, and in this it is also a parable for our times. It will be a classic, a cherished book passed on from generation to generation."
— Riane Eisler, author of The Chalice and the Blade

For more on Even the Stones:

tinyurl.com/edge3007

—— <> ——

Poseidon & Cleito

by Andrew J. Peters

He became a god. Her story was forgotten.

From the shore of a frozen steppe, an outcast hunter embarks for the otherworld to ask his ancestors how to bring the mammoth back to the fields of sedge. In a shining, island kingdom of wonders, the daughter of a high priest fights for her claim to wealth and power after her father is assassinated by the king. Together they will build an empire recalled as an ancient legend and a cautionary tale. But how did he become a god while she became a mere footnote in history?

Poseidon & Cleito is the engrossing first book of a fantasy trilogy of myth and legend exploring the rise of the lost civilization of Atlantis. In the best traditions of an epic journey, one man's struggle to discover his place in the world takes him across perilous seas into the epicenter of political strife in a foreign land. But a legend is not made of deeds alone... Fans of Guy Gavriel Kay's historical fantasy and David Gemmell's Troy series will enjoy this fantasy novel as it sets out to reimagine the inception of a Greek myth.

Praise for Poseidon & Cleito

Poseidon is a mighty barbarian leader, and Cleito's a commendably strong woman with a ruthless streak. Alternating between Poseidon's and Cleito's points of view also gives the story a wonderful counterpoint while illuminating two very separate cultures.... A fresh twist on

an old sea myth, complete with magic, intrigue, and plenty
of old-school adventures."
— KIRKUS REVIEW

The story is well written and the cast interesting, while
the complexity of the political relationships, especially with
the uncle, are quite well drawn."
— Margaret McGaffey Fisk

For more on Poseidon & Cleito:

tinyurl.com/edge6018

For more EDGE titles and information about upcoming speculative fiction please visit us at:

www.edgewebsite.com

Don't forget to sign-up for our Special Offers